UNDER THE CANYON SKY

Guarding the Treasure

Books by Dick Brown

Under the Canyon Sky Series
Book One: Canyon Crossroads
Book Two: Heart of Gold
Book Three: Guarding the Treasure

UNDER THE CANYON SKY

Guarding the Treasure

Dick Brown

SPEAKING VOLUMES, LLC
NAPLES, FLORIDA
2024

Guarding the Treasure

Copyright © 2024 by Dick Brown

All rights reserved. No part of this book may be reproduced or transmitted in any form or by any means without written permission.

As a work of fiction, the characters, places and incidents are either products of the author's imagination or are used fictitiously. Many incidents are created for dramatic story-telling purposes; however, some events are loosely drawn from history. Any resemblance to actual persons, living or deceased, buildings, business establishments, organizations, events or locales is entirely coincidental.

On the other hand, certain background incidents, historical events and characters are real. Teddy Roosevelt did indeed visit the Canyon on three occasions. Buffalo Bill stood in awe on the South Rim. Steam locomotives transported visitors to the very brink of the Canyon. Publishing magnate William Randolph Hearst raised wild speculation with his significant property purchases on and below the rim. And the Colorado River still glides quietly along in some places and roars loudly in others.

ISBN 979-8-89022-141-4

This historical novel is dedicated to the pioneering men and women who had a hand in the Grand Canyon's transition from unbridled backcountry to one of America's greatest national parks.

Acknowledgments

My very special thanks to my wife Donna who accompanied me on many of the Grand Canyon's grueling backcountry trails, exploring abandoned copper mines, trudging along on endless field trips, and patiently enduring my time away while I plunged into periods of historical research. And then at home, conducting critical reviews of manuscript drafts, cautioning me not to stray into a monotonous history report, offering her thoughts and perspectives, and giving me emotional encouragement and inspiration every single day, all the while keeping the home fires burning.

I also acknowledge my friend Gary Fogel, an author in his own right, for his constructive critiques and encouragement during the development of this trilogy.

And finally, I thank my publisher and editor for believing in this project and making this story come alive on the printed page.

Preface

The wonder, intrigue and stunning beauty of the Grand Canyon are beyond measure. This historical novel brings to life the struggle of nineteenth and twentieth century pioneers against monopolistic corporations while enduring rapacious government control. It is a human-interest story where the Canyon itself takes on a life of its own. The story underscores the obsession of the Santa Fe Railway and its captive enterprises to drive the independent entrepreneurs—the men and women who opened the Canyon for all to experience—out of business and off the land. Despite constant badgering and accusations of being squatters and trespassers, the canyon pioneers still managed to leave their indelible mark on this grand stage. What we see today at the Grand Canyon is not only the work of nature but the work of brazen pioneers who chiseled trails out of stubborn rock, erected primitive tourist lodges on the rim, discovered rich copper deposits below the rim, and guided daring mule riders to the river. This is their story—a story of passion, dreams and challenges.

Chapter One

A LEGEND AND LEDGES

Don't go where you imagine the path leads; instead go where there is no path and leave a trail for others to follow

Kirby and Sabrina O'Brien relaxed at their Circle K Ranch, which encompassed the old stage stop known as Little Springs, about twenty miles northwest of Flagstaff, Arizona. They both found news of a recent gold discovery in the eastern reaches of the Grand Canyon rather perplexing.

"Sabrina, how do you explain ol' Lucas Randall finding gold nuggets on the Jackson Trail? You must have dropped some in your excitement?"

"Kirby, I'm sure I did. Dark, muddy water gushed everywhere. The first rusty coffee can fell apart in my hands. Some nuggets swept by me, but I thought I retrieved them all when the weather cleared. My guess is Lucas gathered enough strays that he thought he found the whole cache. I wonder if he noticed parts of rusty tin cans that also washed down. After so many years, I'm surprised he found any nuggets at all."

"Let's play along with his reveling," said Kirby. "Your secret is safe with me. By now, ol' Lucas is in his late seventies. After all his years of probing rocky nooks and scrounging through washouts with his beer-drinking jacks, he deserves some measure of notoriety and celebration. I've met this canyon character several times over the years. He almost rivaled Clancy Jennings in telling wild stories. I remember one that he swears is true."

Sabrina settled back, ready for some armchair entertainment.

"Lucas remembers watching two river-runners in a flat-bottomed boat attempting to navigate around a mass of boulders in Whiskey Rapids. I think this river fiasco occurred just before the turn of the century. The way Lucas tells it, the boat already looked like a battered and splintered wreck."

Sabrina interrupted. "I can understand wanting to cross the river in a smooth section but why would anyone want to ride the river lengthwise? Why would anyone ask for such trouble?"

Kirby continued. "Yes, the way Lucas explained it, the men instantly plunged themselves into trouble, in fact, a watery disaster. These daredevils noticed Lucas and his two jacks, Chester and Otis, standing on the shore, waiting for the show to start. With a ready audience, the men set about running the rapids, trying to hug a northside channel and immediately slamming their boat against a half-submerged rock. Lucas said he saw an oar break and its oarlock rip out of the sideboard. One of the men used the broken oar as a prybar to free themselves from this imposing obstacle. The boat swirled into the main channel, only to smash into a midstream boulder, breaking the other oarlock. Lucas said he watched the boat slide sideways downstream, reaching the lower end of the rapids, narrowly escaping another series of rocks. He saw one of the men fish an oar out of the water, enabling them to paddle ashore. They then set up camp after that terrifying ride."

Sabrina added, "I still wonder why anyone in their right mind would try to journey down this raging river. Just because that explorer, what's his name, Powell, did it, I guess others think they can do it too. Like Lucas and his astute burros, I would rather keep my feet on firm ground and not challenge an angry, unforgiving river. After all, it is in shallow streams and on dry land where one might chance upon gold."

* * *

With Ryan Perkins' literary skills, and Sabrina's coaching and financial support, Monte Bridgestone's book landed on the *New York Times* bestseller list. Sabrina had arranged for Clint McCarty, one of the last living canyon pioneers, to write the foreword. Some of Heidi Sherman's best historic photographs graced the center section. Clint's foreword read, in part:

"Those who knew Monte Bridgestone are better for it. Like all of us pioneers, we cherished the Grand Canyon and took care not to do her too much harm. More than anyone else, Monte and I opposed the Santa Fe Railway and Trails West Company and their exclusive arrangements to capitalize on this awesome national treasure. Monte spent most of his life exploring below the rim. He opened Grand Canyon for anyone willing to step over the edge. The pages that follow tell the story of one man—a legend in his own lifetime—who loved the Canyon and helped bring it within reach of everyone. Monte Bridgestone and his gripping, emotional saga will live in your dreams and in your hearts for all time."

Ryan crafted the text to improve the book's readability so well Monte himself did not recognize the minor editorial changes. The book told Monte's story in his own words. The New York-based publishing house released the book in major cities along the route of the Santa Fe Railway, including the hotels and restaurants of the Trails West Company. And the Starlight Lodge and the Canyon Queen Hotel maintained a ready supply in their gift shops.

Jeremy Livingston closed Monte's book and set it on an oak table. "Monte, this is a great story; it brings back many memories of our trail-building and mining days."

"He's right Monte, a great book indeed," chimed Rachel, Jeremy's wife. "I read it too. I don't know if all the stories are true, as many are before my time, but they certainly captivated my interest."

The Livingstons spelled the O'Briens whenever they needed to tend to Circle K ranch chores. No one wanted to leave their ailing canyon pioneer alone.

Monte stared at the table. "I still can't believe there's a book telling the story of my fellow pioneers settling here." Monte winced as another pain shot through his stomach.

"I wish I could see the Canyon from my ranch here."

Jeremy gave him some assurance. "Monte, I know you relish sitting at Summit Point and gazing at the great wonder of nature below. It's rather late today, but we'll get you over there in the morning. My brother Dexter will be here to help."

"Thank you, appreciate it. By the way, what is Dexter doing these days?" Monte often thought about the brothers during their trail-building days.

"Oh, you would be surprised; he is working as a carpenter, helping to build boats for a new river outfitting company, Western River Adventures, I think it is called. He is not planning to run boats down the Colorado, but instead manage the scheduling and provisioning to ensure safe experiences for paying passengers. This is a new canyon tourist enterprise hoping to launch next year. Quite a change from building the Summit Trail or racing down to the Shooting Star when we heard that mysterious mine explosion, right?"

Monte nodded, then launched into his recollection of hearing that terrifying sound resonate among canyon walls while his crew worked below the saddle. "I remember charging down the trail to where Kirby, Dexter and you labored to put the finishing touches on the trail. Thunder came to Kirby's mind. We all high-tailed it to the mine. When we arrived, we found dust and smoke billowing from the mine entrance. I smelled gunpowder and immediately suspected sabotage." Monte paused until another pain subsided.

Jeremy broke into the conversation, "Yeah, I recall the explosion created a giant cavern where the tunnel wye used to be. Monte, you pointed to the ceiling and a newly exposed vein of pure copper."

"That's right; the culprit who set the explosion did us a huge favor." Monte went into deep thought for a moment. "I always suspected Ben Saxton but we could never prove it."

Jeremy changed the subject. "On a happier note, Monte, I remember the days when we ran strings of jacks loaded with rich copper ore to Summit Point. It always felt good to reach the rim as Mark Warren and I knew we completed the first leg of the long trip to a smelter. I figured every climb to the rim contributed to a productive mining operation. I also remember you lecturing Kirby, Mark and I about not overloading our burros."

"You fellas needed lecturing at times. You always tried to overload those poor jacks, despite my reminders. Ah, I remember those days." Monte drifted into a dreamy state of mind as Jeremy and Rachel tiptoed out of the room, suspecting a forthcoming nap for the exhausted pioneer.

* * *

Sabrina finished her errands in the Village, her last stop being the freight depot where she noticed Teresa Cordova dismounting her horse. Teresa came from a long line of stagecoach drivers operating in southern Arizona Territory.

"Teresa, hello, do you have a few minutes? My name is Sabrina O'Brien; I don't think we've formally met but I've seen you a few times over the years."

"Howdy, Sabrina; I've seen you a few times too. It is high time we got to know each other."

The women leaned on the hitching post while their mounts shuffled their feet. "This is my second Serendipity. I still miss my first Serendipity. You say you have seen me before? Where? I'm usually hunkered down at my Little Springs ranch or visiting Summit Point, one of our favorite canyon haunts."

Teresa decided to open up about her sightings. "This is Hank, my trusty four-footed friend. You won't believe this but I spotted you many times at Little Springs when I worked as a stage driver. I've always been curious about why you tried to hide in the barn loft. An outlaw might do that. Perhaps a shy person too."

Sabrina explained. "This is embarrassing. My first husband died in a terrible accident at our Winslow ranch. My second marriage to a no-good bum only lasted a few months. Not until I married Kirby O'Brien did I come out of hiding. Up until then, I did not want anything to do with men, or anyone else, so I just avoided being seen at the stage stop or whenever I went prospecting below the rim."

"Prospecting?" Teresa suddenly realized Sabrina is the notorious horsewoman. "You know, we used to call you the Mystery Lady. I think I saw you once on the old stage road near the tourist camp operated by the late Clancy Jennings. I worked as a postrider back then. For a while, I watched you walking along with a chestnut mare and a mule, both heavily loaded."

"Oh, my original Serendipity and my mule Jenny! We didn't think anyone saw us; makes me wonder who else caught us trudging along the old stage road. I'm now on my way back to our Circle K Ranch. You should visit Kirby and I sometime."

Teresa enjoyed their talk and the opportunity to finally meet the person behind the long-standing mystery. "I will do that, Sabrina; I need to go to Flagstaff next month. I'll stop by your place on my return."

* * *

The survey team picked up Kirby at the Circle K and drove to the site of the future Pioneer Museum. While a flagged survey stake and the ceremonial cornerstone still marked the spot where Monte thrust his shovel into the caprock, the architect and the contractor needed an official survey with control lines and boundaries. The team consisted of the survey chief who ran the transit and level on a tripod and a rod-and-chain man for measurements. Kirby hung around the site as an interested observer.

The plans called for the north wall of the museum building to cling to the edge of the rim. As the rodman walked backwards along the caprock, stretching his chain from the flagged stake at the northwest corner, he moved toward the northeast corner. Just then, he stepped over the edge and fell about thirty feet, landing on a narrow ledge. Kirby and the survey chief rushed over to see the rodman writhing in excruciating pain and holding his leg.

"Mr. O'Brien, I have a long tow rope in my truck." He scampered back to grab the rope, and back to the spot where his partner tripped and fell.

"Lower me down. I will see what I can do for him," said Kirby, in a rather shaky voice. The chief tied a loop around Kirby and played out the rope as Kirby rappelled down the rock face. When he cut away the bloody trouser fabric on the rodman's lower right leg, he exposed a ghastly sight—a bloody bone protruding from muscle and skin.

The chief yelled, "How is he?"

"Not good, two broken bones, one sticking out of his leg, the other partially exposed. I am fashioning a tourniquet out of my belt." Kirby had an idea. "See if you can build a stretcher out of your tripod and anything else you can find, and retrieve this rope, tie one end to your truck and the other to the stretcher. And hurry!"

The poor fellow glanced at his leg, grimaced, and groaned, "How bad, how bad is it? Kirby did not know what to say but the look on his face told the story.

"It's bad; try to stay calm and we will get you out of this mess."

Using his transit tripod, an old, frayed piece of canvas and some twine, the chief quickly rigged a crude stretcher, tied one end of the lifeline to his truck, the other to the stretcher, and let it down to the ledge. Kirby rolled the injured man, screaming with pain, onto the stretcher and signaled to the chief to start hoisting while he held the fellow out from the wall. The chief jammed his truck into reverse, jerking the line, then put a steady strain on it. With the stretcher about ten feet from the rim, the canvas ripped open. The rodman slipped out and plummeted toward Kirby, bounced off his right foot and tumbled over the side. The man died instantly when his body thudded onto another ledge three hundred feet below. The chief used the rope to haul Kirby to the surface. Doc Callahan of the Park Service clinic diagnosed Kirby's right foot and declared his ankle broken.

* * *

The surveyor dropped Kirby off at the Circle K and continued his return to Flagstaff where he reported the accident to authorities. Sabrina heard the truck roar out the gate, dropped her dish towel, ripped off her apron, and ran out to see Kirby hobbling along on crutches.

"Oh no, what happened to you?" Sabrina helped him to the house.

"It's a long story. Our surveyor's helper fell into the canyon and died. I suffered some fractured bones in my right ankle while trying to rescue the poor soul. Doc Callahan at the clinic says I need to stay off my feet for a few weeks. Ironically, it is the same foot that Monte injured many years ago."

Kirby sank into his rocking chair as Sabrina returned to her kitchen to make some hot apple cider. By the time she returned with a steaming mug, Kirby had fallen asleep. She would have to wait for details on the fatal accident and what needed to be done next.

* * *

A week had passed since Kirby struggled up the driveway to Sabrina. The swelling had subsided and he learned how to use his crutches to avoid putting weight on his fractured ankle joint. He also learned park officials retrieved the rodman's body and the survey chief planned to resume work next month. Sabrina insisted that Kirby stay home, but he argued they needed to get back to Monte's ranch and relieve the Livingstons. He could rest there with Monte just as easily as at the Circle K. And Sabrina could look in on the survey work as Kirby stayed with Monte.

Using a wagon would be too jolting on Kirby's foot injury. Although the O'Briens purchased a bright red fifty horsepower Ford Roadster two years ago, they often preferred the lazy wagon ride to the Canyon. But in the interest of time and comfort, Sabrina drove while Kirby relaxed in his reclining seat.

Jeremy saw them coming. Sabrina pulled up close to Monte's ranch house to shorten Kirby's workout on crutches.

"What happened to you?" Jeremy rushed over to help Kirby stand.

"I'll tell ya later. How's Monte doing?"

"As well as can be expected. His stomach pains are more frequent. I'm glad you are here. I've been hauling him to Summit Point but it is really you two who he wants with him there."

Monte staggered into the room. "Kirby, why are you on crutches?"

Kirby explained the accident at Inspiration Point and the unfortunate loss of one member of the survey party. He added that he and Sabrina would take over for Jeremy and Rachel, and assured Monte that his Summit Point visits would not be impacted.

* * *

One day, Monte, Kirby and Jeremy sat on the caprock at Summit Point, reminiscing about their trail-building days. Monte opened the discussion.

"I could not have built that trail without you fellas. You never hesitated dragging juniper logs down to where we needed to build cribbing or hauling rocks for retaining walls on our switchbacks. I wish I could have paid you more but at least it tripled the rate for lumbermen and cowboys."

Kirby, with a wide grin, interjected, "Monte, it did not go unnoticed that you selected the highest point on the South Rim of the Grand Canyon for the trailhead!" Jeremy added, "Dexter and I marveled at how you struck such an extreme course to Windsong Mesa, building a trail that literally clutched vertical ramparts and spiraled down terraced slopes."

"Yeah, but we did it and what a team we made," added Monte.

Jeremy jumped back in. "There's one thing that has bothered me for years." Looking directly at Kirby, he continued. "During our mining days on Windsong Mesa, Kirby, I could not figure out why you always volunteered to make the water runs to Arrowhead Spring, a labor-intensive, time-consuming operation. Then one day it dawned on me; you hoped to meet a very special lady down there."

"You and me both, Jeremy," added Monte. "It took several months before I discovered Kirby's secret encounters with the Mystery Lady, all the while filling water barrels and strapping them onto jacks. That explains—ah, ooh, that was a bad shooting pain—his insistence on taking charge of our water-hauling operations."

Monte's health continued to decline and his regular Summit Point visits became less frequent. On what turned out to be one of his last visits, he commented to Kirby. "Sitting here, I feel one can reach the outer limits of sight and sound. What I mean is this place inspires reflection and vision. Kirby, you would not have had to haul water to the rim if we just had a reliable source here. That river down there is not the solution, too far and too much elevation to overcome."

"I've thought about that, especially during my long days waiting for Sabrina to show." Kirby continued. "Most of the rainwater and snowmelt up here drains away to the south. If only we had some high land to the south to send water up this way."

"We do! San Francisco Peaks!" exclaimed Monte. "Maybe we could collect water from the snowpack there and run a gravity pipeline to the South Rim. You need to find an engineer—uh, oh that hurt—to do a feasibility study and determine if there is enough elevation and pressure to deliver water to the rim." Monte suffered one of his worst pains ever. "Kirby, get me, uh, get me back to the ranch. I'm really hurting this afternoon."

Under The Canyon Sky: Guarding the Treasure

* * *

Monte Bridgestone died in view of his beloved Grand Canyon during his final outing at Summit. A brilliant sunset cast the entire canyon in reds, oranges and yellows. With Kirby and Sabrina at his side, Monte spoke his last words, "For me, with my dearest friends at my side, there is no place I would rather be. By day, this Canyon is a glorious panorama of wild colors and teasing shadows; by night it is a canopy of shimmering stars." Sabrina gazed at the sunset. When she looked back at Uncle Monte, she realized death had claimed a canyon legend. Kirby whispered, "He is now with the stars."

Following funeral services at the Community Building in the Village, the Knights of Pythias conducted graveside services at Pioneer Cemetery. They laid Monte to rest beside Anna and son Ben. Kirby O'Brien had the honor of presenting the eye-watering eulogy.

"Monte Bridgestone served as the unofficial guardian of the eastern end of the Canyon, first for the Forest Service, and later for the Park Service." Kirby glanced at Sabrina, then continued. "He opposed the government giving the Santa Fe Railway and Trails West Company total control of canyon country. He spent half a century exploring mesas and side canyons below the rim, mining high-grade copper ore, building tourist enterprises, and living on the edge. A quest to unlock the Canyon's hidden secrets propelled him through life. His energy seemed inexhaustible, exceeded only by his love of the Grand Canyon, which he adopted as his own. By his reluctance to talk about himself, history has lost many thrilling adventures, although many are captured in his book. As a master trail-builder, Monte brought the Canyon within reach of all of us here today and generations to come."

Eyes welled with tears. Everyone knew when Monte Bridgestone died, a legend died.

Sabrina stood before the crowd to deliver her own personal comments. "I did not know Uncle Monte as long as many of you. I am the only one who called him uncle as I regarded him as family. To Uncle Monte, never a master with words, descriptions of the Canyon's extent and majesty seemed futile, even impertinent. He watched every change of season, the dawning of each new day, the passing of every hour as new elements of grandeur showed in the side canyons. He marveled at color changes on cliff walls, exposing new dimensions in the Canyon's dizzying depths. This is Monte Bridgestone's home."

Sabrina, after choking up, collected herself. "I remember Monte's last visit to Summit Point. I asked our master trail-builder what stirred him the most about the Grand Canyon. He said, 'Its immensity, stillness and wild beauty.' Then I asked Monte what would you say to future generations who visit this very spot. He thought for a moment, then said, 'Don't go where you imagine the path leads, instead go where there is no path and leave a trail for others to follow.' I cherish those words and have arranged for them to be etched onto a copper plate to be bolted to his headstone."

"I believe Uncle Monte is watching now, from a place where he has a commanding view, where he continues his oversight of the eastern reaches of his favorite part of this, his Canyon."

* * *

With Monte's passing, his Coconino Basin ranch fell into disrepair. Livestock wandered off to greener pastures and someone stripped the trading post of any valuable wares. Kirby and Sabrina had retrieved Monte's collection of copper rocks and canyon artifacts that once occupied a room at the Grand Canyon Hotel. They would one day go on display in the Canyon Pioneer Museum. Kirby had already moved most of the ranch furniture to the Circle K.

But there remained the matter of what to do with Blackie, Monte's old Hudson touring car. Its gears had jammed six months ago, and Kirby could not budge the car from its parking spot outside the dilapidated garage. The auto had two flat tires, cracked leather seats, and a dull black exterior covered with pine needles. Before leaving Monte's old ranch, Kirby looked inside the Hudson one more time, just to make sure he left nothing of value.

He checked under the seats and in the trunk. He turned to leave, then remembered the glove-box. Tucked among a few unimportant papers, Kirby found an unopened letter, postmarked Carbonville, Utah. He could not imagine who Monte knew in Utah, but resolved not to open the long-lost letter until he arrived home.

At the Circle K, Kirby handed Sabrina the mysterious letter. "Did Monte ever mention knowing someone in the Utah community of Carbonville?"

"No, not that I recall." Sabrina held the envelope up to a light. "There is a handwritten letter inside. Since we are operating as unofficial executors of Uncle Monte's estate, we are in the right if we open it. Look, he posted it on March second nineteen thirty."

She used a kitchen knife to slit the envelope.

"Oh, it's from ol' Francois LaRue! Remember him? Monte forgot this letter. It looks like the work of a jittery hand." Sabrina added, "I'll try to read it."

"Monte, mon ami, I'm sure you never thought you would hear from me again. I'm now in failing health, too many years working in the coal mines up here. Not good for an old codger like me to spend long days breathing coal dust. I'm eighty-five years old and I feel it. The company is about to send me to Glenwood Springs, Colorado, where local citizens converted an old hotel into a sanatorium, same place where Doc Holliday spent his last days back in eighty-seven."

"Kirby, this does not sound good. At this writing, Francois is near death. There's more." Sabrina wiped her eyes, but tears blurred her vision.

"Let me take it from here." Kirby started to read. "Let's see, Doc Holliday, okay, here we go."

"I never got any financial backing for that North Rim railroad. The timing was just not right. Even five years ago, there was still no serious development on the North Rim. So, I went back to the only life I knew—mining. But at my age, it has been back-breaking work. I hope you are doing well on the South Rim but it is probably different now, the Canyon being a National Park. Please give my regards to Clancy and Clint and any other pioneers that may still be thereabouts. Oh, and that mystery lady, Sabrina; I wonder what ever happened to her. You can write to me at Glenwood Springs. I expect to be there in hospice care in a week or two. Yours truly, Francois."

"Hospice care, what's that?" Kirby seemed confused.

"It's hospital care for the terminally sick. I wish Uncle Monte had remembered this letter. I'm afraid by now Francois is long gone. And now both are gone."

* * *

Sabrina O'Brien donated large sums to frontier hospitals, nursing homes, and the future canyon museum she had promised Monte. She still reeled from the loss of her dear friend. "Kirby, the living testimonials to Uncle Monte are so great; I don't think of him as having passed away. He is still with us in spirit."

"Yes, he is, and once built, the Grand Canyon Pioneer Museum will transport visitors to a bygone frontier, tugging at their hearts and touching their soul."

Kirby knew the museum remained an important mission for Sabrina, but a string of bureaucratic issues delayed its construction. With somber determination etched on his face, he vowed to help Sabrina navigate the Federal bureaucracy and, if necessary, oversee the museum's development himself.

"Since the Geology Museum also occupies Inspiration Point, maybe the Pioneer Museum will attract just as much attention." Kirby nodded his agreement. "In some respects, I wonder if Summit Point would be a better location," sighed Sabrina. Kirby promised her dream to honor Monte and his fellow pioneers would not go unfulfilled.

The two had been conducting a plan-in-hand review at the museum site. But now the sun was low on the canyon horizon. As Kirby rolled up the architect's drawings, Sabrina looked up to see an orange glow on the North Rim in the area above Skeleton Creek, too far north to be part of the sunset building to the west.

"Kirby, look at that! Looks like a fire!"

"That looks bad, Sabrina. I heard a subsidiary of the Union Pacific Railroad built a lodge over there a few years ago. Maybe it's on fire." Memories of Monte's Grand Canyon Hotel burning down flashed through his mind.

They stood gazing at the North Rim for about half an hour as the fire flared into a raging monster with smoke billowing above the darkening rim. Before leaving Inspiration Point, they looked back across the canyon one more time to see the sky glowing red, partly due to the setting sun, but mostly due to the fire on the rim.

A week later they learned that a massive blaze gutted the two-story North Rim Lodge. Apparently sparks burst from a fireplace on the first floor and ignited wooden furnishings, then the fire spread rapidly throughout the building. The structure featured exterior walls with Spanish-style stonework and an observation tower on the roof. The fire destroyed two adjacent luxury cabins of similar construction, but with no casualties. The wood interior of the lodge became a colossal disaster. Its heavy timbers and framing smoldered for days. Only blackened chimneys and foundation piers remained standing in the thick bed of ashes.

* * *

On her way back from Flagstaff, Teresa visited Sabrina at her Circle K Ranch. Kirby herded cattle miles away. "I remember this place as the Little Springs relay station on the stage road with a hay barn, corrals, and livery stables for changing horses. Back then Augustus and Martha Klostermeyer operated it for the Grand Canyon Stage Line."

Teresa had not changed much since those days of driving four-in-hand stagecoaches. Her cascading black hair framed her dark eyes. While still quite spirited, she lacked certainty in how she wanted to live the rest of her life, a life which up to recently had been that of a loner.

"The Klostermeyers are great folks and took me in when I really needed a place to live," explained Sabrina. "Getting up in years, they decided it was time to move to town. We bought the ranch, so it worked out well for everyone." She changed the subject. "Teresa, at the risk of getting personal, have you been single all these years?" The women walked over to the corral where Hank munched on some hay.

"Yes, I have been somewhat of a loner but that is going to change soon. I have not shared this news with anyone yet, except Roscoe Andrews, but I have recently become engaged to marry Tomas Garcia. Since I have no family, Roscoe, my former co-worker and stage driver for many years, has volunteered to give me away. We have not set a date yet."

"Teresa, that is great news. Congratulations! Maybe the wedding can be right here at the Circle K." Sabrina suddenly had an idea and could not hold back. "We have Thanksgiving coming soon. Let's stage a big Thanksgiving celebration and a wedding ceremony right here at the ranch, nothing formal, just a reunion of canyon friends and family enjoying a country-style dinner of roasted turkey, potatoes, beans and pumpkin pie."

"I'd like that very much, Sabrina. Tomas and I have been wrestling with ideas on when and where we should get married." With a plan coming together, Teresa seemed relieved. Clearly, she and Sabrina seemed well on the way to becoming good friends.

The two watched Hank finish his supper. "How is Hank on canyon trails?"

"What? Oh, I don't think he's ever been below the rim if that is what you are thinking. I haven't either," confessed Teresa.

"You mean despite all these years driving tourists to the brink of the Canyon and serving as a Federal postrider between the Village and Clancy's place, you have never ventured below? You and I need to plan a trip." Sabrina seemed shocked that this outdoors lady had yet to experience the inner canyon. "I'll give you an introductory tour, say down the Pioneer Trail, across the Tonto and up the Summit Trail."

"Sabrina, I am not sure Hank would go along with such an adventure. I'm game but perhaps an initial ride halfway down a canyon trail and back would be better." Teresa noted Hank's ears twitch when she said canyon trail.

"Teresa, okay, we can work on a canyon trail ride later. Let's start planning for our Thanksgiving shindig." The two pioneer women hugged and said their goodbyes. Sabrina watched Teresa and Hank pass through the ranch gate and mosey along the old stage road. She then rushed back into the house to begin making an invitation list.

Chapter Two

CANYON COUNTRY TALES

Hugs and apples apply throughout life

Longtime stagecoach driver Roscoe Andrews arranged for padre Fernando Benavides to conduct the simple wedding ceremony for Teresa Cordova and Tomas Garcia at the Circle K Ranch. Besides Sabrina, Kirby and Roscoe, witnesses included Jeremy and Rachel Livingston with son Cody, Jeremy's brother Dexter, Chad and Heidi Sherman as the picture-takers, Mark Warren, Moonflower Yazzie, Ryan Perkins, and the venerable Jesse Parks.

The wedding took place outdoors on the expansive veranda of the Circle K's ranch house. Everyone gathered around as Padre Benavides began the simple ceremony. "Folks, welcome one and all. We are gathered here on this beautiful October afternoon to celebrate one of life's greatest moments, that is, to unite a man and a woman in marriage. I now ask, who gives the bride away?"

"I, Roscoe Andrews, have the honor of giving Teresa away."

"Very well. Let's get started. Teresa Cordova, do you take Tomas Garcia as your wedded husband to love, honor and trust for the rest of your life?"

"I do," confirmed Teresa.

"Tomas, do you take Teresa as your wedded wife and promise that no matter what challenges lie ahead, you will face them together in love, in honor and in trust?"

"Yes, I do," confirmed Tomas.

"Then in witness of those present here on this special day, and with the power vested in me by the Catholic Church, I pronounce you husband and wife."

Everyone clapped and cheered, offered their congratulations and best wishes to the newlyweds, then slowly drifted into the ranch house dining room.

After a filling Thanksgiving dinner, folks sat in rocking chairs and on stools on the veranda, watching a herd of grassland grazers on the other side of a split-rail fence. "Sabrina, don't take this the wrong way but the Circle K brand on your horses reminds me of outlaws running rebranded horses on the Coconino," said Teresa. "Ol' Levi Jackson used to warn me about encountering dangerous horse thieves on the stage road."

"Levi warned me too. Stealing horses is an unpardonable sin," said Sabrina. That casual mention of horse thieves threw the entire gathering of canyon trailblazers into a long Old West storytelling session, one wild tale of the Old West after another.

Sabrina continued, "Two drunk outlaws once confronted me below the rim." That revelation startled Kirby.

"You have never mentioned that to me, Sabrina. Folks, I'm still getting to know my wife of three decades."

"Kirby, I chose to not tell you all these years because I'm too embarrassed about so easily getting myself into such a dangerous situation. I just managed to escape a rockslide at Doubtful Canyon when two drifters, who called each other by their last names, Morton and Sykes, stumbled into my camp."

"Those scoundrels? Slim Broadway told me about them and later their names came up regarding other suspicious activities," said Kirby.

Teresa then surprised everyone. "I killed Morton after he took a shot at me. As a Federal Agent delivering mail or not, I had the right to defend myself. As for his sidekick, investigators found his body in the ashes after the Grand Canyon Hotel fire. He had a Bowie knife sticking out of his chest. I've always suspected that Morton killed Sykes."

Chad Sherman also had an incident with the two outlaws. "As you know, Heidi and I operate the Cliffhanger Photo Studio on the rim. One day, while delivering some prints to the Canyon Queen Hotel, I stumbled upon a daring daylight robbery underway in the lobby. Morton and Sykes had just forced the hotel clerk to open his vault and relieve him of visitor valuables and cash. I recognized them from a wanted poster and foiled their escape by tripping them as they ran out the main door. I just happened to be in the right place at the right time. The loot scattered all over the steps but those two outlaws got away."

Sabrina jumped back into the conversation. "I recall Francois LaRue claiming to know another shady character. Francois knew a woman with a strong penchant for drinking and gambling, and just rabble-rousing on the wild side. That shady lady, Martha Canary, better known as Calamity Jane, raised quite a ruckus back in our Frenchman's Dakota days. He said Calamity could out-drink, out-spit, and out-cuss any man in Deadwood. Francois never referred to this wild woman as being on the wrong side of the law; she just wanted to make a name for herself in dime novels. I doubt she ever knew he named his mule Calamity Jane!"

Teresa, who has worked as a stagecoach driver for several overland mail companies, opened with a tale about stage robberies. "Let me tell you about an attempted robbery I experienced in my younger days. My five passengers found themselves tossed on the floor in a heap when I brought my stagecoach to an abrupt stop at Picacho Pass, northwest of Tucson. I had no one riding shotgun with me that day so I had no chance against four banditos wearing gunnysacks to mask their identities. The leader ordered us to step down and raise our hands. I had no choice but to abandon my Winchester on the driver's seat. I lowered my hands to test the seriousness of these desperados. The cocking of the leader's six-shooter sent my arms back up."

Everyone on the veranda listened intently, even six-year-old Cody Livingston.

"The banditos searched our luggage, the box under the driver's seat, the undercarriage, and the boot but they found no strongbox onboard. The gang's leader became furious and asked where we hid our strongbox. I said, 'it's on the other stage.' He grinned and announced that they would hold us there until it showed up. I noticed every horse had its feet wrapped in gunnysacks, obviously to make it nearly impossible for a posse to follow. After thirty minutes I confessed 'It's no use fooling you any longer. There is no second stage.' This is when the situation took a turn for the worse."

"Did they shoot you?" asked Cody.

"No, but one of the banditos pointed his shotgun at me. Another ordered my passengers to line up alongside our stage—in reality, the second stage!"

"They held us captive for another hour, enough time for the first stage to deliver its shipment of gold coins to the bank in Tucson. The banditos finally gave up, but this Wild West episode is the reason I left the southern runs across New Mexico and Arizona and moved north to cooler and safer stagecoach operations."

While Sabrina and Rachel served pumpkin pie and coffee, Ryan recalled writing about two train robberies as a *Frontier Times* reporter: one near Prospector Flats, the other near Canyon Diablo.

"After the train departed the Village with Canyon Queen lodging proceeds onboard for depositing in a Flagstaff bank, two robbers flagged the train down just outside Prospector Flats, pretending to want to board as paying passengers. They escaped with the loot. Rampant speculation in the Village pointed to Morton and Sykes as the culprits."

"My other story involves the westbound Frisco freight train near Canyon Diablo and some train robbers, dumb and sloppy, executing their risky night-time heist. One wonders if they knew the Arizona territorial legislature made train robbery a hanging offense several years earlier. Sheriff Clint McCarty witnessed several hangings of train-robbing desperadoes."

Kirby looked around at his guests. Ryan, known to be a prolific storyteller, had their undivided attention.

"The robbers set a bonfire on the tracks to stop the train and uncouple the express car which usually had an armed messenger inside, especially when carrying payroll shipments. In those days, they randomly placed the express car in the boxcar lineup. As they hurried in the dark, the robbers mistakenly uncoupled the wrong cars and set about placing dynamite on what looked like the express car, intending to blow the locked door off its hinges. Meantime, the engineer, fireman and brakeman cleared the bonfire off the track and started the train rolling again, with the real express car in tow. Upon its arrival in Flagstaff, Sheriff Clint McCarty organized a posse to chase down the bandits. They reached the stranded railcars by the break of day. The train robbers' tracks went off in several directions. McCarty's posse split up, but the empty-handed bandits escaped."

"Folks, I don't have any spectacular stories to tell like most of you, but here's one of my favorite stage road memories," stated Roscoe Andrews.

"As a stagecoach driver, I often had four-in-hand, but on occasion, six-in-hand. Either way, perched high in my seat, I had a great view of teamwork. With four horses in harness, you wonder if the two at your feet are doing their fair share of pulling. Are they just going along for the ride? What about the two in the lead? They are frothing at the mouth, sweating profusely, and are running as fast as their legs can go. Are they pulling the entire coach? No, all four horses are pulling together. Sometimes I stopped, jumped down from my perch, and gave each horse a hug and an apple. When we got underway again, it just seemed like each team member took the job in stride! I think hugs and apples also apply throughout life."

Up to now, Jesse Parks, a retired banker living on a nearby ranch, sat quietly, engaging in little conversation. Now an old man, in fact, the oldest in the group, he decided to join the discussion.

"Folks, many of you do not know me very well but I want to thank Sabrina and Kirby for inviting me to this wonderful gathering. I had grubstaked many a canyon prospector, joined Buffalo Bill Cody's entourage when he visited the South Rim, and rode in Griggs' autocar in the Great Race to the Rim."

"Cody? I'm named after Buffalo Bill Cody," interjected young Cody Livingston.

"And a fine name it is, Cody. It's getting late and I'll be starting back soon but before I go, I think it is important to remember our own Old West legends—our canyon pioneers. I knew them all and I reckon you remember most of them too."

Sabrina interrupted with a great idea. "Let's name each pioneer but add one or two little-known facts about them as we go through the list. I'll start with Levi and Molly Jackson. Levi guided hundreds of Mormons on the Honeymoon Trail. After that, Kirby worked for Levi building the Jackson Trail and working some mines at river level."

Ryan added, "We all knew Clancy Jennings as quite a colorful character. My research confirms Clancy served in the Civil War. He never held the military rank of Captain although he loved to use the title. He enlisted in the Confederate Army, but enemy forces captured him. Ol'

Clancy spent nearly two years in Union prisons. He never talked about his war days."

Kirby took his turn. "We will never forget Buckey O'Neill. While I helped him build his log cabin on the rim, which is now part of the Starlight Lodge, Buckey told me he always wanted to be a journalist and in fact he started out in that profession, first working as a reporter for the *Tombstone Epitaph*, then as a court reporter in Prescott, then as editor of the *Prescott Journal-Miner*, and finally as owner of the stockman's journal *Hoof and Horn*.

"Speaking of log cabins, added Mark Warren, "Clint McCarty told me his old hotel in the Village used to be the Red Horse Station on the stage road. I'm sure Roscoe and Teresa are well-acquainted with that stage stop. Clint also told me the contractor for the Canyon Queen Hotel did not harvest ponderosa logs from canyon forests but instead imported them by rail from Oregon!"

"The mention of hotel building brings back great memories of Monte and Anna Bridgestone," said Mooney. "I was part of the team that built the Grand Canyon Hotel; well, I was just the camp cook, but I was there. During breaks Monte used to tell me how he and his brother were among the first prospectors to scour the carbonate fields outside the boom town of Quartzville in Gunnison County, Colorado. They mined silver, not copper, and one of the silver mines was actually named Flagstaff!"

"So far we have not mentioned Stuart Casey," added Jeremy. "He explored side canyons on both sides of the river." Dexter added, "Don't forget Slim Broadway, he was with him from the beginning and both died below the rim, Casey in a rockslide, Slim from a rattlesnake bite on the Tonto."

Heidi had the final word. "Like Ryan, I've done some research, mine on two Canadians who also became canyon pioneers. Did you know that Francois LaRue hailed from Quebec and Cole Campbell from Nova Scotia? Following his canyon mining days, Cole ramrodded development of Flagstaff's water system using a series of deep wells, storage tanks and piping networks. Francois, following his copper mining days, journeyed to Utah where he worked in the coal mines. There is a lot of mystery surrounding this wayward Canadian. I found one reference saying he was married to the daughter of Chief Spotted Tail, maternal uncle of Crazy Horse. But I have serious doubts about that. I also learned LaRue was married twice in Quebec, had a daughter with his first wife, and four sons with his second wife. He never talked about leaving a family behind in Canada."

"Well, that's a wild report on our French-Canadian friend," said Jesse. "And an intriguing conclusion to our tribute to our canyon legends and their place in historical collections and in our memories of Old West stories, whether true or not."

* * *

After their guests departed, Kirby and Sabrina relaxed on their veranda, gazing at the rising moon. "Kirby, sorry about not telling you about my uncomfortable encounter with Morton and Sykes. I should never have allowed myself to get into such a predicament."

"You sure surprised me. I remember asking how you managed to get across Doubtful Canyon," said Kirby, then with a slight grin he added, "I wonder what other surprises you have tucked away."

"I have two more! I attended President Teddy Roosevelt's famous address on the South Rim. No one recognized me in the crowd. Of course, hiding under my slouch hat helped some," confessed Sabrina.

"You were there? I was too! Okay, that's one secret. What's the other one?" asked Kirby.

"Later that same day, I stood ten feet from President Roosevelt as he listened to Clancy Jennings' spiel about beer-drinking burros at an old saloon on the rim. Did you know the very site we have selected for the Grand Canyon Pioneer Museum was once the site of the Road-to-Ruin Saloon? And guess who owned the burros? Lucas Randall!"

Kirby shook his head. "Sabrina, you never cease to amaze me. I missed the President's visit to Summit and did not know about his stop at Inspiration Point. More important, I missed running into you—twice!"

* * *

Kirby and Jeremy stood at the site of the abandoned Grand Canyon Hotel, watching the demolition work by the Park Service's contractor. "Jeremy, I'm glad Monte is not here to see the destruction of his pride and joy. He worked so hard to establish a tourist foothold here on the rim." Kirby pointed behind them. "I understand Monte's bungalow in the trees over there is also on the contractor's work list."

Jeremy reminded Kirby of another project at hand. "Now that your ankle is fully healed, we also have a job to do. Remember Monte's special request he made to you when reviewing the museum plans? We need to retrieve the winch on Windsong Mesa, the mine cart and a section of track from the upper tunnel, and some other mining equipment from inside the mine. It will be like hauling that copper block for the Chicago Fair."

Kirby agreed. "You are right, Jeremy; we cannot put this off any longer. It is obvious the Park Service is anxious to return the mesa and the rim to its original pristine condition. Let's get started before the government changes its mind about retrieving historical mining artifacts."

Kirby and Jeremy decided to start with the most difficult task, the Shooting Star ore cart. It had the farthest to go but its six-inch wheels could not roll on the trail's rough surface. Fortunately, Jeremy found the old Chicago Fair flatbed on Monte's old homestead. The ore cart's rectangular wood box, bolted to a steel frame, just fit on the flatbed. The men used Jeremy's strongest mule, Bernardo, to pull this piece of canyon mining history out of the tunnel, up the Redwall path to the mesa, then all the way up the Summit Trail. The hauling process required two weeks of intermittent hard labor, mostly by Bernardo.

"Kirby, we did it! That was the difficult part of capturing Monte's collection of mining equipment. Let's get some of the demolition crew to help load this on our wagon."

With the ore cart on the wagon, Kirby, Jeremy and Bernardo pulled the flatbed cart back down to the mine. The winch had a concrete base that needed to be chipped away from the mesa limestone. Once free, they lifted it onto the flatbed. Hauling this to the rim took only a few days. Kirby mentioned several times along the way how much Monte admired how easy the winch lifted bucket-loads of ore up the mineshaft. "The ore bucket!" Kirby just remembered they forgot to retrieve the ore bucket that rested at the bottom of the shaft.

"Jeremy, we need to go back in the mine for that heavy iron bucket. We should have done that after removing the ore cart."

"Kirby, relax, we can still get it. We'll just drop a heavy rope down the shaft. I'll go back down to the lower tunnel and tie the rope to the bucket, and Bernardo can pull it up to the surface."

With the bucket tied securely on the flatbed, Kirby, Jeremy and Bernardo made their third trip up the Summit Trail, a three-day grueling exercise with many breaks.

"Hello fellas! Surprise!" Sabrina jumped off her sitting rock and gave Kirby a hug. "What's this big pot?"

"It's not a pot, it's a bucket for hoisting copper ore up the Shooting Star mineshaft," answered Kirby. "It's part of our museum exhibit, and what are you doing here? I thought you were back at the ranch."

"I had some things I wanted to check at the museum site. Hello Jeremy. How's the family?"

"Doing well. I'm headed back to our place as soon as we con these demolition men into helping us load this piece of iron onto our wagon."

"Kirby, you know I've never been inside the Shooting Star Mine, or for that matter, any mine; how about a tour next time you go down?"

"That will be tomorrow, say mid-morning, if it's alright with Jeremy and Bernardo." He glanced over to his partner who nodded in the affirmative. "We still have a ten-foot section of track, a coil of winch cable, and some remaining pickaxes, shovels, and lanterns to recover. And I don't want to leave this loaded wagon here too much longer."

Sabrina had a question. "Kirby, where are we going to put all this stuff while the museum is under construction?"

"I've been thinking about that. To keep it secure maybe we should store it at the Circle K. Too risky leaving it at Monte's old homestead. I guess we could ask the Park Service about temporary storage but—" Sabrina interrupted.

"Let's decide when we come back tomorrow, but I think Monte would like it to stay in our hands," concluded Sabrina. "See you tomorrow, Jeremy."

"Kirby, while you were below the rim, I watched the contractor dismantle the second story of the old hotel. It's too bad she could not be salvaged but there's that big burned-out section."

"Yeah, I feel the same way. I reminded the foreman that Hearst promised us twenty medium-sized logs for use as vigas in the museum. I see a pile off to the side. At least we'll have saved part of the hotel."

Kirby stared at the operation for a few minutes then announced, "It's time to go."

* * *

Kirby and Sabrina met Jeremy and his mule at the Summit trailhead. After three hours trekking down the trail, they arrived on Windsong Mesa.

"Jeremy, if you could gather up a stretch of cable and lash it on Bernardo, then check the old cookhouse and shanties for anything of value to the museum, Sabrina and I will start down the east wall. Come join us in the upper tunnel where we'll be pulling up railroad spikes on a section of the track."

"See you in a while," answered Jeremy.

"So, Kirby this is your old water-hauling route down the Redwall. I remember watching you many times leading a string of burros down to the spring."

"Yes, I've traveled this path many times. We'll not be going all the way. We're coming up to a cutoff leading to the tunnel entrance and dump," explained Kirby. "But you can see Monte's Arrowhead Spring where I waited for you to show. You made my day when you caught me filling water barrels."

"You made my day too. Dump? What do you mean dump?"

"This is where the low-grade ore diggings were dumped over the side. We used the ore cart to haul the mine discards along the track and into the gulley. Here's a lantern we'll bring back with us. Let's see if it will light."

Kirby, with the lantern burning bright, guided Sabrina along the tunnel, into a large chamber, and beside a covered shaft. "Be careful here, these boards are old and the shaft is fifty feet deep. If you look up, you can see daylight."

"Hello up there," shouted Sabrina, "Jeremy can you hear us?"

"Yes, I'm coiling up about twenty feet of winch cable. See you soon."

"So, Sabrina, this is the part of the mine that produced the best ore, some as high as seventy percent copper and some pure metallic copper. The high-grade ore went up the bucket hoist. The useless rock went to the dump via these tracks. We have other tunnels and shafts but you are seeing the best part of the Shooting Star Mine."

"Kirby, is this the track we need to haul out of here?" She scanned the length as far as she could see in the dark tunnel.

"We're only after a ten-foot section at the entrance. If you would douse this lantern and set it aside, as it is going up with us, I'll start prying up these miniature railroad spikes."

"I'm sure the spikes will go with us to be used in new ties for the rails at the museum. See? I know a little bit about railroad tracks."

Kirby grinned, then grunted as a miner set on soundly securing the rails had pounded the spikes deep into the juniper ties. After the fourth tie, Jeremy arrived to take over. Kirby and Sabrina, hand-in-hand, walked out onto the dump to get another view of Arrowhead Spring.

"That fern-covered grotto is not only special to us, but special to Monte as well. He claims it was one of his favorite spots below the rim. He told me he often checked on it with his field glasses. He also confessed, to my great surprise, that he spotted us there on three separate occasions."

"What? He saw us there?" Utterly shocked, Sabrina added, "I thought we were completely out of sight. That was our secret meeting place! Now I'm guessing he already knew our romantic relationship was well underway."

"What are you two talking about?" Jeremy just finished pulling the tenth spike free and gathered the two rails.

"Oh, nothing, just commenting on this inner canyon view," responded Kirby.

"Okay you two lovebirds, we need to haul these rails up to where Bernardo is waiting. Sabrina, if you can carry the spikes and that lantern, Kirby and I can each carry a rail." The threesome started up the Redwall.

"Jeremy, where's Bernardo? I hope you tied him to a post."

"I did; that rascal has a habit of unhitching himself," admitted Jeremy. "And it looks like he did. Let's search the mesa for a mule with a coil of cable on his back. By the way, I found two pickaxes, a rusty shovel, and a lantern half-full of kerosene next to the cookhouse. Once we find Bernardo, we can pack up and be on our way. I'll call him; he'll come to me."

Kirby and Sabrina searched the northern portions of the mesa while Jeremy searched the southern end including part way up the trail. Two hours later he returned to where Kirby and Sabrina rested near the open shaft. They had returned an hour earlier.

"I found him! He decided to get an early start and was already a half-mile up the trail," explained Bernardo's owner. "Give me ten minutes and I'll help load him up with our mining equipment. It's going to be dark on the upper trail. Good thing we have two lanterns."

With two rails and mining tools strapped to his sides, Bernardo struggled to negotiate the sharp switchbacks. Kirby led the way with one lantern, Jeremy kept a tight hold on Bernardo's rein, and Sabrina brought up the rear with the other lantern. With fading light, they all stumbled a few times.

After five hours trudging, mostly in the dark, the entourage arrived at Summit Point. They built a campfire, unloaded Bernardo and placed their mining artifacts in the wagon. Kirby drew a canvas sheet from the wagon and spread it on a bed of ponderosa pine needles. The horses that he and Sabrina rode to Summit had small overnight bedrolls and saddlebags with antelope jerky, water and jackets. They watered their animals, threw some more wood on the fire, and retired for the evening.

* * *

Rudely awakened by the clatter of the demolition crew arriving at the hotel, Jeremy stood up and stretched. "Bernardo and I are headed out. I assume you two are headed for the ranch. Do you need help harnessing your horses to the wagon?"

"Thanks, Jeremy, we can manage. We'll be on our way soon too." Kirby wanted one more look at the demolition work before leaving.

Once on the road, Sabrina broached a subject she had put off discussing because it involved a bundle of papers Monte had given her. "Kirby, you know those papers we received from Monte? Until now, I've been unable to muster the courage to look into them. It brings back memories of our dear friend, but I think it's time to see what we have in our hands. I suspect we'll find the original homestead certificate and other papers Monte thought important to keep."

"Let's take a look when we get home," said Kirby. "Since the homestead is now abandoned, there may be questions about ownership."

After taking care of their horses and other ranch chores, Kirby and Sabrina untied Monte's papers and spread them out on the kitchen table. A last will and testament immediately caught their attention. Other papers included an affidavit by son Ben signing over his homestead to his father, Anna's death certificate, an operator's manual for Monte's

Hudson autocar, old bank statements, many mining claims, sales receipts for Summit properties, and a dozen prospecting journals.

"Kirby, look at this will. It shows you and I as beneficiaries of all Monte's assets, including real estate and personal property. I guess that means we have inherited his forest homestead. Monte should have told us about this."

"I recall Monte saying the homestead included one hundred and thirty-five acres and it butted right up to the Coconino National Forest fence line. Those officials may be chomping at the bit to annex the property. Since it is abandoned, they may already have taken custody." Sabrina sighed after that meandering assessment.

Kirby added, "I think we need to visit the Forest Supervisor's Office in Williams."

"Maybe not. Kirby, we don't really want the property, do we? If we try to donate it back to the government, they may want us to first remove all manmade facilities, return the land to its natural state, and even pay for survey and legal fees. Instead of visiting the Forest Supervisor, maybe we should visit Jesse Parks for advice."

"Sabrina, the next time we are in Flagstaff, let's stop by the County Recorder's Office and see how the property is listed. You know your way around in county records. You could determine if the homestead ever got recorded in Monte's name."

"That's definitely the first thing we should do, Kirby, before we get the Forest Service stirred up." With no rush to take any other action, Sabrina breathed a sigh of relief. She added, "Besides, it is time to get back on our museum project."

A few days after their return from Summit, Teresa and Tomas stopped by for a brief visit. Tomas, a park geologist, had a few days off from his job at the geology museum. Kirby took advantage of their social call and solicited Tomas' help in unloading the wagon and moving the mining equipment into a spare barn stall.

Chapter Three

MUSEUMS AND BRIDGES

Tenuous steel threads tensioned to the breaking point

Kirby and Sabrina drove their Roadster to the South Rim to meet with Park Service officials, including Ranger Tomas Garcia, at Inspiration Point. "Kirby, the living memories of Uncle Monte are so great, I don't think of him as having passed away. He is still with us in spirit."

"He certainly is, and once built, the Grand Canyon Pioneer Museum will transport visitors to a bygone frontier, tugging at their hearts and touching their soul."

They arrived early and found Tomas waiting in the parking lot. "Good morning, O'Briens! I hoped you would arrive early; there has been a development. Some senior managers are having second thoughts about two museums in the same general location."

"What!? That can't be! At the groundbreaking ceremony, even the superintendent was excited about locating the Pioneer Museum near your Geology Museum. We even had preliminary approval of the architectural drawings!" exclaimed Sabrina.

"It's not your design, it's a matter of congestion, sharing one parking lot, and fitting into the park's mission," explained Tomas. "Here comes Chief Ranger Roland Hawley."

"Hello Chief, let me introduce you to Kirby and Sabrina O'Brien. They are the benefactors for the proposed Pioneer Museum."

"Pleased to meet you. I've studied your site plan and your design. It's a good thing your surveyor is on hold because we're thinking about changing the museum location to a different site. It has nothing to do with the rodman's death here but we can offer a couple sites in the Village, back a safe distance from the rim."

Kirby countered, "But Chief, we made a promise to the late Monte Bridgestone. You heard his passionate speech at the ceremony. He was excited about representing all the canyon pioneers. It was especially important to him that the museum be on the rim, more importantly right here on Inspiration Point, with commanding views of Angel's Gate and the Navajo Palisades, and even a teasing glimpse of the river!"

"Well, you are going to have to convince my boss. It's not that we do not appreciate your generosity in privately financing construction of the museum; it's the concern for tourist congestion and having co-located museums with conflicting missions," explained the chief.

"Conflicting missions?" blurted Sabrina. "They both serve Grand Canyon. One educates visitors about the oldest rocks on the planet and the other honors the pioneers who helped open the Canyon so visitors could experience those rocks first-hand." Sabrina continued, "Our architect is waiting for your final approval of the design, our surveyor is ready to get back to work, and I'll soon have a building contractor needing a construction permit."

Tomas added, "Sir, I think the two museums will feed off each other. The shared parking lot facilitates visits to both museums. We have a rare opportunity here—a canyon pioneer in her own right willing to privately finance this project. It would be a shame if her dream to honor Monte and his fellow pioneers went unfulfilled. Both facilities, albeit three hundred feet apart, deserve a front row seat on the rim."

Chief Hawley stood gazing at the Canyon, trying to imagine the two buildings among the pinyons and junipers. "I will discuss the matter with the superintendent and he will get back to you in a few days." With that terse statement, the chief left the premises.

"How do you think this will turn out, Tomas? Do you think the project will be allowed to go forward?" asked Kirby.

Before he could answer, Sabrina thanked Tomas for his support. "This is the perfect place for the new museum, not tucked away from the rim, off the tourists' beaten path. All we can do now is wait for the superintendent's decision."

As the O'Briens turned to leave, Kirby had a thought. "Sabrina, something else must be going on here. You have a solid plan but there must be another issue that is troubling park management." Kirby shook his head in disgust. "What could it be?"

* * *

The superintendent got back to Sabrina in a few weeks, not a few days. He called for a meeting to review the whole museum concept. By then, three feet of snow buried the South Rim. It would not be until Spring when survey work could be resumed. But the winter months provided an opportunity to nail down the location, foundation details and utility connections, while also fine-tuning the architect's design. When the roads became passable, the Park Service scheduled a meeting, facilitated by Tomas.

As the couple pulled into Park Headquarters in the Village, Kirby had a revelation. "Sabrina! I think I know what is behind the Park Service's hesitancy in allowing us to proceed with museum construction!"

"What's that, Kirby?"

"Clint McCarty! He is not a canyon pioneer held in high regard by the Park Service. I remember Monte and Clint in many heated arguments about Clint's quest to control development of the entire Canyon. And his anti-Park stance is well known."

"Maybe we can change the superintendent's mind by emphasizing the good things Clint did for Arizona and the Grand Canyon."

As they stamped their feet, the superintendent's secretary met them at the door. "Good morning Mr. and Mrs. O'Brien, can we get you a cup of coffee?"

"Yes, thank you. It's a cold morning."

"I agree," stated the superintendent at his office door. "Sorry for taking so long to get back to you. I have studied your architect's plans and can give you my final approval. And I agree the two museums can co-exist at Inspiration Point. I was not as opposed as I let on. However, I still have a problem. I have read Monte's book, including Clint McCarty's foreword."

Kirby glanced over at Sabrina and nodded. Just then the secretary arrived with three cups of coffee on a tray.

The superintendent took his cup and looked directly at Sabrina. "I take exception to a statement McCarty made here." He pointed to the sentence and read it. 'Like all of us pioneers, we cherished the Grand Canyon and took care not to do her too much harm.' That is far from the truth. You must know he was a real thorn in our side for years, and before us, the Forest Service. McCarty claimed thousands of acres of Grand Canyon for himself. He manipulated our national mining laws for personal gain, essentially blanketing choice geography with claims for purposes other than mining."

Sabrina knew she had done nothing wrong but felt the kind of foreboding that comes before a stern lecture.

"McCarty was, correction, is a devious man. He constantly battled rangers and government agents. He wanted to dam the river and supported funding for test borings at potential dam sites! He opposed Grand Canyon National Park from the very beginning and carried a personal vendetta to oust our first National Park Service director! One year, as a Senator in Washington City, he succeeded in deleting all funding for this park from the Interior Department's appropriation bill!"

"What? McCarty did all that? I had no idea," stammered Sabrina.

"So, Mrs. O'Brien, I am going to approve your Pioneer Museum with the condition that it contain no reference to Clint McCarty, no photographs, no personal artifacts, no writings, no listing on placards."

"But sir, Clint McCarty helped build trails, expose mineral resources, encourage tourism—" The superintendent cut her off. "This is my final word. Now, you can proceed with your survey, hire your contractor, and build the Grand Canyon Pioneer Museum. And thank you ma'am for your support and understanding. We look forward to the ribbon-cutting."

Kirby and Sabrina left the building, both pleased and perplexed. "Kirby, how can we leave out one of the key pioneers? Clint was Monte's partner for decades."

"Sabrina, don't forget they had major falling outs over the same issues the superintendent just reiterated. Maybe he'll have a change of heart or maybe the situation will change under a future park administration. The important thing is we have permission to move the project forward, and in our originally planned location!" concluded Kirby.

"That meeting was so intense I didn't touch my coffee," said Sabrina.

"I didn't either," returned Kirby.

They walked along the rim, in fact, to the exact spot where the Road-to-Ruin Saloon once stood. Below their feet, snow still lay tucked in shaded places; a solid blanket of white masked the North Rim. They breathed in the solitude and quiet of this immense spectacle.

"Sabrina, look at this breathtaking canyon. It would take two lifetimes to take it all in," announced Kirby, squeezing her hand. Sabrina added her own clever line. "We are two lifetimes."

Kirby changed the subject. "While Teddy Roosevelt admonished the thought of seeing the works of man's heavy hand in the Canyon, if you look closely, there is a sliver of the river showing between canyon walls." He pointed to a recently constructed manmade structure. "I'm talking about that swinging suspension bridge that replaced the rickety cable car crossing."

The Park Service erected the bridge in the same location as the old cableway and designed it to support mules and pedestrians. Finally, a safe structure bridged the Canyon, forming a much-needed connection between the South and North Rims, and more importantly a river crossing to access Trails West's Dancing Ghost Ranch on Skeleton Creek. And it will be visible from a stone terrace on the north side of the future Grand Canyon Pioneer Museum.

"Kirby, the last few months have been so nerve-wracking that I think a vacation is in order. Let's go down there. Let's cross that ol' bridge and stay a few nights at that dude ranch. I've never been there. It would be a nice break after these tense times."

"Believe it or not, I've never been there either. We can ask Jeremy to mind the ranch for a week or so, and head for the inner canyon. It's been years since you and I relaxed at river level." Memories of their first time together in the sand dunes at Whiskey Rapids raced through Kirby's mind.

* * *

Chief Ranger Hawley burst into the superintendent's office. "Sir, I just received a report from the field that two support cables snapped on the downstream side of the swinging suspension bridge! Also, a few hanger rods broke loose and some floor planks buckled. A string of five heavily loaded pack mules were northbound while strong gusts spiraled down the inner gorge."

"That bridge is rated for only one mule crossing at a time! Any injuries or losses?"

"No sir. But the wrangler has asked Trails West for a few days off. Repairs are already underway. It will take five or six days to string new cables and replace some rods and planks."

"Very well, keep me informed. I've never trusted that frail bridge. Post a notice about it being limited to single mule crossings. My predecessor told me that bridge has been known to capsize in high winds. We may need to replace it someday."

* * *

Jeremy and Rachel agreed to manage the Circle K for a week while the O'Briens vacationed at the Dancing Ghost Ranch. They journeyed to the Village and rented two saddle horses at the Pioneer trailhead.

"Kirby, I can't recall if we've ever traveled this trail together, in fact, I can't remember the last time I went down by myself. Obviously, it's been many years."

"It's been years for me too. Here's my plan. We'll take the Pioneer Trail down to Canyon Gardens, take a short break there to water our horses, then continue down to the river where we'll travel east on the newly-constructed River Trail to the bridge. Just crossing on the suspension bridge will be a new experience for both of us."

Along the whole route, Kirby noticed a pack train following them. "Sabrina, there's a wrangler with a string of ten mules slowly closing from behind."

"I've noticed the mule train too and I see the spring runoff has begun. Look at that river; it's running high and wild!" Sabrina felt some trepidation as the bridge came in view. "Kirby, just how safe is a suspension bridge? I'm worried about these horses being spooked. I hope the walkway is sturdy and solid."

"We'll soon find out. We need to time our crossing well ahead of the pack train so our combined weight does not overload the cable suspension system." Kirby's voice carried a touch of apprehension as the bridge came into sight.

"When we passed opposite Skeleton Creek Canyon five minutes ago, I could not see the dude ranch. I guess it is tucked up in the canyon some distance. But now I see the bridge! Looks rather flimsy!" remarked Sabrina.

Kirby, noting a touch of the same apprehension in Sabrina's voice, observed, "That wrangler and his string of heavily loaded mules is right behind us. I think we should let him pass. We're in no hurry but he sure seems to be."

"I agree. Let's see how his mules handle the crossing. They have probably done this many times before," remarked Sabrina.

Kirby and Sabrina guided their mounts to a wide section on the River Trail, with a great view of the bridge.

"Good day, folks. Appreciate you letting my mule train cross over first. We're running rather late today." The wrangler kept his mules going at a steady pace, encouraging them with words only mules understood.

Sabrina scanned the heavy packs as they went by. To her, every mule seemed grossly overloaded. Their bulky leather side bags squeaked with every step and the belly straps seemed to squeeze the mules without mercy. She never loaded her mules to that extreme. Sabrina also noted each mule had a bridle and bit, with a three-foot rope from the bit to a strap on the rear of the mule ahead. She wondered if one mule fell, would it take the whole train down. She watched with great anxiety as the mule train entered the bridge.

"My word, Kirby, look at the plank walkway bounce! The mules are setting up some sort of wave action!"

"I see that," said Kirby, "And the mules are forcing the entire walkway into a series of waves; you can see them roll along the bridge planks with each mule that steps aboard; on top of that, the wave action seems to grow as it rolls to the north terminal."

The creaking of boards and the humming vibration of overstressed cables panicked the lead mules which tried to squeeze past the wrangler's mule. The twangs of snapping cables, tenuous steel threads tensioned to the breaking point, spelled disaster for the bridge. Kirby and Sabrina witnessed a horrifying scene—the total failure of the suspension bridge. So many cables snapped that the bridge dumped the wrangler and his entire string of mules into the roiling Colorado. A seventy-foot plunge into ice-cold water.

Three mules in the string, still tied together, broke out of their bridles and managed to scramble onto Skeleton Creek's delta but the rest, including the wrangler, who minutes earlier wished them a good day, drifted downstream. Kirby and Sabrina stood helpless on the trail about eighty feet above the water, unable to rescue the thrashing mules, unable to inform authorities, unable to get anyone's attention on the north side of the river.

The O'Briens, with their vacation plans abruptly cancelled, had no recourse but to return to the Village and report the terrible accident to Chief Ranger Hawley.

Kirby's good friend, Mark Warren, conducting an inspection of the area around Francois LaRue's old river camp for the Park Service, looked up to see a mule wrangler, his mule, and several tangled pack mules flailing in the rapids. "Help, mister, help!"

Mark, without taking time to don his cork life jacket, jumped into his flat-bottomed scow and rowed with all his might to rescue the ill-fated wrangler. His boat surged and bucked, plowing through waves of frothing, cold, brown water, then slammed broadside into a midstream boulder. Before he could gain control, it capsized and broke apart on the rocks. Mark tried to swim ashore but the current pulled him under. He bobbed up in the center of the channel, sputtering and gasping for air. By now the unidentified wrangler and his mules with their water-logged packs had drifted around the bend. His energy near spent, Mark too disappeared around the bend.

Mark had made many successful river crossings and short downstream runs over the years. At Casey Crossing, he often ferried supplies and grub across the river using canvas boats to reach the north side and the asbestos mines on high bluffs. He worked at the Shooting Star Mine, including driving pack trains up and down the Summit Trail, and he served on Monte's crew building the Grand Canyon Hotel near Summit Point. But on this day, the thundering river swallowed Mark Warren.

* * *

When Kirby reported the collapse of the suspension bridge, he learned about another pioneer museum delay, this one by Washington City bureaucrats who balked about private funding. Apparently, they read about Sabrina's generosity in the superintendent's monthly report and felt totally uncomfortable about accepting funds not appropriated by Congress.

Sabrina, both furious and disheartened, stormed into the Chief Ranger's office. "Hawley, we had an agreement! We both know it could be years until the Park Service budget included a line item for museum design and construction! I'm willing to finance the entire project now and assure it will meet your specifications. I respectfully request that you convey this assurance to your colleagues in Washington swivel chairs."

"Ma'am, I will ask the superintendent to persuade his superiors that we need to proceed with construction. Spring weather is here and the time for construction is upon us. As an aside, the Park Service will now be seeking emergency congressional funding approval for a new steel bridge across the river. That should be the concern in Washington City, not turning down offers for private funding of projects."

"I most certainly agree, sir."

"In addition, Sabrina let me thank you and Kirby again for your eyewitness report of the tragic bridge failure. The information will be very useful to the designers of the next bridge."

Sabrina left the office feeling much better about her museum project and pleased to learn Park officials planned to erect a rigid steel bridge where the old suspension bridge collapsed.

* * *

Inspiration for the architect's museum design dates back eight hundred years when the Anasazi built vibrant settlements in canyon country. Their buildings included thick walls of irregularly shaped limestone, flat roofs supported by vigas or log rafters, and small windows. The Spanish architecture of the Southwest also influenced the designer. Kirby vowed to help Sabrina navigate the continuing Federal bureaucracy, even if he needed to oversee the museum's development himself.

One mild spring day, Sabrina invited Teresa and Tomas Garcia to the Circle K ranch. She had an ulterior motive: entice Teresa to run the future museum's gift shop. She also wanted to show the final plans to someone other than the Park Service, even though Tomas worked as the resident geologist in the adjacent Geology Museum.

"Here they are, Kirby. The Garcias of Grand Canyon Village have arrived."

"Welcome back to the Circle K, Teresa and Tomas. Please come in. Would you like a root beer soda? Kirby bought a case in Flagstaff last week."

"Yes, Sabrina, Tomas and I would both enjoy a bottle."

"How's the Pioneer Museum coming along?" asked Tomas.

Kirby had a quick answer. "Sabrina is anxious to show you the plans. As you know, she has final approval from the Park Service now. The surveyor will complete his work next week and we'll soon be soliciting contractor bids for construction."

Sabrina spread the architect's drawings on the dining room table. "As you can see from this site plan, the building will be perched on the very edge of the Canyon, just like your geology museum, Tomas. It will share the parking lot and have a large stone terrace with heavy oak benches on the west side and rock-lined walkways in front. On permanent display will be a stagecoach, a Studebaker wagon, an ore cart on a section of track, a reconstructed rock monument with a mining claim visible inside, and more oak benches."

"Very impressive, Sabrina," commented Tomas.

"Now for the building construction itself. It will be designed to blend into the surroundings. It will honor the first inhabitants of this hallowed place. I'm referring to the Anasazi cliff dwellings built with irregular-shaped native limestone and the flat-roof, pueblo-style buildings typical throughout the Southwest. There will be high, small windows on the south side for some natural light. This type of architecture uses ponderosa vigas which Kirby salvaged from the Grand Canyon Hotel fire. The vigas will penetrate the rock walls. And the exterior doors, with wrought-iron hinges and handles, will be crafted from heavy oak." Sabrina paused to catch her breath.

"I like the idea of honoring the Anasazi and their canyon homeland," added Teresa. "They spent their lives here and it is said their spirit remains a part of the rocks, the sky and the river. After all, a place where people once thrived and survived is never said to be abandoned; the spirit of these canyon ancestors remains centered here forever."

Kirby took over and explained that the interior includes separate rooms for mining, trail-building and tourism, plus a great room with ponderosa log pillars and vigas visible in the ceiling.

"Before I describe the mining room, allow me to point out a very special feature, similar to what you have, Tomas, in the Geology Museum," said Kirby, "And that is five giant, tempered-glass windows on the canyon side of the great room for stunning panoramic views."

"Now for the mining room," said Kirby. This will feature an ore bucket, mining tools, including pickaxes, shovels and wheelbarrow, and even a winch with some hoisting cable. We looked for the Shooting Star Mine's gasoline-powered blower but it has vanished. There will be ore sacks filled to the brim with colorful copper ore, kerosene lanterns, empty giant powder crates, and wall exhibits showing assay reports, mining claims, and underground plan and profile maps of the Shooting Star Mine. If we can find an old canvas boat, we'll add that to the exhibit because many canyon prospectors and miners used these craft to cross the river."

"Kirby, let's go back to the great room. Part of it will be devoted to a photograph gallery and gift shop. There will be a sales counter with a mechanical cash register and shelves with stacks of our *Monte*

Bridgestone – Pioneer of the Grand Canyon book, as well as picture postcards and folded trail maps." Sabrina looked directly at Teresa. "I'm hoping I can convince the Park Service to hire you, Teresa, as the gift shop manager."

"I'd be honored to work in the Pioneer Museum. I accept if they will have me," said Teresa. "Tomas, we could be working side-by-side in the two Grand Canyon museums!"

Sabrina turned to Kirby. "You are the trail-builder here. Would you go over the part of the museum dedicated to trail-building?" She proudly added, "Kirby here helped Levi build the Jackson Trail, helped Clint build the Pioneer Trail, and helped Monte build the Summit Trail."

"Of course, this is my favorite part of the museum. It will feature tools like drills, jacks, rod-and-feathers for splitting rock, miner's spoons for loading powder holes, and even a few empty powder kegs. There will be a few juniper logs used for shoring, and iron rods, some with heads for pounding, some with eyes for threading cables."

Teresa just remembered she and Sabrina were going to plan a trail ride. "I have not been below the rim yet but Kirby, I appreciate all your hard work in blazing a way for canyon fans to venture below and experience the Grand Canyon from what must be a totally different perspective. Sabrina, I am looking forward to my first trail ride."

"Now that we are past winter, Sabrina, let's plan that trip," said Teresa. "And Kirby, looking at these drawings, I see there is another part of the museum devoted to tourism, partially made possible by the trails you helped build." That observation set the stage for a tourism discussion.

"Thanks for that lead-in, Teresa. What you are looking at here are reminders of early tourism here at the Canyon. This section will display canteens, knapsacks, walking sticks, binoculars, stage schedules and rates, hotel signs with room rates, and livery signs for saddle horse rentals and carriage rides. There will be stalactites and stalagmites from the Windsong caves and a collection of water barrels, items of which I am intimately familiar, that were used for hauling drinking water from Arrowhead Spring to the Grand Canyon Hotel. This was the hotel's only water source. Village hotels had water delivered by rail."

Kirby continued. "Sabrina and I had an idea of including some relics from some of Clancy Jennings' tourist tales. They are certainly part of the lure and lore of the Canyon. We're thinking about battered pans and rusty rifle parts, even bullet holes in a tree trunk and a scattering of empty Twin Oaks whiskey bottles. That plan is still in the development stage."

"Kirby, we haven't mentioned the interior décor but to promote an Old West theme that visitors expect, there will be bighorn sheep horns, deer and antelope antlers, and Navajo rugs. Also mounted on the walls will be historic photographs showing mining operations, different views of canyon trails, hotel complexes, and the pioneers who opened the Canyon for others to see and experience. My all-time favorite photograph is one of Monte and President Teddy Roosevelt having lunch in the Grand Canyon Hotel dining room."

Sabrina continued, "Below the Grand Canyon Pioneer Museum sign there will be another sign with the museum motto 'Explore. Dream. Discover.' Maybe in the vestibule, another sign 'To all who enter, that they may know something of the life and times of the early canyon pioneers'. I haven't decided yet how we will honor our pioneers by name; perhaps a copper plaque dedicating the museum to Levi, Monte, Clancy, Francois, Casey, Buckey, Clint, Cole and Slim."

"Whoa! Sabrina. Remember what the park superintendent said about Clint McCarty. There is to be no mention of him in the museum."

"If that was just a personal feeling expressed by the current superintendent, don't worry," said Tomas. "I heard he is to be reassigned to Washington City soon. The Park Service rotates these prestigious management positions every few years."

* * *

So far, Grand Canyon National Park's experience with river crossings has not gone well. The privately-owned cableway lasted ten years but the Park Service's first single-span suspension bridge lasted only seven years. It obviously lacked structural rigidity and the load capacity to carry continuous mule trains. Running one or two mules across at a time seemed safer.

As an eyewitness to the recent bridge collapse, Kirby frequently responded to Park Engineer Steven Baxter's requests to observe the design of a four-hundred-foot replacement bridge. For this new bridge project, the Park Service planned to combine the attributes of suspension cables with riveted steel. The engineer had an approved budget of fifty-two thousand dollars for design and construction. The plan called for locating the new bridge in the same spot as the old cableway and the swinging suspension bridge.

"Come on in Kirby; take a look at what we are planning here."

"Mr. Baxter, you know I do not have an engineering background. I know mining and I know trail-building, but nothing about structural steel or long suspension cables. But I do know mules and horses and I have some suggestions for the wooden walkway, as well as the approaches at the two terminals."

"Great, Kirby, but I'm not at that point in the design yet," said the engineer as he smoothed out an overall drawing of the bridge. "By the way, I understand you are going to monitor the Pioneer Museum construction. Let me know if I can help at all. Later, as Park Engineer, I may be called to do a final inspection before the Park Service accepts the building for occupancy."

"Thank you, Steve. When we get to reviewing the bridge construction phase, I will also have some ideas for you on how to get materials from the South Rim to the bridge site."

"Okay, Kirby, here you see the bridge spanning the river, the two terminals and an array of cables anchored to rock walls and supporting the riveted steel framework. I think you saw the walls suffer whip-lash when the cables snapped on the first bridge."

"I did, Steve; it was a frightful sight and happened so suddenly. How will this long steel structure come together?"

Steve pointed to forty ten-foot sections. "These are riveted together along the entire length of the bridge. You say you know mules and trails. Do you think mules can carry ten-foot pieces of steel around trail switchbacks and under rock overhangs?"

Kirby had an answer. "That was one of my construction phase ideas. Use mules to carry tons of pieces down the Pioneer and River Trails into the inner gorge. You certainly can't use boats to haul bridge parts. It's primarily a mule bridge. Let's have mules help build it! And they work cheap. Just feed them hay and water, and you'll get a full day's work out of each mule."

"Okay, that's the plan. What do you suggest for transporting four five-hundred-foot cables to the bridge site? Each one weighs a ton." Steve had been struggling with this challenge for quite some time.

"I have many Havasupai and Navajo connections and can help assemble a large work party. You'll need to hire, let's say forty tribal members, and space them every fifteen feet along the cable. Of course, they need to work in unison, all lifting at the same time, all resting at the same time. This way, with each team member shouldering his share of the load, the cables can be snaked down the trails to the construction site."

"Perfect, that should work, Kirby. You are starting to think like an engineer."

"Steve, I'm looking at your bridge floor, the walkway of horizontal cross-planks. Just before the old bridge collapsed, I saw these roll along the bridge like a series of waves. The wrangler and his mule string rode these waves like a boat shooting rapids. To further strengthen the walkway, I might suggest running a plank tread longitudinally along the length of the bridge. It will further stiffen the overall structure and it will be easier on the feet of mules and horses."

"Another great idea, Kirby. You are a big help. I'm sorry you and Sabrina had to witness that tragedy but you being in the right place at the right time is greatly benefiting this new design. We're jumping around a bit but what are your ideas for the north and south terminals?"

"Okay, these ideas may add some additional cost to the project. The north terminal, as you can see on your site plan, is right up against the vertical rock wall, with no place to go. I suggest excavating an immediate turn on the upstream side in a descending curve around and under the bridge to link up with the short pathway to the dude ranch. The south terminal will not be as easy. While watching the mules before the accident, I worried about how a rockslide could decimate the south end of the bridge and any pedestrians or mule riders who might be in the way of falling debris. To get around that hazard, I suggest tunneling through that rock buttress. Make it straight in line with the bridge. It would be the connection between the River Trail and the new bridge. Those are my long-winded ideas." Kirby felt he had just made some valuable suggestions to the bridge design.

"Kirby, I should make you my assistant engineer. You've got some great ideas and I'll consider them all. Thank you."

"Steve, I have a ranch to run and a museum to get built. No time for an assistant engineer job, but I'd like to continue stopping by your office from time to time. I just might dream up some more projects for you to pursue. Park visitation is on the rise, and you may need more facilities to meet demands, more buildings, more utilities, more roads and trails, and maybe even a second bridge across the river!"

Chapter Four

RETURN OF A PIONEERING WOMAN

Exploring narrow paths widens one's perspective

Kirby and Sabrina visited the Pioneer Cemetery to pay their respects at the Bridgestone family plot, where Monte, Ben and Anna rest in peace. Kirby had written a tribute to Monte that he wanted to read aloud, even though it was only the two of them standing graveside.

"No canyon pioneer more exemplifies the American pioneering spirit on the South Rim than Monte Bridgestone. He was a man poor in material things but rich in ideas, adventure, tenacity, and courage. He saw failures as opportunities: shallow copper showings on Windsong Mesa meant dig deeper; tragedy meant rethinking safety strategies; low lodging numbers meant a chance to make the stay more intriguing. For Monte, failure never meant surrender. He always persevered in the face of adversity."

"That was very touching, Kirby. I'm tempted to add another copper plate to his headstone but there's just not enough room for your special tribute. Today, we also pay tribute to Anna who stood by Monte's side through good times and bad, and to his son, Ben, with whom they had so very little time together."

"While we're here, Sabrina, there are two other pioneers to whom we should pay our respects. One I think you encountered on several occasions, both on the rim and below the rim, and that is the venerable Clancy Jennings. He was a prospector and trail guide, but above all, a storyteller. Notice his headstone and footstone are nearly ten feet apart to accommodate his tall tales. The other canyon pioneer is Stuart Casey.

He suffered an agonizing death in a rockslide while prospecting alone and was first buried at the head of the Pioneer Trail, then later moved here."

"I don't think I ever met Casey, but I've heard about the good things he did for Arizona as a territorial legislator and about his contributions to the development of the canyon's mineral resources as president of the Grand Canyon Mining District." Sabrina then commented, "It is so fitting that he now rests in peace here on the South Rim."

"Where is Levi Jackson?"

"Not here; he is buried in a Mormon cemetery in Taylor, southeast of Winslow."

* * *

The day had come for Sabrina and Teresa to venture into the Canyon. It would be Teresa's first time over the edge. Sabrina wanted to get an early start, hoping to beat Trails West's popular mule trains. Before they arrived at the Pioneer trailhead, two strings of saddled mules had already trod from the mule barn to the corral where wranglers matched dudes with mules. As they passed the corral, Sabrina overheard a middle-aged father discussing with another about putting his wayward teenage son on a mule. "I just told him, don't come back until you make something of yourself."

"Did you hear that, Teresa? Quite a send-off for a young dude."

"I did and assumed he was joshing. I'm paying attention more to how Hank will take to a descent into the Canyon," stuttered Teresa, her voice trembling like a juniper in the wind.

"Just follow Serendipity's lead. She has more horse sense than any of those mules headed down the trail. One thing you need to know; mule trains have the right-of-way over hikers and backpackers on these trails, and the mules have a habit of leaving a mess in the same place on every trip. I was planning an earlier start to avoid the crowd—and fresh messes—but it seems we're all headed down at the same time. I wonder if your Hank will follow suit."

The ladies pulled off to a flat overlook to let the first mule string pass. They watched as each mule clattered over loose gravel, waterbag slung over saddle horn, each dude with one hand holding the reins, the other with a death grip on the horn, and the stiff leather chafing their backsides. Hank followed Serendipity with ease and no sign of being skittish between two mule trains.

"Teresa, we're coming to a place where wranglers always halt their mule trains and cinch-up every saddle. This is our chance to get ahead of the pack."

"Great, Sabrina; Hank and I are getting used to the switchbacks and rock overhangs. Quite different than riding across sagebrush or through forests. You know, exploring narrow paths widens one's perspective. Let's put some distance between those mule trains."

They stopped briefly at McCarty's Canyon Gardens camp where a small creek trickled along a tortuous path to the river. Sabrina noticed several mining claim markers in the area. As they mounted up, the mule train caught up to them.

"Teresa, I'm rather certain that these mule strings are headed for the river but the suspension bridge is out so I guess they just want to see the mighty Colorado as they ride along the new River Trail. Once the new bridge is built, Trails West's Dancing Ghost Ranch will be their destination. I suggest we take a short diversion across the Tonto to a place with a stunning view of the inner gorge. It's known as Plateau Point."

"Sounds good to me and I'm sure ol' Hank here will enjoy the level terrain of a plateau."

"Kirby and I have been to the point several times. You'll be impressed. First, you can see a stand of isolated boulders along the path ahead. Kirby tells me this is where Slim Broadway was fatally bitten by a rattlesnake. They were journeying on foot. Slim died within minutes of the strike. Among all his prospecting and mining exploits, Slim helped build the Pioneer Trail we've been traveling; in fact, he named it!"

"I never met Slim but I understand he was a canyon pioneer in his own right," commented Teresa, adding, "I hear a roaring sound ahead, like a noisy gasoline engine; do you see anything?"

"Teresa, I believe that is a biplane! I've heard of them but never seen one before. He's dropping into the gorge. Like the ravens and turkey vultures, he's probably getting a spectacular view. Let's get out to the point."

"What a view of the Colorado River! I've only had glimpses of it from the Canyon's East Rim. And look, that plane is contouring along the river, maybe only a hundred feet above the rapids. Sabrina, I know you brought me out here for a special look into the gorge, but seeing our first plane is also very special."

The biplane disappeared around a bend in the river and Plateau Point returned to its quiet, sublime mood, except for the dull roar of Bighorn Rapids to the west. The women dismounted and sat marveling at the ancient black walls, with vertical bands of pink and gray, keeping the river constrained on its downstream rush.

"Teresa, those black rocks had me fooled for years. And I was not alone. Their sparkling teased every prospector into thinking they contained gold or silver. We eventually learned the flecks were mica, not gold. We called them black diamonds!"

"I can't see any diamonds from here, but the magnitude and sheer splendor of the inner gorge are most impressive. Sabrina, this is a view of Grand Canyon that every visitor should experience."

"I agree, as long as the visit is on foot, horse or mule. There's some talk about building a cableway from the rim to this point at the top of the gorge. That would be a travesty. I hope the idea is quashed before anyone puts pencil to paper. Now it's time to backtrack to the Pioneer Trail and resume our descent, that is, after watering our livestock at Canyon Gardens."

The next stretch of the Pioneer trail featured a series of steep corkscrew turns. Here one of the mule trains, probably the second, caught up to them. Sabrina motioned for the string of mule-riding dudes to pass. The wrangler nodded and continued to guide his party down the trail. The women watched the mules carefully stepping around rocks and teasing their riders by nibbing a leafy bush just over the edge. Suddenly a chorus of shrieks and screams rose from the mule train.

"Teresa, something has spooked the second mule, probably a rattlesnake. The mule bucked that young lady out of her saddle and stirrups and then rolled on top of her!" Sabrina and the wrangler quickly dismounted. The thousand-pound mule rolled down past the switchback and landed on his feet at the next level. The other dudes and damsels watched in horror.

The wrangler, petrified that anything could spook his time-tested mules, stood stone-still as a pink rattlesnake slithered into some bushes. Sabrina and Teresa tended to the damsel in distress, now holding her right arm and writhing in pain. A quick look by Teresa, who had witnessed many broken bones in her stagecoach-driving days, and she knew immediately the young woman broke her arm.

"What's your name?" asked Teresa, while the wrangler checked his mule for injuries.

"Bridget, Bridget Hamilton. Agh! I think, agh! I think my arm is broken."

"You are right, in fact, in two places. I can immobilize it with an agave stalk and some twine in my saddle."

Sabrina cautioned, "Stay calm, Bridget, we're here to help. Is there anyone else with you on this trip?"

"No, I'm, agh, traveling alone."

Yelling down to the wrangler, Sabrina asked, "How's the mule?"

"Jumpy is okay!"

"His rider is not. Her arm's broken and she has some nasty scrapes and bruises. I have an idea. We were on the way to the river like you. My horse is used to trailing a mule on backcountry trails. If we can get Bridget back in the saddle, Teresa and I will guide her back up to the rim." Sabrina then turned to Teresa. "We can complete our venture into the canyon depths another day. The Six-Gun Creek confluence and the raging river can wait. Let's get this young lady to the park clinic."

The wrangler, most grateful, asked Sabrina to apprise the mule barn manager of the accident. He would follow up with a detailed report. He helped Bridget back up into the saddle, then continued guiding his mule train down the Pioneer Trail, almost as if this dude injury is a common occurrence and getting his mule train to the river is far more important.

"Hey wait, who should I say will be filing a report?"

"Arnie Turner, the wrangler for today's second mule string. Thanks for all your help." Sabrina wondered how he would have handled the situation if she and Teresa were not there.

"Bridget, this is important. Hang on to the saddle horn with your left hand. You don't have reins to worry about." She cautioned, "We'll go slow so as not to jostle your right arm too much."

With Sabrina leading on Serendipity, Bridget following on Jumpy, and Teresa trailing on Hank, the rescue party started its long climb back to the rim. Five hours later, they reached the trailhead, dropped off their injured mule-rider at the clinic, and returned the mule to the barn, followed by a coffee break at the Canyon Queen's café.

"Sabrina, you are more than welcome to stay overnight with Tomas and I. Park housing is not nearly as comfortable as the Circle K ranch, but it's getting late, and you are still a long way from home."

"I accept your hospitality. Kirby expects me to be away a few days anyway. We're headed to Flagstaff next week to visit Bergner Construction about our museum project. This has been a long day but now we know Hank has no problem with steep trails and you can now say you have been below the rim!"

"Thanks to you," acknowledged Teresa. "Bergner Construction; that's one of Ernst and Otto Bergner's enterprises, right?"

"Yes, two of Ernst's sons are operating their construction branch. I'm hiring them to build the Grand Canyon Pioneer Museum."

Sabrina had an idea while she and Teresa enjoyed some fresh-brewed coffee at the Canyon Queen. "We should issue a certificate to Hank. It could read 'By the renowned Order of Master Mule Skinners, the mule known as Hank faced the narrow trails of the Grand Canyon, descended and ascended its sheer walls, endured its changing moods, and tolerated the whims of his gentle, faithful owner, Teresa Garcia.' Hank can then officially boast of his feat forevermore."

Their coffee mugs barely hid their wide grins.

* * *

Before visiting the Bergner brothers, Kirby and Sabrina drove their Roadster out to Summit to check on the hotel demolition work.

"Kirby, it's gone! The Grand Canyon Hotel is completely gone!"

"At least the logs I requested have been set aside; looks to be about thirty or forty in the pile. Some are slightly charred but I think we'll find enough good ones for the museum vigas."

That reminded Sabrina about her contract with Bergner Construction. "I need to add a clause in the contract about hauling those logs to the museum construction site."

Monte's homestead bungalow and his old Summit Hotel also suffered the hand of the demolition crews. Workers restored the entire area to its original natural state. Except for a sign marking the Summit trailhead and some ponderosas stripped of their lower branches, little evidence remained of one of the Canyon's earliest tourist establishments.

"It's sad, in fact rather depressing," commented Sabrina. "The glory days of the Grand Canyon Hotel and the Canyon Copper Company are now part of history, and we'll preserve that era in museum exhibits. Kirby, I'm sure this place brings back many good memories for you."

"Yes, I helped build the hotel, in fact, I think I recognize some of those logs piled over there. I also helped build the trail and spent several years working in the Shooting Star mine on Windsong Mesa. Ah, the good ol' days." Kirby's mind flashed through all the good times with Monte, as well as his water-hauling days when he met Sabrina during her rock-scratching days. He then became very quiet for several minutes.

"Okay, Kirby, snap out of it. We have a museum to build." As they climbed back into their Roadster, Sabrina made a mental note to remind Bergner Construction about relocating the logs from Summit Point to Inspiration Point, the sooner the better.

Under The Canyon Sky: Guarding the Treasure

* * *

Kirby maintained an unusually high interest in the new suspension bridge design and made frequent trips to the Park Engineer's office to check progress. Steve Baxter always welcomed his comments and suggestions. This time Kirby had a rolled set of Pioneer Museum drawings under his arm.

"Hello Kirby, good to see you again. What are you doing back in the Village?"

"Steve, I'm on my way to the superintendent's office to get a permit for construction. The superintendent already approved these museum plans, but I brought them along anyway, just in case he has any new concerns."

"We have a new superintendent now, just reported aboard last week. He wants me to handle the construction permit process now. I don't need to see your plans. Your builder is Bergner Construction, right?" Steve started filling out the permit. "They built our clinic, our addition to our headquarters building, and our new ranger station at the south gate. You and Sabrina have a very good contractor. Here's your permit."

Steve had the anchor system design for the new suspension bridge on his mind. "Kirby, when you saw the old bridge fail, did the cables pull parts of the rock wall down or did the cables just snap at the anchor point? I'm trying to design a better support system for attaching to the north and south terminals."

"Sir, it all happened so fast; I'll never forget the horrifying sight of whip-lashing cables and mules plunging into the river. I think most of the cables snapped due to overstressing but on the north side I saw one of the anchors rip completely out of the wall, rock slabs and all. You can probably see the hole it left."

"Thank you, Kirby, I know what I need to do. I'm going to require that the construction crew jack-hammer deep holes into the granite walls and then backfill the holes with concrete footings to hold deep-set anchor bolts. Our riveted steel design for the major structure and the design for the heavy plank walkway are complete. And now I think we have a real solution for attaching steel cables to rock walls. The design is coming along very well. Stop and visit any time you're in the area. It's always good to bounce ideas off a friend, albeit an eyewitness to the bridge disaster."

"Okay, Steve, see you next time and thanks for the permit."

"Kirby, next time please bring Sabrina along. She may have some thoughts on the design since she also witnessed the bridge failure."

"I'll do that. She may also have a color scheme in mind when you paint the steel structure. I'm guessing russet brown to blend with the muddy Colorado or black to blend with the rock walls. She's very sensitive to having man-made structures blend into the natural environment." Kirby turned to leave.

Steve shouted, "Wait Kirby, you forgot your plans."

"Thanks, I've had a lot on my mind these days."

* * *

For three months, Bergner Construction cluttered a large portion of the parking lot with trucks, trailers, machinery and building materials but the museum construction proceeded very smoothly, from footings in the caprock to vigas in the roof, with one exception. The first load of viga logs rolled off Bergner's newfangled truck-trailer rig during a tight turn on the road from Summit. After that incident, Kirby assumed the role of unofficial project supervisor, including the loading and unloading of ponderosa logs.

One day, early in the project, Kirby and Sabrina discussed some design changes with the project foreman, Harvey Klostermeyer, son of Gus and Martha, prior owners of the Circle K Ranch, seventeen miles northwest of Flagstaff.

"Harvey, I like your suggestions. We totally forgot to include space for a museum office and storage room," admitted Sabrina. "Also, Harvey, your idea of a foyer is most appreciated, especially during winter months when visitors come trudging through snow at the entrance," added Kirby.

"Folks, those additions will add some square footage to the thirty-by-fifty-foot floor plan but consider that part of the building as Bergner Construction's contribution to this most worthy project," offered Harvey. "And, despite the economic depression our nation is fighting, we'll hold the cost to the original thirty-thousand-dollar budget we negotiated."

Sabrina was elated. "Sir, we will place a copper plate near the entrance, 'Constructed by Bergner Construction, Inc., Flagstaff, Arizona' in appreciation of your fine workmanship and generosity. Your construction is a marvelous blend of plate glass, stone masonry, ponderosa vigas, copper sheeting, and black granite flooring."

"Thank you, ma'am, much appreciated. By the way, please wait until we finish construction, including lining the walkways with native stone, positioning all the remaining oak benches, and clearing the parking lot before moving your outdoor centerpieces in front of the building. We note that your site plan allocated space for a stagecoach and a wagon."

"Duly noted, Harvey," said Sabrina and Kirby in unison. They walked around to the canyon side of the building.

"Look how the museum is precariously perched on the edge, similar to what the Anasazi may have done."

"And they probably had cantilevered vigas and rock buttresses similar to this." Kirby seemed infatuated with vigas and most pleased that ponderosa logs from the Grand Canyon Hotel could be reused in the museum structure. "And Sabrina, your idea of this stone patio with heavy oak benches adds character, a nice touch on this north side. And you've specified oak benches for the south side as well."

"Yes, and after Bergner vacates the premises, I look forward to seeing the stagecoach, with tack and harnesses, the winch with some hoisting cable, the ore cart on rails, full of turquoise blue copper ore, and the Studebaker wagon in their assigned places. And Kirby, as the real prospector in the family, you need to create a mining claim marker in front of the museum."

"I have some ideas for that. There may be a way to show claim papers inside. I sense you are anxious to jump into the interior design for this project, which means revisiting our floor plan with respect to visitor traffic flow from station to station and arrangement of materials within each exhibit—a monumental task—with placards describing the artifacts. You might ask Teresa and Mooney to assist," said Kirby. "I certainly will help with the larger artifacts, including the canvas boat the Casey family donated."

* * *

Sabrina indeed did solicit the help of Teresa and Mooney in implementing the interior design and staging the various exhibits.

"Mooney, let's start with the mining exhibit which includes pickaxes, shovels, kerosene lanterns, empty giant powder crates, and wheelbarrows, plus ore sacks filled to the brim with colorful copper ore," directed Sabrina, pointing to the artifacts stacked in a corner.

"I'll help you with the canvas boat, Mooney; let's lean it against the wall. I can't believe prospectors made it across the river in this flimsy craft," said Teresa. Wall exhibits included framed assay reports and mining claims, plus large, heavily annotated Shooting Star Mine plan and profile maps.

The next room, devoted to building canyon trails, featured tools like rod-and-feathers for splitting rock, drills, jacks, and miner's spoons for ladling blasting powder out of kegs.

"Ladies, it will take all three of us to place these juniper logs that Monte and Kirby used for shoring," said Sabrina. "And along with them goes these iron rods, some with heads, some with eyes." Mooney built a small rock cairn while Teresa mounted trail signs and survey maps on the wall. "I like this one," giggled Mooney. "I wonder if it's real. It reads 'Trespassers will be shot; survivors will be shot again.' Seems more appropriate for a mining claim but I guess it would easily apply to a private trail as well."

The three women completed the mining and trail-building exhibits over a ten-day period. Next came the exhibit that highlighted early canyon visitation and tourism. Stage and train schedules and fare postings, hotel signs with room rates, and livery signs for saddle horses and carriage rides all demonstrated how early visitors journeyed to the South Rim.

"Girls, we need to be careful with how we display this next group of keepsakes. Monte collected them from the Windsong Caves. I'm talking about stalactites and stalagmites. We need to get the spelling and tags right. I'll get Kirby to check our work later. There was a day when the caves were as big an attraction as the Canyon itself," explained Sabrina.

Mooney added, "And for those who don't dare go underground, like me, we have canteens, knapsacks, walking sticks, and field glasses. And this box is labeled story relics. I have no idea what that means."

"Oh, the relics are related to Clancy Jennings' wild tales. You'll find a battered pan, rusty rifle parts, and even bullet holes in part of a tree trunk in that box. Some empty Twin Oaks whiskey bottles too, Clancy's favorite," explained Sabrina. "Next to the relic box are several water barrels that our miners used for hauling drinking water. Kirby and I have one in our kitchen as a memento of when we first met."

Teresa reviewed a list of other items related to tourism. "Sabrina, it's going to take another week, maybe two, to stage this exhibit. I see it includes a gift shop and a photograph gallery."

Sabrina agreed. "Yes, the gift shop is especially important to tourists. I'm happy that you and Mooney have volunteered to oversee the sales counter and cash register for the Park Service. Besides folded trail maps and road maps, and picture postcards by professional photographers, this is where there will be tables stacked with the *Monte Bridgestone – Pioneer of the Grand Canyon* book. And we'll store some books on shelves too."

"As for the photo gallery," continued Sabrina, we have framed historic photographs to be hung on the walls. These show the mining operations, different views of various trails, all the pioneers who opened the Canyon for others to enjoy, plus some distinguished visitors."

"And here are some additional items for the walls," said Mooney, "bighorn sheep horns, deer antlers, and my favorite, Navajo rugs. I presume most of these will be in the main lobby and viewing area, opposite the big windows where the Canyon can be viewed from an indoor vantage point."

The work on the exhibits went on for weeks but in the end Sabrina's promise to Monte became a reality, a great museum paying homage to the pioneers of the Grand Canyon. Now it was nearly time for the ribbon-cutting and grand opening.

A week before the planned ceremony, Sabrina and Kirby drove to the museum for some final checks. Walking to the main door, Sabrina suddenly stopped.

She gasped. "Oh no! Where's the Studebaker wagon? That wagon descends from the company who built the original Conestogas!"

"It was here yesterday when I was working on the mine monument," said Kirby. "I'm sure I saw it. Maybe it was stolen overnight. Let's report this to Chief Ranger Hawley."

Later that morning, they learned Hawley's rangers stopped two young men driving out the main gate. The strange sight caught their attention, an auto pulling a horse-drawn wagon. Hawley had the thieves in custody and his rangers arranged to get the wagon returned to the museum.

Kirby wisely decided to add chains and locks to the stagecoach, ore cart and wagon. While Sabrina made last-minute checks on her museum exhibits, Kirby put the finishing touches on his mining claim marker, a reconstructed rock monument with a glass viewing window to show a mining claim certificate inside.

The day before the grand opening, someone vandalized the marker, perhaps in protest by someone who never wanted mining claims peppering side canyons, springs and viewpoints. Perhaps souvenir hunters considered the certificate as an authentic historical document. "Sabrina, I can't fix it in time. Maybe it was not a good idea after all, especially trying to show a claim paper inside, normally in a sealed can or jar."

Despite difficulties with the mine marker and the historic wagon, the opening ceremony went off without a hitch. The Park Superintendent stood at the entrance sign 'Grand Canyon Pioneer Museum' with its motto underneath, 'Explore. Dream. Discover.' and announced,

"Now we have a new facility here on the rim to provide a deeper understanding of the human history and heritage of our cherished Grand Canyon." He seemed rather nervous and hurried, being new and unfamiliar with the early days of the canyon pioneer.

The superintendent continued, "I now want to introduce the project benefactor, Sabrina O'Brien, and allow her to cut the ribbon and say a few words."

"Ladies and gentlemen, museums must tell stories, must explore and expand a visitor's curiosity, and must serve as a place to get explanations and understanding of our pioneers' work. This museum does just that. I want to thank Bergner Construction who completed the construction of the Grand Canyon Pioneer Museum on schedule and within budget."

She continued, "Now, as I cut this ribbon, I dedicate this museum to Levi Jackson, Clancy Jennings, Francois LaRue, Stuart Casey, Buckey O'Neill, Clint McCarty, Cole Campbell, Slim Broadway and Monte Bridgestone." Pointing to the main entrance, "All their names are etched into that copper plate to the right of that doorway."

The crowd cheered, the doors opened, and everyone elbowed their way inside, almost all gravitating toward the five giant plate-glass windows and the panoramic view that lay beyond.

Kirby hugged Sabrina, and congratulated her on keeping her promise to Monte. "He would be most pleased with this magnificent tribute to the canyon pioneers, and its mission to explore, dream and discover."

* * *

Among the crowd that day was an old lady and her grandson. He had read about the museum opening in the *Frontier Times*.

The grandson approached Sabrina and introduced himself as Louis Jackson. "Ma'am, I'm here with my grandmother. She is 86." He pointed to a petite lady with a long gray braid. "I don't think you have met her but she would like to meet you when you're free."

Sabrina asked, "Who is your grandmother?"

"Molly Jackson."

"Levi Jackson's wife?"

"Yes, he was my grandfather. He died about fifteen years ago at age ninety." Sabrina walked over to Molly and gave her a bear hug.

"Molly! I am so honored to finally meet you. I encountered Levi several times on the Coconino! Welcome to the Grand Canyon Pioneer Museum. We just dedicated it to Levi and his fellow canyon pioneers."

"Sabrina, that's why we traveled all the way from Taylor, a very long drive even by auto, to be here today for this special ceremony."

"Molly, I hope you and Louis can stay a few days. You could be Kirby's and my special guests at our ranch in Little Springs."

"Kirby O'Brien? Kirby is your husband? He was Levi's favorite prospecting partner. Yes, we'd love to stay with you."

"I'll ask Teresa, my assistant here at the museum, to join us. She also knew your husband. We could probably talk for days."

Kirby, glancing over to Sabrina, broke away from a group at the viewing window and joined her.

"Kirby, you won't believe this but this grand lady is Levi's widow, Molly Jackson. She and her grandson are going to spend a few days with us at the Circle K."

"Molly! Levi talked about you all the time. What a pleasure to finally meet you."

"And you," said Molly. "Levi talked about you all the time too."

* * *

The reunion at the Circle K evolved into an oral history session with Teresa, somewhat of a history fan herself, taking notes.

"Sabrina, before we get into my trip down memory lane, you need to understand I was Levi's second wife. Before me, he was married to Jenny Lewis."

"We understand. We'd love to learn how you and Levi met and about your lives together after his prospecting and mining days."

"I can give you some background on Levi before we met but you may already know some of it," explained Molly. "Teresa, I'll go slow so you can take notes."

"Levi was among the first Mormons to caravan across the country to the Salt Lake valley. When he reached his early twenties, Brigham Young encouraged him to join the California Gold Rush, presumably to find gold for the church. He was so successful he bought a cattle ranch in southern California. That's where he married young Jenny. Levi did not talk about her very much except that she was shy and wary of moving away from her family. Nevertheless, they married, sold the ranch, and settled along the Virgin River near a farming community that became St. George in Utah Territory. I believe she died giving birth."

"Sorry to hear that; it seems Levi was not too far from the Canyon at that point in his life," surmised Sabrina.

"He skirted it many times. Perhaps you have heard of the Honeymoon Trail," continued Molly. "It served as the link between the St. George Temple and settlements in the Little Colorado River valley, including the crossing on the Big Colorado at Lee's Ferry. Young Mormon men and women, who were directed to colonize the area, would travel this long, grueling wagon road to the temple to join in eternal marriage, then return to the Little Colorado Valley, a six-week round trip. Water sources along the way were few and unpredictable."

Molly enjoyed talking about her early days. "I was born in Salt Lake City but met Levi in the Joseph City Ward. He was the guide on many caravans through Paiute and Navajo Country. I think the wagon road was so primitive it seemed more like a trail, and so nicknamed the Honeymoon Trail. Levi guided young couples along the trail for years. We were married in Joseph City but we solemnized our wedding vows in St. George. After that, Levi settled down with me and we established a ranch at a bedrock crossing on the Little Colorado."

"Ah, that was Jackson Crossing! Levi raved about your beautiful home there," said Kirby. "Now you are getting to the part where Levi ventured into the Grand Canyon for some prospecting."

"Yes, Kirby, Levi dreamed about finding gold like he did in California. He was obsessed with finding gold, not just in canyon rocks but as lost treasure too. As you know, he barely found any copper worth mining," explained Molly. "I tolerated his canyon treks for a few years. I understood a man's need to get away from ranch work and be alone for a while. Thank goodness he had you, Kirby, as a mining companion. I waited patiently as you fellas finally realized the diminishing chances of gaining any prosperity from your copper claims. All the while, I dreaded the lonely nights and I missed Levi's help in running our livestock and gardens."

"I'll bet you were happy when he put his pick and shovel down for the last time and quit mining altogether," said Sabrina.

"And that's not all; we soon quit ranching too. We had good times and bad, bad being the lack of water. We often found the Little Colorado streambed bone dry. Other times it was a flashflood. We moved to Moenkopi where Levi traded with a Hopi chief named Tuba who, incidentally, Levi converted to Mormonism. Water was more reliable due to many springs in the Moenkopi area so we settled near Tuba City, an adjacent Navajo community, and that's where our family grew larger."

Teresa interjected, "Folks, could we declare a break? Sabrina, do you have some more notepaper?"

"Certainly, and this would be a good time for supper. I might suggest we close our discussion for tonight and resume in the morning. Molly, I could use some kitchen help. Care to join me?"

"I'm coming. Louis, Kirby knew your grandfather very well. Perhaps he has some wild stories to share." Molly headed for the kitchen.

"Molly, I see you like long braids too."

"Yes, Levi loved long hair and so do I. A single braid off to the side works well for me, except when I'm bending over a horse trough or a kitchen sink."

"I have the same problem but that's okay. I've always had long hair like you. Now, if you would help me set the table and serve dinner, we can sit comfortably and perhaps enjoy some lighter conversation, although we're all enjoying your life story."

After dinner, Molly started feeling poorly. She may have been overtired from her long journey to the Canyon and then down to Little Springs or just over-excited about sharing her life and times with her beloved Levi. Either way, she retired early to one of the O'Brien's guest rooms.

* * *

Kirby and Sabrina had already served breakfast to Teresa and Louis, but Molly had yet to show. A knock on her door failed to get her attention.

"Louis, is your grandmother in the habit of sleeping late?" asked Sabrina.

"No, in fact she is an early riser. But she seemed very tired during this entire trip, except when we were talking about my grandfather. Are you worried? Should I check on her?"

"I say let her sleep some more," stated Sabrina, trying to hide any concern. "Her journey down memory lane yesterday must have been mentally draining."

After another hour, Molly still failed to show.

Chapter Five

CARAVAN OF WORKERS

A national experiment to restore self-confidence in oneself and the nation

Sabrina and Louis, coffee cups in hand, stared out the dining room window, watching Kirby and Teresa feed the ranch livestock. Some of the buildings and corrals reminded Teresa of how the ranch looked when it served as the first way station on the stage line to the Canyon.

"Louis, I'm worried about your grandmother." Sabrina sipped her hot coffee.

"She never sleeps this long. I should check on her again." Just as Louis reached for the guest room door, it creaked open and Molly, rumpled and haggard, appeared.

"Granny! We've been wondering when you would wake up. It's already mid-morning!"

Following a yawn, came the words, "Coffee smells good. This visit has been harder on me than I ever expected. I'm still exhausted; Louis, I think we should start back soon."

Sabrina had something to say about that. "Oh no, not yet, Molly. First, I need to fix you some bacon and eggs. We've already had breakfast. Second, we need to wrap up your life story with Levi."

Sitting around the dining room table, Sabrina asked Teresa, "Where did we leave off?"

Teresa checked her notes. "Molly and Levi abandoned their home at Jackson Crossing because the Little Colorado had only two modes of operation, flashflood or bone dry, and moved to the Navajo community of Tuba City."

"That's right, Teresa, we lived among the Navajo. Levi spoke their language well and was always welcome in their hogans. His Navajo name was Hosteen Shush which means Strong Bear," said Molly, as she gathered her thoughts.

"Tuba City was our home for many years. Our four married children and their families also lived there. Levi made a living as a trader with the Paiute, Havasupai, Navajo and Hopi. When the government uprooted Mormon families to make way for a larger Navajo reservation, we all scattered. We received some compensation for improvements we made to the land, but barely enough to make a fresh start. Levi and I relocated to Joseph City, named in honor of Joseph Smith, founder of the Mormon movement. That colony sat astride the Little Colorado. Like at Jackson Crossing, it ran as a braided wash trying to make its way from the flatlands to the Big Colorado, although flashfloods kept destroying diversion dams in the colony. We finally got away from that pitiful river by moving one last time, south to the farming community of Taylor, named after John Taylor, third president of the Mormon Church. Sorry, that's more info about Mormon settlements than you probably wanted to know. Whew, I'm out of breath!"

"And that's where Levi is buried, right Molly?" asked Kirby.

"Levi's health began to fail in Taylor. He lost his sight, first just one eye, then the other, during his last years. He lived a long life, reaching age ninety," explained Molly. "Yes, Kirby, he is in the Taylor cemetery, probably waiting for me."

Sabrina wanted to make sure Molly knew something about the relationship between Monte and Levi. "Molly, did you know Monte saved Levi's life? He was prospecting at river's edge when Levi floated by, yelling for help while floundering in the Colorado."

"Much after the fact, he finally got around to telling me. He also mentioned he had to immediately turn around and rescue Monte who then fell in the river. He said they looked like drowned river rats sprawled on the rocky shoreline."

Kirby had a question too. "Molly, do you realize most of Levi's prospect holes were on the north side of the river? He had a flimsy raft that we used to get across."

"That I did not know!"

"He used to warn us about the danger of running into outlaws on the Horsethief Trail, which included the Jackson Trail," added Teresa.

"And on the Coconino," added Sabrina. "I ran into Levi a few times where the Moqui trade route crosses the stage road. He was shocked to see a lone woman rider out there."

"Well, you folks have more secrets about my Levi than I do, but I'm thinking we should end this round of Jackson recollections. I'm still not feeling well." Turning to her grandson, "Louis, how's our gas supply for driving back to Taylor?"

"Getting low, granny, we need to stop in Flagstaff. If not there, in Winslow."

After a round of hugs and well-wishing, Louis helped Molly into their auto and waved goodbye. Kirby and Sabrina watched them drive out the ranch gate and down the road until out of sight while Teresa threw a saddle on Hank.

"It's time for me to go too. Sabrina, I'll put my notes in good order, file the original in our museum archives, and get a copy in your hands. I need to check on Mooney at the museum and see how Tomas is doing. Thank you for inviting me to this historical reunion. I love history and this meeting with Molly Jackson has been most interesting. We're so lucky for this chance to get to know her. She's quite a pioneer lady."

Under The Canyon Sky: Guarding the Treasure

* * *

A month after Molly's visit, Sabrina received a letter from Louis announcing that Molly died in her sleep and is now buried next to her beloved Levi. Louis also explained that he is lonely and depressed, and unable to see his way forward.

"Kirby, this is very sad news. The trip was so hard on her and yet she was thrilled about describing her life and times with Levi." Kirby added, "For me, this is especially a great loss. May they now both rest in peace."

Sabrina and Kirby journeyed back to the Canyon, Sabrina to check on the museum, now an official Park Service operation, and Kirby to call on Park Engineer Steve Baxter who enlightened him on President Franklin Roosevelt's plan to put young single men to work. Unemployment remained very high, and household incomes very low, as there seemed to be no end to the economic depression.

"Kirby, the President launched the Civilian Conservation Corps, a jobs program designed to put unemployed young men, ages eighteen to twenty-five, to work on public works projects that promote conservation of natural resources in rural lands, like here at the Grand Canyon."

Kirby asked, "Are these the same conservation boys who blasted the River Trail out of solid rock?"

"The very same, in fact, we're expecting a caravan of Army-style trucks packed with young men and tools any day now. These workers receive room and board but only thirty dollars a month. Twenty-five dollars is automatically sent to their families at home to help them survive during these lean times while also stimulating the depressed national economy. Two added benefits of the program are to raise public awareness of our natural resources and to train young men in special skills."

Louis Jackson came to Kirby's mind. "Steve, what kind of work are these conservation boys expected to do, besides blasting trails out of rock walls high above a raging river?"

"These boys can select the type of work they want to do. Here in the park, we use them for erosion control, washout repairs, roadwork, picnic shelters, campgrounds, tree-planting, fire lookout construction, and you'll like this, the tunnel you suggested at the south portal of the new bridge. By the way, the bridge is now under construction and your ideas for hauling tons of steel components on mules and using Native American teams to carry long cables down the trail are working out just fine. And tell Sabrina we are going by her suggestion; the steel portions of the bridge will be painted black."

"Steve, I have a suggestion for another worker," said Kirby. "His name is Louis Jackson, grandson of the venerable canyon pioneer Levi Jackson. He's about twenty, unmarried and available for work."

"We can use all the help we can get. If he's willing to do hard labor in this glorious canyon, I suggest he consider applying." Steve had an additional thought. "Mention of his connection to a canyon pioneer would be a plus on his application."

Louis Jackson became one of the conservation boys at the Grand Canyon. The Army moved enrollees from induction centers to work camps, in Louis' case, from Winslow to the South Rim. He became part of the national experiment to restore self-confidence in oneself and the nation. He quickly snapped out of his depressed state and happily accepted an assignment to a team that hand-crafted the long wall of tight-fitting native limestone rocks along the rim from the Starlight Lodge to the Canyon Queen Hotel, replacing a dilapidated wood fence. Louis felt the Corps offered a tremendous variety of job opportunities. His team also widened the Pioneer Trail, including the construction of four rustic rest-houses using native stone and timber. Working with the Park

Service, the conservation boys removed McCarty's old buildings at Canyon Gardens. In the Village they built one of their first projects, the two-story Community Building, and they completed Trails West's project of reducing the McCarty Hotel to the original single cabin that once stood at the Red Horse stage stop.

* * *

After four months, the Park Service contractor completed the new bridge, now dubbed the Black Bridge. Engineer Steve Baxter was pleased with his design and personally supervised the construction. As a further precaution against swaying, Steve ordered wind cables with guy wires. Finally, the conservation boys had easy access to the other side of the river, enabling them to establish a base camp on Skeleton Creek near the Dancing Ghost dude ranch. From there the boys worked on the trail to the North Rim and upgraded the original trans-canyon telephone line by stringing twenty miles of new wire on six-foot iron poles.

With completion of the new bridge, Sabrina and Teresa rescheduled their ride down the Pioneer Trail. This time they avoided all mule trains, passed the spot where they rescued Bridget, and reached Six-Gun Creek with its meager contribution to the thundering Colorado.

The wide span of the river amazed Teresa, maybe four hundred feet across whereas from places on the rim it looked more like forty feet. "This river looks like it's in a big hurry," observed Teresa, "It churns and slides, and look at the whirlpools out there! It's a wonder Levi survived his accidental ride down the main channel."

"Kirby showed me places upstream where some rapids are six or seven feet high!"

The women, anxious to see the new bridge, proceeded along the River Trail. The conservation boys used jackhammers to carve the trail out of sheer granite walls, several hundred feet above the river. As the women approached the new steel suspension bridge, the area looked quite different to Sabrina. Now there was a one-hundred-foot tunnel that opened directly onto the bridge.

"Teresa, this tunnel was Kirby's idea. It should be named O'Brien Tunnel. He also suggested the wood planking design you see on the walkway. Is Hank ready for his first river crossing?"

"You and Serendipity go first; Hank and I will follow." Teresa herself felt some trepidation but Hank, trudging between high guardrails, showed no fear. "The other end of this tunnel looks like it ends in midair, high above the current."

The new bridge validated Steve Baxter's engineering expertise, no undulating flooring, no sideways swaying, and no bouncing when hoofs put pressure on the structure. The women landed on the other side of the Colorado for the very first time, journeyed downstream a short distance, then paused near a gravesite.

"Look Teresa, a Park Service trail foreman is buried here," said Sabrina. "According to that marker he died of injuries received while blasting this trail, struck by a falling boulder during the excavation work."

They rode past some Anasazi ruins and then turned into Skeleton Canyon.

"Whoa!" shouted Sabrina, "What's this? Looks like an Army camp!" Spread before them lay a sprawling tent camp for the conservation boys. Teresa counted thirty tents, in two rows, with ten more larger tents off to the side.

"There's the Dancing Ghost Ranch where we're booked for an overnight stay," said Sabrina. They led Serendipity and Hank to their quarters, a small corral with hay and water, then reported to the registration clerk who announced the family-style cantina would open in thirty minutes, ready to serve beef stew and fresh-baked rolls. The women checked into their cabin, one of five quaint stone and log structures, not unlike the Pioneer Museum. It had two benches of similar construction and newly planted shade trees irrigated by the gurgling waters of Skeleton Creek. Cage structures at the base of their trunks guarded against beaver damage. "I predict these young cottonwoods will someday reach thirty or forty feet above the canyon floor," announced Sabrina. Several deer nibbled vegetation nearby.

After dinner, the women followed the creek to the river, listening to croaking frogs and clicking crickets along the way. Dusk, a magical time in the inner gorge, created a golden glow between towering cliffs. Sabrina promised herself she would return with Kirby. The women sat gazing at the Colorado, watching driftwood bobbing in the current, a good time for girl talk as dusk transitioned into night.

Teresa opened the conversation. "Sabrina, you and I have something in common. We're proof that women can work in occupations other than running a household. Tell me about your family."

"I was born in a big Texas city. I don't have any siblings. All through my high school years, I dreamed of living on a ranch, raising cattle, and driving herds to market. My parents wanted me to be an urban housewife. I rebelled, met and married my first husband in Waco and settled at our ranch south of Winslow. Brent fell while working on our barn roof and died from his injuries. On a whim I married again but that lasted only three months. During divorce proceedings, he cheated me out of the ranch so I ended up clerking in Flagstaff. It was a matter of survival but I hated being stuck in a dingy office. I eventually escaped to this Canyon. What's your story?"

Teresa tossed a stone at a drifting log, and hit it! "I was born on a ranch south of Abilene and was the youngest in our large Hispanic family. My education ended at the sixth grade because I was needed for ranch work. My father and brothers all worked as seasonal stagecoach drivers on runs across southern New Mexico and Arizona. I've always been intrigued by Old West history, including train robbers, saloon brawls, and legends of lost gold. I learned livery and stagecoaches at age eleven while riding with my father. Eventually I drove my own stagecoaches. I simply had no time for married life. I wanted to be in the driver's seat and always on the move."

"So, that ol' stage line serving the Canyon also served as our early connection to each other. We are both intrigued by legends of lost gold, both interested in preserving history, both enjoying the great outdoors," concluded Sabrina.

Teresa added, "I have a feeling you know more about lost gold than you admit, but I'll leave it at that."

Suddenly, they heard a bugle sounding taps! "Sabrina, I believe we have invaded the rigid life of an Army camp, not unlike the forts I supplied during my stage-driving days, totally unexpected here at the bottom of the Grand Canyon."

"Okay, conservation boys, that is your call for lantern lights out, not ours," commented Sabrina. "However, we got the message; it's time for us to also retire for the evening. It's been a very long day."

After being rudely awakened by the camp bugler sounding reveille, Sabrina and Teresa caught breakfast at the cantina, saddled their livestock, and embarked on the arduous climb to the South Rim. Looking back at Skeleton Canyon from the River Trail, with its Army-style taps and reveille calls, Sabrina thought about Louis Jackson and whether he had adapted well to such a regimented life.

***

"Kirby, wait till you see the Black Bridge! It's magnificent."

After Sabrina's trip with Teresa to Dancing Ghost Ranch, she booked a two-night stay for Kirby and herself. This time they hired saddle horses at the Pioneer trailhead and hit the trail before the first dude inserted his foot in a stirrup. After five hours in the saddle, the O'Briens reached the Black Bridge.

"It looks just like Steve Baxter's drawings!" exclaimed Kirby. "The riveted steel structure, the rockwall anchors, the south tunnel and portal, all just as I imagined they would be in real life. The tunnel excavation work was handed to the conservation boys since they already had air compressors and jackhammers on site."

They crossed the bridge and hitched their horses at the Dancing Ghost Ranch office. After registering for their cabin, Sabrina and Kirby followed Skeleton Creek to the Civilian Conservation Corps headquarters tent. There they encountered Army Lieutenant Mark Rogers who supervises the young civilians and their project assignments.

"Good afternoon, Lieutenant. I am Kirby O'Brien and this is my wife, Sabrina. We live on a ranch northwest of Flagstaff but have a long history here at the Grand Canyon. Sabrina stayed at the Dancing Ghost Ranch about two weeks ago and came across your camp. This is my first time."

"Well, welcome to our conservation camp; how can I be of service?"

Kirby explained, "The grandson of our dear friend, now deceased, Levi Jackson, recently enrolled in the Conservation Corps. We'd like to visit him if he happens to be in camp."

Lieutenant Rogers asked, "What is the grandson's name? I'll get my orderly here to check our roster."

"Louis Jackson," answered Sabrina. "I think he enrolled for six months."

The Lieutenant added, "Our program allows up to four six-month terms. Sounds like he's in his first term. This camp operates here on Skeleton Creek during the period October to March, but when it gets hot down here at river level, we move the camp to the North Rim for the period April to September. Here comes my orderly."

"Sir, we show Louis Jackson's first term on the South Rim but then he enrolled for another term on the North Rim. He's also scheduled for a third term beginning in October right here."

"Well, there you have it; he'll be working here soon. Can I interest you in a brief tour of the camp?"

Sabrina jumped at the opportunity. "Yes sir, we'd like that."

The tour included a walk down the long line of tents, a visit to the kitchen and mess hall at the south end, and a look at officer quarters and the infirmary at the north end. Kirby learned that they first gathered driftwood along the Colorado for fuel, but the sparks raised havoc with the canvas tents. He learned that mules started hauling more coal, already used in the camp blacksmith shop, from the South Rim for fuel.

Kirby and Sabrina retired in their cabin for the night.

After breakfast at the cantina among Trails West mule riders, the O'Briens tended to their horses in the corral and watched dudes mount up for their return trip. As that mule train departed, two supply trains arrived. A string of ten heavily loaded brawny Army mules with two packers arrived first. Then a Trails West string, with packs that looked almost as heavy, arrived. These mule trains were the lifeline for Dancing Ghost Ranch and the Civilian Conservation Corps.

Kirby called over to a packer. "What's a typical load, one hundred and fifty pounds?"

The packer answered, "About that, sometimes two hundred."

"Kirby, at the breakfast table this morning, a couple raved about their visit to Zuni Falls, a spring-fed waterfall one hundred feet high and about six miles up Skeleton Creek from here. It's in a secluded side canyon that leads to the falls and a mound of travertine covered with moss. They said there's a cave with dangling lush ferns behind the falls. Sounds like a desert oasis!"

"I know you love waterfalls. I'm guessing you want to ride up there for a look."

"Let's saddle up!"

Kirby and Sabrina followed a trail that eventually reaches the North Rim. They found some conservation boys working on lower parts of the trail but maneuvered around them with no trouble. When they turned west into a side canyon, they could hear water splashing.

"Let's climb up there and sit on a rock for a spell, Kirby. You know I am mesmerized by waterfalls and never have I seen one this spectacular." After an hour gazing at the water cascading over moss-covered rocks, it was time to ride back to the dude ranch.

At the mule corral, still raving about Zuni Falls, a packer reminded them that the falls are sacred to the Zuni. He added, "They believe their ancestors emerged from that special place. The Hopi also have sacred places like the Zuni in this Canyon."

On the way back to their cabin, Sabrina commented, "Kirby, I wonder if we have done enough to respect the culture and traditions of Native Americans. We've blazed all these trails and have dug holes hoping to find valuable minerals, all with total disregard for those who came before us. This whole canyon could be sacred to native peoples."

"I share your concerns, Sabrina. In some respects, we have invaded their territory and have done little to protect areas where Native Americans have left their mark. We set aside this wondrous canyon under the initial premise of protecting antiquities, but we seem to have moved away from that."

As Kirby and Sabrina continued their stroll through the conservation camp, Sabrina remembered Mooney talking about a project underway at the east end of the Canyon. "Kirby, there is a project under construction that will pay tribute to all the tribes who have lived, and are still living, in this region. It's a lookout tower with a commanding view of Navajoland. Mooney says some of the Grand Canyon Hotel logs were also saved for that project, probably as vigas for the kiva they are building at the base of the tower."

"That's good news and it is in the same spirit as the Pioneer Museum in trying to preserve that part of canyon history. So, Monte's logs will also live in tribute to Native Americans." Kirby's thoughts strayed into the days when Moonflower Yazzie and he helped build the old hotel. He suspected that Mooney arranged for some hotel logs to be integrated into the tower and kiva design.

Just then, someone from behind commented, "Oh, you're talking about the Desert View Tower! Sorry, I was not eavesdropping but when you mentioned Navajoland, you caught my attention. My name is Jim Nez. My brother and I are members of the Conservation Corps here, still on light duty after our accident on the River Trail."

"Greetings, Jim. We are Kirby and Sabrina O'Brien, visiting the camp and dude ranch for the first time. We heard the conservation boys had a terrible accident on that trail construction. Sounds like you were part of that?"

"Yes, we are Navajo and are known to work in high places without fear. Here comes my brother, George. We are jackhammer operators and suffered some injuries when the rock terrace gave way and we fell a few hundred feet toward the river."

"George, this is Kirby and Sabrina O'Brien on a visit down here."

Sabrina asked, "Jim and George, we'd like to hear more about what happened that fateful day on the River Trail. Kirby and I have traveled that trail and witnessed the collapse of the old swinging bridge. In fact, Kirby assisted in the design of the new bridge and the tunnel. You conservation boys excavated Kirby's tunnel!"

Kirby whispered, "Stop saying that, Sabrina. It's not my tunnel, just my idea."

George Nez returned the conversation to the River Trail. "Our accident was not as bad as that bridge failure but was just as frightening. Jim and I had separate safety lines, working in tandem. Our positions were precarious and awkward—sitting in slings, safety harnesses around our waists and shoulders, goggles impairing our vision, miner's helmets with scratchy chin straps, hissing air lines hanging from the compressor high above, and wielding heavy jackhammers tethered to our harnesses—all this with an angry river growling below. They say Navajo have little fear of heights; in fact, many Navajo have been hired as steel workers on high New York City buildings. It's not true; we all have a fear of falling and that we did."

Kirby interjected, "I have built several trails here at the Canyon, some by just pick and shovel, some by blasting with giant powder. We could have used jackhammers in those days, but none existed. I heard you conservation boys used over fifteen tons of blasting powder and dynamite to carve the River Trail out of solid granite."

"That's true, Mr. O'Brien, we did a lot of blasting but also a lot of jackhammering," commented Jim. "We had some training in jackhammer use by a hard-rock miner working on the Boulder Dam project. At times we were dangling mid-air off the side of the cliff from a taut-safety line; other times we had our feet on the terrace we were cutting so the line was slack."

"And, of course, we always had the air hose from the air compressor to contend with; quite a tangled mess. The rock was very hard, black granite with sparkly specks," added George.

"Oh, I know that rock very well from my prospecting days; we called it black diamonds!" blurted Sabrina.

"What? You were a prospector, Mrs. O'Brien?" George had run into male prospectors but never a woman prospector.

"Don't get her started, George. She'll regale you with stories from her years of roaming side canyons down here," cautioned Kirby.

Getting back to the high-line tragedy, Jim explained what happened. "George and I were standing on the rough-cut ledge we had just created. Our safety line had plenty of slack as our feet were set on what we thought was firm rock. Then it happened. There was a sudden cracking sound, like a clap of thunder close at hand, and a two-hundred-foot-long section of the terrace or trail bed dropped out from under our feet. Jack, a conservation boy tending the air compressor on top of the cliff, got tangled in my safety line when it was pulled tight and went over the cliff. He landed in the river and was killed by falling debris. George and I, with jackhammers in hand, dropped with broken hunks of granite falling all around us. We were quickly jerked to a stop about ten feet above the river, dangling from our safety lines. Our air lines snapped but our ropes held. Other boys rushed to the point where our lines were fixed to firm ground and started pulling us up."

"Thank goodness you were saved. Sorry to hear Jack did not make it. Were you injured by falling debris?" asked Sabrina.

George answered, "Lucky for us, no direct hits by your black diamond rocks, Mrs. O'Brien, just nasty scrapes, cuts and bruises, but also severely pulled muscles from the sudden jerk of our safety lines."

Jim added, "Needless to say, that part of the River Trail had to be rerouted higher up the cliff. Perhaps you have noticed where the trail goes back up a few hundred feet before going back down toward the river. That rise on the trail is above where the big section fell into the Colorado."

"Jim and George Nez, thank you for sharing your story," said Kirby. "We wish you both safe and happy days ahead. We'll be journeying back along that River Trail in the morning, on our way back to the rim."

* * *

As Kirby and Sabrina departed on their return trip to the South Rim, they paused on the Black Bridge. Fortunately, no other traffic appeared in either direction. Then came a sight neither had ever seen. Three rowboats, each with two fearless thrill seekers, passed under the bridge. There was an oarsman amidships sitting backwards, and a fellow in the stern, hands gripping the gunwales, and facing downstream, presumably serving more as a lookout than a passenger.

"Well, that's something you don't see every day, especially on this river," said Kirby, adding "These rowboats seem rather frail for running rapids, a sharp-pointed bow with a deck and splash guard, spare oars fastened outboard, and another deck behind the rider."

"Let's get across and ride down the River Trail to see how these boats handle Six-Gun Rapids," urged Sabrina.

At the rapids, the first two boats slipped past mid-stream boulders with ease.

Kirby had a thought. "Sabrina, it seems to me the fellow rowing should be facing downstream. I know nothing about river running but it would be best if the fellow with the oars sat facing the direction of travel, like driving a car. He would have much better visibility to make quick decisions on the best route and gain finer control in rough water with the broad stern adding stability to the boat."

"If only he could have heeded your suggestion, Kirby; look at that last boat scraping its side on a jagged rock. Now it has a long gash on its sideboard."

The O'Briens continued up the Pioneer Trail, ending a very interesting visit in the inner gorge.

Chapter Six

CHALLENGING THE RIVER

A new breed of canyon creature, the river rat, invades Granite Gorge

Decades after John Wesley Powell's runs through the Canyon and the railroad survey that encountered Levi and Kirby prospecting at river's edge, only a few more daring souls attempted runs on the Colorado. Largely undocumented and rather controversial, they often served as the subject of lively campfire stories bandied about by deer hunters and beaver trappers. By the mid-thirties, river-runners called themselves river rats. Some trips served to test boat designs and techniques for running ferocious rapids. All-in-all, about ten runs took place, including a geological survey, a mysterious run by a honeymoon couple never seen again, and the rowboats that Kirby and Sabrina encountered.

"Sabrina, I keep thinking about those three boats we saw challenging the rapids at Six-Gun Creek," mused Kirby. "I'd like to learn more about this river-running sport from Dexter Livingston, Jeremy's brother. He's involved in developing a river boat design for Western River Adventures, a new tourist enterprise. It appears commercial trail-riding enterprises may be joined by commercial river-riding enterprises in Grand Canyon. Let's invite Dexter to visit us here at the Circle K."

"Great idea. I'd like to learn more about this new breed of canyon creature, the river rat, invading Granite Gorge. Let's go a step further; let's make this an O'Brien-Livingston gathering and have Jeremy, Rachel and Cody join us as well."

Kirby agreed. "Let's do it!"

* * *

Ten days after receiving invitations, the Livingston wagon rolled through the Circle K Ranch gate, with Dexter and Jeremy in the driver's seat and Rachel and Cody in the back seat.

"Welcome Livingstons. It's so nice to see you again. And Jeremy, right off the bat, please again accept our thanks for looking after the ranch when Kirby and I have business at the Canyon," said Sabrina.

"Our pleasure. By the way, we're combining this visit with a run into Flagstaff for groceries," explained Jeremy. Everyone moved onto the O'Brien's sprawling veranda.

"They call this the Great Depression. Nothing great about it. With the drought, our well is going dry and our vegetable garden is a disaster," said Rachel.

Sabrina piped up, "No need to drive into Flagstaff. This is Little Springs and it is harvest time! We have good water and a lush vegetable garden and orchard. Let us load you up before you leave."

"That is very kind of you, Sabrina; we are having a rough time this year." Rachel looked at Jeremy. "But we'll make it."

"Dexter, what is this we hear about you working on boats for carrying passengers down the Colorado? Not long ago, Sabrina and I watched a group of boats tackle the rapids at Six-Gun Creek. One of them side-swiped a rock."

"Western River Adventures is not operational yet. With the Depression and all, progress is slow. But we envision a need for paying passengers to ride with experienced guides in well-built boats to take them to parts of Grand Canyon few have ever seen. You no doubt know there are plans evolving to dam parts of the river for hydroelectric power generation and water storage. Before the river gets tamed too much, we'd like to allow as many adventurers as possible to experience one of America's wildest rivers."

"Dexter, we know Boulder Dam is nearing the end of construction, but are there plans for other dams?" asked Sabrina, with deep concern in her voice.

"That dam is truly a concrete monster at Black Canyon. Like the Civilian Conservation Corps, it has provided thousands of jobs during these hard economic times," confessed Dexter, "And that's a good thing, but I have mixed feelings; the river will never be the same. Its precious waters are already pooling behind the concrete arch. To answer your question, yes, another dam is being proposed upstream at Bridge Canyon."

"Kirby and I, and Jeremy too, are most familiar with the eastern reaches of the Canyon. We've never been to the western reaches. We know there is so much more to the Canyon than what we have experienced. Dexter, I guess river-running is a good way to see what lies further downstream." Sabrina appeared to be shocked that another dam may further strangle her wild river.

"We at Western River Adventures are very concerned," started Dexter. "As we speak, test holes are being driven into solid rock by gasoline-powered drills, despite nationwide gas shortages. This whole operation reminds me of Clint McCarty's grandiose schemes to sell unproven mining claims to dam builders, or should I say canyon flooders. He was in it for the money and cared little about the environmental and cultural impact due to hydroelectric power generation. But that's another story."

Dexter continued. "If built, the Bridge Canyon Dam will be a seven-hundred-foot-high arch of concrete in Lower Granite Gorge, two hundred and thirty miles from Lees Ferry. We've studied the feasibility reports. It would back-flood the gorge ninety miles upstream to a point just below where the tributary coming down from Kanab and Fredonia joins the Colorado. The reservoir would flood thirteen miles into the protected lands of Grand Canyon National Park, drowning natural landmarks like Lava Falls and the lower portion of Havasu Creek with its turquoise blue waters, essentially the entire lower canyon."

"That's terrible," shrieked Sabrina, "We can't let this happen! Kirby, has Park Engineer Baxter mentioned this?"

"No. We should go visit him to see what he knows. Maybe we should also have a few words with the Superintendent. I bet he will claim innocence and explain the Bureau of Reclamation is the primary driver for building dams and reservoirs on the Colorado. I always thought running a river-level railroad through the Canyon was a bad idea, but this is far worse."

"Rachel and Cody, let's go raid our garden. We have all kinds of vegetables. And Cody, bring those baskets; we have apples and pears just waiting to be picked," said Sabrina. "You've come at a perfect time, a beautiful fall day, and we need a break from that depressing discussion about dams."

* * *

Jeremy and Dexter wanted to reminisce about the good ol' days with Monte but Kirby wanted to learn more about river-running, especially the boats.

"Dexter, tell me more about your boat design."

"We are improving on the design of the slender flat-bottoms you saw. Our new boats will be wider, with a broad stern and pointed bow, splashguards fore and aft, and gently curved hull stem to stern. They will plow into waves stern first with the oarsman seated amidships in his cockpit facing the direction of travel."

"More like facing his danger," commented Kirby.

Dexter continued, "Based on early reports, we understand running stern-first into rough water is best for visibility and stability."

"That was my observation at Six-Gun," interjected Kirby.

"We hope to have two passenger seats behind the oarsman but that's still to be worked out as it will be the narrowest part of the boat."

"Sounds good to me," added Jeremy, despite having never seen a boat on the river.

"Kirby, we will be one of the first commercial river-running companies in the Southwest. After a few test runs by our river guides with our new boats, you and Sabrina might want to consider a voyage down the Colorado. It would give you a clearer appreciation for the damage these dams might do."

"Dexter, I would consider such a run but I'll never get Sabrina to go along. Let's hold that thought for a while. Meantime, I see a lot of fruits and vegetables coming our way."

Rachel called to Jeremy. "It's time to load the wagon. Sabrina has been most generous."

Sabrina added, "You can't go yet, we have a nice lunch prepared. So come on inside after the wagon's loaded."

Sitting around the dining room table, the conversation drifted back to dams in the Colorado River corridor.

Dexter re-opened the discussion. "You know it is rather ironic. Powell became the first to run the river through Grand Canyon and his ideas for protecting the West's limited water resources were incorporated into legislation that established the Reclamation Service, today's Bureau of Reclamation, which authorized Boulder Dam in nineteen twenty-eight."

"You are right, Dexter. It is ironic that the first river-runner's ideas led to creating large-scale water storage projects in the American

West," added Kirby, "And not only that but this action set the precedent for the Bureau becoming a major hydroelectric power producer."

"Call me old-fashioned, but why do we need electricity anyway? Windmills drive our wells and kerosene fuels our lanterns." Sabrina clearly remained upset about damming the precious waters of the majestic Colorado. "I do not understand society's unquenchable thirst for electricity."

Rachel added, "With Dexter's news of the Bridge Canyon Dam, it seems the Bureau places power production above protection of the Grand Canyon, whether upstream or downstream of these big dams."

"Well, I'm not going to sit here and let the Bridge Canyon project go through," exclaimed Sabrina. "I'm going to initiate a public outcry such as the Bureau has never seen. I have not run the river but I know what it is like to lay on soft sandy beaches, listen to the gurgle of the river, and the call of the canyon wren. I don't want to see this disturbed by man-made flow adjustments to meet power demands or to see water pooling behind dams and inundating wildlife habitats and cultural resources, especially in a national park. I'm sorry Kirby, but I plan to become very vocal on this issue; if I have to, I will lead an anti-dam movement. Boulder, unfortunately, is here to stay but Bridge Canyon doesn't stand a chance."

After Sabrina's tirade, no one else had anything to say. Dexter did not dare mention rumors of future dams in Marble Canyon and Glen Canyon. Kirby walked the Livingstons out to their waiting wagon as Sabrina set about clearing the table.

"Sorry about Sabrina's behavior. I've never seen her this upset."

"It's getting late and we need to get home before dark. Please thank her again for the fruits and vegetables, and a fine lunch. We are so lucky to have friends like you," said Rachel.

As the Livingston family started back up the old stage road, Kirby went back inside. Neither he nor Sabrina had anything else to say that evening.

* * *

While pouring cups of coffee for Kirby and herself the next morning, Sabrina apologized for her outburst during the Livingston visit.

"It is just insane to think the government is contemplating the destruction of part of the Canyon that it worked so hard to protect," said Sabrina, "I've always been a passionate defender of the Grand Canyon and now I am absolutely outraged by the Bridge Canyon proposal. I'm not sure I can even find it on a map but if it is predicted to impound water ninety miles upstream, what a travesty it would be."

Kirby set his coffee cup down and put his arm around her waist. "I have an idea; let's ride up to the Village, rent two saddle horses and ride out to the West Rim. I understand there is a new equestrian trail that crosses McCarty's old claims. We could stop at every viewpoint to get a better feel for a part of Grand Canyon National Park we have never seen."

"Then after that," Kirby continued rather facetiously, "Being thoroughly conversant in all things West Rim, we pay a visit to Steve Baxter."

"I'll go for that plan, even though the West Rim hardly reaches as far as the proposed dam," admitted Sabrina, "But a visit with the Park Engineer may shed some light on crazy dam proposals. Surely, he has been in meetings with the Bureau." Both Kirby and Sabrina wondered if Clint McCarty is still scheming in the background.

The equestrian trail ran parallel to a gravel road and offered stunning vistas at every scenic overlook. The first one provided a raven's eye view of the Village and the Pioneer Trail switching back and forth on its tortuous path into the canyon depths. They passed an unsightly shack, boarded up and locked, with a keep-out sign, clearly a mining claim, with a rope ladder slung over the rim. They then arrived at the Powell Memorial where a brass plaque showed the date nineteen twelve, presumably when the marker was established. The trail then hugged a wide curve where one could look straight down into the abyss. Where visible from the next series of overlooks, the river snaked its way through the gorge. Sabrina thought she could hear the rapids. At the end they came upon an old miner's cabin constructed of large chunks of limestone caprock. This point offered a great view downriver, several miles of glittering ribbon headed in the direction of Bridge Canyon.

On the return, Sabrina commented, "The West Rim is just as scenic as the East Rim. Now I understand why Francois LaRue raved so much about his part of the Canyon. Seeing where he lived and prospected gives me a much better feel for what lies downstream and could be flooded if the river were stopped in its tracks at Bridge Canyon."

"Let's see if Steve is available at Park Headquarters," said Kirby.

Sabrina added, quietly, "I promise, I'll be civil."

* * *

"Kirby, it's about time you brought Sabrina along; Ma'am, I've been dying to meet you," said the Park Engineer. "Great job on the Pioneer Museum. It's getting as much visitation as the Geology Museum. What can I do for you two?"

Kirby started the conversation. "Steve, we have questions and concerns about the proposed Bridge Canyon Dam and how it could negatively impact the Canyon."

"Oh, that. I'm not in favor of the project but it may be out of our hands. The Bureau of Reclamation seems dead set on making it happen, despite National Park Service opposition."

Sabrina jumped into the discussion. "Mr. Baxter, you are the Grand Canyon National Park resident engineer; don't you have a say in how such a dam can impact the protected lands and river you oversee? We heard this dam could back water across the park boundary and many miles upriver!"

"That is true, Sabrina, and we have expressed those same sentiments. They are in the early stages of core-drilling. It may turn out the core samples reveal rock that will not support such a massive concrete monolith."

"So, Mr. Baxter, you are hoping the core samples fail, but what if they pass? Are we just going to let a big monster dam cripple the river and ruin Granite Gorge in the name of electric power generation for distant cities?"

"Sabrina, it's not just cities. Have you two heard of the Rural Electrification Administration? It was created by President Roosevelt and Congress six months ago with the goal of bringing electricity to America's rural areas. At first, power companies have been slow to come around, seemingly unwilling to string miles of wire over farmland and backcountry for the few farms and ranches along the route. It is hoped the project will offer some relief to the nation's unemployed but very few of the unemployed in rural areas possess the necessary electrical trade skills. Fortunately, the situation is turning around and it now appears the program will be a great success."

"Ah, electricity; who needs it?" Sabrina became increasingly frustrated. "With all due respect, sir, you are changing the subject. This Bridge Canyon monster could set a bad precedent. What if the next proposals start eyeing the upper reaches of the Canyon, like Marble

Canyon or Glen Canyon? It's like dams squeezing our national treasure to death, drowning our beloved Grand Canyon!"

"At the risk of making you angrier, Sabrina, there indeed are vague rumors to that effect."

Before Sabrina could say another word, Kirby tried to steer the conversation back to Bridge Canyon Dam. "Steve, I have a favor to ask. Would you kindly keep us updated on Bridge Canyon? We are very concerned about impacts downstream but more so upstream of the dam. It could devastate the cultural landscape, Anasazi sites, Hualapai and Havasupai tribal lands, springs and waterfalls, plant life, and wildlife like desert bighorn sheep and ringtail cats. As you know, Grand Canyon is sacred to many tribal nations in the region. We must respect their culture, their traditions, and their lands. We just can't imagine another lake flooding another ninety miles upstream, including thirteen miles into the protected lands of this national park."

"Kirby, in appreciation for all your help on the Black Bridge, I'll do what I can. By the way, I'm going to have the conservation boys give the bridge a second coat of paint. As for Bridge Canyon, keep in mind, any information I feed you will be unofficial." Steve added, "On a personal note, I completely concur with you and Sabrina, not on rural electric issues, but on river dam issues."

"Thank you, Mr. Baxter. I apologize for my outrage and we appreciate your time." Sabrina, not totally satisfied, at least got her points across.

As they left Park Headquarters, Kirby commented, "If a powerline comes close to the Circle K, maybe we should subscribe."

Sabrina glared at him. "How can you even think that at a time like this? We have a canyon dam to fight."

Under The Canyon Sky: Guarding the Treasure

* * *

When the O'Briens returned from Grand Canyon Village, they found a postcard in their mailbox at the gate.

"Kirby, Louis Jackson sent us a postcard by mule! Here's what he writes: Greetings from the bottom of Grand Canyon. I'll be at the River Camp October through March, beginning with a most unusual assignment—construction of a large, irregularly-shaped swimming pool fed by Skeleton Creek. As if the Canyon is not deep enough, we conservation boys are making this part eighteen feet deeper! Love LJ."

"Sabrina, imagine that, a swimming pool at the bottom of the Canyon!"

"When we were staying at the Dancing Ghost Ranch, I recall seeing an official mailbag slung over a packer's saddle horn. I'll bet every visitor takes a few minutes to send mule mail to folks back home. It's good to hear from Louis," commented Sabrina, "We were so busy with the museum during his first six-month term with the Civilian Conservation Corps, we failed to search him out on the South Rim. His second term was on the North Rim and now he's stationed at the River Camp. Sounds like his winter will be spent digging everything from gravel to boulders washed down from the North Rim over the centuries. Next time we visit the Dancing Ghost Ranch, we might test the waters in their swimming hole."

* * *

As an initial step in Sabrina's anti-dam campaign, she distributed Bridge Canyon Dam flyers in the two museums, community building, hotel lobbies, post office, railway station, and visitor center. She also wrote protest letters to area newspaper editors and members of

Congress. This action attracted the attention of the Park Superintendent who requested her presence in his office. On a cool mid-October morning, Kirby and Sabrina pulled into the parking lot at Park Headquarters.

"Good morning, Mr. & Mrs. O'Brien, the superintendent is expecting you. Please take a seat and I'll see if he is ready," said his secretary.

"Ah, Kirby and Sabrina O'Brien. You sure can make life difficult for me but first let me affirm our appreciation for your support for the Pioneers Museum. It's a beautiful facility and attracting a lot of attention. Your misguided flyers scattered about the Village are also attracting attention."

"Sir, we cannot just stand by and watch the Canyon be destroyed by hydroelectric power generation dams and reservoirs. We were both in the crowd and heard first-hand what Teddy Roosevelt said about the Grand Canyon. 'Leave it as it is. You cannot improve upon it. The ages have been at work on it, and man can only mar it.' I'd say Bridge Canyon Dam will definitely mar the Canyon."

"You don't need to cite that for me, ma'am; you can see I have it on a plaque on my office wall." The superintendent pointed to his plaque, then glared at Sabrina.

"Sir, I would like to know what the Park Service is doing about this planned assault on the Colorado River. I hope you are speaking against the dam in meetings with the Bureau of Reclamation. Bridge Canyon Dam will back water into the park!"

The superintendent stood up, "Not far enough to see from any of the overlooks! No one will notice the difference from the rim where most visitors view the Canyon!

Sabrina countered, "Mr. Superintendent, that is not the point. The cultural and environmental damage would be irreparable. Grand Canyon National Park, which you oversee, is the only thing standing in the way of the Colorado becoming a proliferation of dams and reservoirs.

Your job is to protect the Canyon, not make it available for electric power generation!"

"Don't tell me what my job is! For your information, we are working with the Bureau's Power Division, the State Water Resources Department, Indian Affairs, and the Hualapai Tribal Council to come up with a viable solution to support the West's insatiable thirst for hydroelectric power."

"Sir, that solution should not include dams in the Grand Canyon."

Kirby tried to calm her down but to no avail. "Sabrina, let's go. You've made your point."

"Not so fast, O'Briens. Before you leave the park, I want you to take down every flyer you posted. They are defacing both government property and concessioner facilities. And I urge you to leave canyon dam issues in the capable hands of federal, state and tribal government agencies."

Kirby and Sabrina left headquarters, feeling they had stirred up quite a hornet's nest. "Sabrina, your tirade reeked of disrespect for the man in charge here. Let's retrieve your flyers."

"If we don't take a stand, who will?" She ripped a flyer off the railway station entrance.

"Wait, before we go, let's visit Steve Baxter in the headquarters annex to see if he has any new information."

* * *

Steve looked up from his desk. "Kirby and Sabrina, you are back already?"

"We were in the neighborhood and thought we'd check on any new developments regarding dam building," responded Kirby.

"Well, your timing is perfect. I recently attended a meeting with the Bureau of Reclamation in Las Vegas. The National Park Service, specifically Grand Canyon National Park, has been kept in the dark for quite some time. I find that rather odd since both agencies have been part of the Department of the Interior for two or three decades now. Before I start, would you like a cup of fresh-brewed coffee? The pot over there in the corner just finished percolating."

Sabrina, juggling three full cups on a tray, took her seat next to Kirby in front of the park engineer's desk.

"Hang on to your coffee cups now. Bridge Canyon Dam has been on the Bureau's drawing boards for the past three years and the Bureau's hints of a future dam in Marble Canyon have been spawning considerable infighting among Reclamation, Park Service, and by far the oldest Interior Department bureau or agency, Indian Affairs."

"What? I can't believe this! Why have these proposals been kept so secret? The general public has a right to know the Canyon is under siege!" Sabrina spilled half her coffee in her lap. She whispered softly to Kirby, "We should put our flyers back up."

"I heard that, and I've seen your flyers. I assume the Superintendent has ordered them taken down. Ah, that's why you're in the neighborhood. Anyway, I believe river dams are not widely publicized right now for fear there would be undo speculation and confusion. Now that you have let one of the cats out of the bag, canyon dams won't be secret for long, instead, highly controversial. Between you and me, you are doing a great service as private citizens. As a Park Service employee, I cannot do that or I'll surely lose my job."

It was time for Kirby to speak up. "Steve, let's get back to Bridge Canyon Dam in a few minutes. But first, what do you hear about Marble Canyon Dam?"

"My information is based on rumor. Even test drilling is way off in the future but here's what I am picking up. It will likely be located about twenty miles upstream of the confluence of the Little Colorado and Big Colorado and . . ."

Kirby rudely interrupted, "Oh, that's Levi Jackson's old stomping grounds—his Little Colorado Mining District; he and I had a number of prospect holes along the river."

"As I was saying, the location means it may possibly back water all the way to Lees Ferry, the only river-level access point for nearly three hundred miles, and may threaten two natural features that Powell called the Redwall Cavern and Vasey's Paradise."

Sabrina jumped in, "Ooh, the fledgling river-running community won't like that! Let's get back to Bridge Canyon."

"Okay, this is where things get complicated and differing agency motives get very tangled. Even so," Steve cautioned, "We are only at the point of test drilling to determine the best locations for dam abutments."

"The Bridge Canyon Dam meeting in Las Vegas included representatives of Reclamation Power Division, National Park Service, which included an assistant director from Washington and myself, Indian Affairs, and Arizona Water Resources Department."

"Surprisingly, Indian Affairs' main interest was maintaining access to hunting and fishing for native peoples, and in the case of the Hualapai, making revenue from non-native recreation seekers since the elimination of rapids renders the river more usable for boating and water sports. All this concern for profit while the tribe continues its fight to reaffirm rights to its reservation, believing it would own considerably more river frontage, all south of the river. Questions arose about whether land finally secured by the Hualapai could be withdrawn for a reservoir. The dam site seems inaccessible on the Hualapai side of the river but it is felt construction roads, for which the Hualapai expect monetary compensation, would eventually facilitate recreation access. Indian Affairs also noted that water may back into Havasupai traditional lands; namely, the lower portion of Havasu Canyon, possibly as far upstream as Beaver Falls."

Steve added, "I was about to stand up for Native American rights when my colleague from Washington stated flatly that the Park Service had no objections to Bridge Canyon Dam!"

"No objections?" cried Sabrina, "This is crazy!"

"I agree," said Steve, "But listen to this. Arizona seemed more concerned about California grabbing all Colorado waters for itself. I sense a water fight coming between these two states. They both seemed to be playing selfish roles. Here's the rub. Arizona, like all upstream states, contributes to the Big Colorado. In Arizona's case, her contributions come from the Little Colorado, the Bill Williams River, and the Gila River, but California contributes nothing; it only takes water and far more than its share. At one point, the Arizona delegate said his state may seek control of the Canyon's water resources on its own and may even use that resource to generate power for its own use."

"Reclamation representatives watched as agency interests became more and more entangled. They expressed concern for rushing into dam projects without proper planning and without conforming to accepted engineering standards and practices. As an engineer myself, I heartily agree. Reclamation added that more in-depth studies and cost and benefit analyses are needed before we begin actual design. It also expressed the notion that increasing power needs would eventually soften the stance of park defenders."

"I'm not softening my position!" announced Sabrina. "On the contrary, all this nonsense has hardened my resolve. I will not allow the Grand Canyon to become home to a chain of lakes in support of hydroelectric power generation. I predict Canyon lovers like me will dig in their heels like a stubborn mule and oppose any dam on the river, especially inside this national park."

"Sabrina," cautioned Kirby, "We are a long way from a chain of lakes as you put it. Bridge Canyon Dam cannot become a reality without public review periods, legislative approvals, negotiation and agreement by all parties involved, and finally detailed engineering design and construction. That will take years."

"He's right, Sabrina, this will be a long project just like Boulder Dam," said Steve. "Let's keep monitoring the process over the coming years."

"Thank you, Steve. On behalf of Sabrina and myself, we appreciate you enlightening us on this assault on Grand Canyon. We need to get back to our Circle K Ranch before dark. See you again soon."

* * *

It occurred to Sabrina that when the Livingstons last visited, they missed raiding her other garden, the one with cucumbers, squash and pumpkins. She sent Kirby off in their Roadster to deliver this forgotten produce to Jeremy's RB Ranch, about thirty miles south of Summit Point.

"Kirby, what a surprise! What brings you out here?"

"I come bearing more produce from Sabrina's garden," answered Kirby as he jumped out of the driver's seat and pointed to some bright orange pumpkins in the rumble seat. "She wanted you and Rachel to have these, squash and cucumbers too. We had a bumper crop this year, despite the lingering drought."

Rachel joined the discussion. "Hello Kirby, not just drought but now we may be facing a cold dry winter. The Farmers' Almanac predicts temperatures well below average and little snow this winter." She motioned Cody over and everyone began carrying groceries into the cabin.

Kirby, noticing the poor condition of the Livingston cabin, asked, "How's your firewood supply?" Looking around, he saw places where daylight squinted between logs due to missing chinking, the roof flapping in the wind in one corner, windows and front door whistling where seals had long disappeared. He suspected the other rooms may harbor the same poor condition, certainly not ready for the bitter cold of winter.

Kirby turned to leave. "Oh, Jeremy, I see you have some cordwood stacked against the south wall."

"Yeah, but that's not nearly enough for the RB Ranch to get through winter. But we have two woodstoves! One has never been installed. Both were here when we bought the homestead. We only need one for this small cabin. Can you use the extra one?"

"Yes, I'll offer forty dollars for it if you move it and help install it at the Circle K."

Jeremy jumped at the chance to sell. "Deal, with winter weather moving in soon, how about if I haul it next Saturday and we set it up then?"

"That's a good plan. See you soon." As Kirby climbed back into his auto, he asked, "By the way, what does RB stand for?"

Rachel answered, "Rock Bottom, and thank you for the grocery delivery. We really appreciate your generosity and compassion."

On the drive home, Kirby kept thinking about other ways he could help his longtime friend. He told Sabrina about the woodstove deal and the exceedingly poor condition of the Livingston homestead. Then he broached an idea.

"Sabrina, we are now in our mid-seventies and beginning to slow down. We have a huge ranch house and could use some help managing our herd of Herefords. The Livingstons are in their mid-sixties and are barely making it. What do you think about inviting Jeremy, Rachel, and their adopted son Cody to move in with us? Together, we can help each other survive these changing times. We have the extra rooms; they desperately need help but are too humble to ask for it."

"Whoa, I know you and Jeremy go way back to your Shooting Star mining days, but this goes way beyond old friendships. I need some time to think about all of us living under one roof. I hope you have not dropped any hints on Jeremy yet. This is a serious decision for us; give me a few days to mull it over."

Chapter Seven

COG RAILS AND CABLEWAYS

Smiles are curves that set relationships straight

Sabrina agreed to the Livingstons moving in with them. They have plenty of extra bedrooms and she could use Rachel's help in the garden and sharing household chores. Kirby could certainly use Jeremy's help on their six-hundred-acre ranch, especially managing their growing Hereford herd, mending fences, and harvesting hay for storage in the barn.

When Jeremy and Rachel arrived with the wagon and wood stove, Sabrina made the offer. Cody stayed home at the RB ranch.

"Okay Livingstons, please join Kirby and I in the dining room. We have fresh-baked cookies, steaming hot coffee, and a proposal." Everyone took their seats. "I'll get right to the point. We are all getting old; I feel it in my bones every day and I'm sure old age is creeping into your lives too. As you can see, we have a very large ranch house, more than two people need. And we have good life-giving water due to dependable springs on our homestead. The so-called Great Depression has been hard on all of us and there are rumblings of impending war in Europe. Rachel, you said it yourself, you are having a rough time on your homestead. Even your well is going dry. Please come live with Kirby and I. We are inviting you to move to the Circle K Ranch as your permanent new home."

Rachel became choked up and tears streaked down her cheeks. Jeremy swallowed his cookie whole, choked and tried to set his coffee mug down without spilling. It sloshed onto the table. He could barely speak with a clogged throat.

"Kirby and Sabrina, you are the best . . . ahem, the best friends anyone could have. We've been having nightmares on how we are going to survive," explained Jeremy. "We too are slowing down. Cody is some help but he's still young."

Rachel jumped in, "What Jeremy is about to say is we accept your invitation. Our homestead is failing, and we are in a desperate situation. With all our hearts and with thanks that will endure for as long as we live, we would love to live with you here on your fine ranch. I promise we will do our share of the work and help in every way possible to make life together a joyous experience for all of us."

"Great, it's settled then," said Kirby, "Welcome to your new home. Jeremy, after we tackle the wood stove project, I suggest we relocate your livestock and any hay, firewood, and perishable food to the Circle K."

"Kirby, we have five horses, including the two hitched to our wagon out there, and fourteen Hereford cattle," explained Jeremy. "Oh, let's not forget our mule, Bernardo. We also have some meager furnishings but decisions on their disposition could wait till spring."

"No problem. Let's merge your Herefords with ours before winter sets in."

"And Cody can help us with the cattle roundup and drive as well as moving household items."

Kirby left the table and came back with four bottles of root beer. "I propose a toast. To the O'Briens and the Livingstons, life-long friends, together on the Circle K Ranch."

* * *

With winter approaching, Jeremy, Cody and Kirby set their mind to installing the wood-burning stove from the Livingston homestead. They offloaded it from Jeremy's wagon and moved it into the great room on the ground floor of the Circle K ranch house. The plan called for positioning this second stove near the stairway leading to bedrooms on the second floor. The stove pipe would also serve as a radiator for both floors. All work stopped when Kirby realized he needed to drive into Flagstaff for sections of stove pipe and a chimney cap. Jeremy and Cody went home, to return the following day.

While in Flagstaff, Kirby bought the latest edition of the *Frontier Times* newspaper. Its headlines 'Cog Railway Planned for Grand Canyon' and the subheading 'Village to Plateau Point' bothered him all the way home.

"Sabrina, look at this, another assault on the Grand Canyon!" Kirby was clearly in a foul mood.

"Now what, Kirby, what could be worse than dams on the river?"

"Cog rails and cableways. We can't deal with this now. We've got to get the Livingstons settled in. After that, let's pay Steve Baxter another visit."

Kirby and Sabrina took a personal interest in protecting the Canyon. They involved themselves in every controversial issue that came along and with each one their trust in park management diminished. Over the years, many issues have surfaced: greedy corporations driving out the pioneers, canceling mining claims that preceded park status, federal officials not enforcing its own rules and regulations, exploiting water resources to power distant cities, and now plans to turn the national park into an amusement park with tram cars providing tourists easy access to the inner gorge.

After spending two days installing the wood stove, the next order of business called for a small-scale cattle drive from the Rock Bottom

Ranch to the Circle K Ranch. The latter encompassed a square mile tract or full section of land. Like professional cowboys, Kirby, Jeremy and Cody handled the round-up and drive with ease.

For two weeks in November, the men made many forty-mile wagon trips between ranches. These included three loads of personal belongings, clothes, important papers, books, canned goods, perishables, and a few heirlooms to the house. Three more loads included hay, bags of feed, tack, and tools to the barn, and two more loads to move Jeremy's firewood to Kirby's woodshed. After all these trips, Jeremy placed locks on the RB Ranch cabin and gate for the winter.

Once settled into the O'Brien homestead, Jeremy wrote to his brother about the move. Dexter responded by passing on to Kirby and Sabrina his appreciation for taking in his brother's family. As a side note he added that three boats he helped build made it through the Canyon a few months ago. It was a scientific expedition carrying two women botanists so Sabrina cannot be the first woman down the river. Sabrina wondered where he ever got that notion. She never considered such a run.

* * *

As early as nineteen twenty, an eastern developer proposed a twelve-mile-long, trans-canyon aerial tramway as a tourist attraction. Not one cable run, but multiple hops using the tallest buttes for tower support, with the south terminal at the Village. Neither Grand Canyon National Park, only a year old, nor the National Park Service, only four years old, had any appetite for such a grandiose scheme. Consequently, the developer's request to conduct surveys received a quick denial.

Kirby remembered the Canyon Copper Company's plan to service the Shooting Star Mine with a tram to lift copper ore to Summit Point.

When the bottom dropped out of the copper market, the company scuttled the plan. More recently, he recalled the Civilian Conservation Corps at the mouth of Skeleton Creek and Trails West's camp below Sunset Point both using a tram to haul food and supplies. However, no one dreamed of carrying human cargo with these aerial tramways. Kirby also suspected that construction of Bridge Canyon Dam, should it ever happen, would surely use aerial trams to lower heavy equipment, concrete and electrical generators down to the damsite.

"Sabrina, before visiting Park Engineer Steve Baxter about a proposed canyon cog railway, I think I will conduct some research on my own, maybe spend some time in the Flagstaff public library to get more conversant in cog rails. I just reread that *Frontier Times* article. It proposes a cog railway from a high terminal on the rim to a low terminal on the Tonto, with Plateau Point Lodge overlooking the gorge. If it's a straight run like an aerial tram, it seems way too steep so I'm guessing it must descend in wide sweeping curves."

"Good idea to do some studying, Kirby." Sabrina had an additional thought. "We may find that Steve himself has been blindsided by this wild idea of a canyon cog railway operating below the rim. I hope we can keep such contraptions out of the Canyon."

* * *

"Sabrina, I'm ready to meet with Steve, but first, here's what I learned in my library study." Kirby bubbled with information on the inner workings of cog railways.

"These contraptions, as you call them, are rather rare, in fact, a novelty, and serve only to climb mountains. The tourist trade in Colorado has a cog railway that ascends Pike's Peak but the situation here at the Canyon is mountain-climbing in reverse."

Kirby thumbed through his notes. "The key to the whole operation is a cog wheel under a narrow-gauge diesel locomotive, continuously engaged in a toothed center rail; two cog teeth are always engaged to assure good traction. So, the cog drive is a matter of smoothly meshing gears. The outer rails serve as a guide and carry the load but have nothing to do with power."

Sabrina rolled her eyes as Kirby continued his technical dissertation.

"The engine is a special design, nothing like what the Santa Fe Railway uses here, to lower one or two passenger cars into the canyon depths and then pull them back up to the rim. The cog and track provide significant braking capability; in fact, both the engine and cars have this safety brake feature. Cog railways can handle grades as much as twenty-five percent."

"Kirby, a cog rail system like you describe would severely detract from the beauty and solitude of Grand Canyon. We need to fight this. Imagine this growling monster snaking its way into the Canyon, crisscrossing the Pioneer Trail in wide sweeping curves, and leaving a hideous scar on the Tonto, all in the name of thrilling lazy passengers in a dramatic descent into the abyss," exclaimed Sabrina.

"And the sight of a lodge at its Plateau Point terminal would be appalling," said Kirby. "I remember when Hearst entertained thoughts of a cog railway from the East Rim into Granite Gorge, replete with palatial palaces at both terminals. Thank goodness he gave up on that plan, but this nightmare sounds like the same kind of tourist attraction. There were also efforts to develop a scenic railway along the East Rim—Anna Bridgestone's dream."

"Teddy would fight these proposals to the end," added Sabrina. "We may need to commit to the same fight. Let's go see Steve in the morning."

* * *

The O'Brien's bright red Roadster reached the Village about mid-morning. The Canyon received a light dusting of snow during the night. Their footprints led directly to the unlocked annex door. They headed straight for the Park Engineer's office.

"Hey, you can't just blaze in here like that; who are you?"

"Sorry, I am Kirby O'Brien and this is my wife, Sabrina. We'd like to see Steve Baxter."

"He's not here. By now he is in New Mexico where he has been assigned as engineer for White Sands National Monument. It's a fairly new Park Service site, about five years old I believe, and has no dam issues."

Sabrina was shocked. "What! He never said anything about a reassignment! Sir, who are you?"

"I'm the new Park Engineer, Russell Cramer; how can I help you folks?"

Kirby answered, "Mr. Cramer, we are interested in the Park's position on the proposed cog railway to Plateau Point."

"Several people have been asking me about that. I read the newspaper article but have not seen the proposal. I'm more concerned with a reliable water supply for the Village than dams on the Colorado. I understand my predecessor's anti-dam stance may have been a factor in his transfer. I won't have a position on a proposed cog railway here in the park until I can get my hands on technical details. I suggest you meet with the superintendent to see if he knows what headquarters is thinking. Sounds like a thrilling cog rail ride might increase visitation."

Sabrina had to ask, "Sir, increasing visitation is not the point. Aren't you concerned about how such a system would impact the scenery and solitude of this place? How a cog railway would scar the Canyon? Would you actually be in favor of a lodge at Plateau Point?"

"My concern right now is water supply which has been severely impacted by this long drought, not some crazy cog railway scheme. At some point, I'll probably get involved in a feasibility study. Now, if you'll excuse me, I need to get back to work here."

Mr. Cramer paged through his calculations on how many Santa Fe water tankers were needed in the coming week. He never looked up when Kirby apologized for the interruption.

"Sabrina, I can't believe this. Steve is gone and without a word. We had grown rather close. He often referred to me as his assistant engineer."

"Kirby, it sounds like his position on the Bridge Canyon Dam project may have led to his transfer, but he only shared that with us. How did the Park get wind of his position? I hope Steve doesn't think we leaked information he shared with us."

"We may never know. And worse, we have no sympathetic ears to listen to our cog rail concerns. I doubt the superintendent would be inclined to meet with us on another assault on the Canyon. Where do we go from here?"

Sabrina sighed, "Home, I guess."

As they walked back to the snow-covered parking lot, Sabrina added, "I did pick up one small clue that may be in our favor. Russell Cramer referred to the proposed cog railway as a crazy scheme. Perhaps when he learns more about it, he'll oppose the project."

"Then he'll also risk being transferred out. Hey look! Isn't that Louis Jackson trudging through the snow?"

Kirby shouted, "Louis is that you?"

Louis came over to greet the O'Briens. "Kirby! Sabrina! What a surprise! I've been thinking about getting back in touch. Did you get my mule mail? I'm still with the Civilian Conservation Corps. We finished all our work in Skeleton Canyon. I'm now back on the South Rim. So good to see you again!"

Sabrina asked, "Louis, do you have time to join us for dinner at the Canyon Queen Café, and an opportunity to catch up on each other? Dinner on us."

"I'm not on duty yet. I'd like that very much."

Kirby suggested getting out of the snow. "This snowfall is getting heavier; let's walk over there now and place our order."

"Louis, the last we heard, you conservation boys were digging a swimming hole at Dancing Ghost Ranch. How did that turn out?" asked Sabrina.

"Very well. Boy, did we take out a lot of rock. It's roughly forty feet by seventy feet and nearly twenty feet deep. Skeleton Creek keeps it full of ice-cold water. I've picked up a lot of skills working in the Corps. Trades that I can use later."

As dinner was served, Kirby asked, "What's your favorite trade?"

"Pipefitting. I've become fairly skilled at assembling steel railings at viewpoints here on the South Rim and also steel poles with yardarms for the trans-canyon telephone line. Seems I've worked on everything from mule corral railings to flagpoles. How are you two doing?"

"Well Louis, Sabrina and I are slowing down. We're in our mid-seventies now and seem to be doing more rim-sitting than trail-riding. You may not know Jeremy Livingston, but we recently have invited he and his family to live with us at the Circle K. They were having a rough time with the depression and drought. It's good to have their help running the ranch, especially when we come up here to the Canyon."

Sabrina added, "And we've been fighting the proposed Bridge Canyon Dam project, and we recently became aware of a proposed cog railway. We just learned today that our good friend Steve Baxter, the

Park Engineer, has been transferred. Perhaps you remember him. He helped you enroll in the Corps."

"I do remember Steve. In fact, I was working on a flagpole outside the superintendent's office window recently and overheard a heated argument between the Supe, that's what we boys call him, and Steve. It was all about Bridge Canyon Dam, but I did not catch any details. Just before I heard a door slam, I heard the Supe shout something about if Steve did not change his attitude about dams on the Colorado, he would be transferred out of here. I guess that happened. Too bad. Steve was a good guy."

Kirby added, "The new Park Engineer just informed us that Steve has been assigned to White Sands in New Mexico."

"Oh, you mean Russell Cramer. He's got us working on all kinds of Village piping systems, pumps and tanks. He's panicking, worried we're going to run out of water any day now. I've been working on a valve manifold to facilitate offloading Santa Fe tanker cars. In fact, my shift is about to start. We pipefitters are under pressure to solve the water shortages here."

"Louis, thank you for joining us for dinner. Let's stay in touch. Sabrina and I also need to get going before this snowstorm closes the roads. Take care."

* * *

Several bitterly cold months had passed with no new developments on river dams or cog railways. Kirby hoped those crazy plans froze over the winter, never to thaw out. Still, he could not get these canyon threats off his mind. He often awakened in the middle of the night worrying about things over which he had no control.

During occasional visits to the Village, Kirby heard complaints of the continuing drought. There had been very little snow that winter and that meant sparse grass on the ranch for his Hereford cattle. Also, among foreign visitors to the Canyon, he heard talk of impending war in Europe. He could do nothing about the drought at home or disputes among faraway countries.

Sabrina heard the same rumors when she visited the Pioneer Museum. Teresa had talked her into volunteering as a guest speaker during their weekly ranger programs at the museum. She loved talking about the pioneers she once knew so well, and each presentation kept her mind off the idiocy of park management and the threat of another mindless war in Europe. Her talks and walking tours through the museum went on through the spring and summer when most tourists visit the Canyon. She often talked about Monte Bridgestone, Levi Jackson, Clancy Jennings and Francois LaRue, all of whom are featured in the museum she founded.

One day at the museum, Sabrina overheard two British visitors talking about war breaking out in Europe. "Excuse me, we do not get much world news here at the Canyon. Did I hear you say there is a war going on overseas?"

"Yes ma'am," answered an elderly gentleman, "As we boarded our ship for America, Germany attacked Poland, then Britain and France responded by declaring war on Germany. A month has passed since then, but we just learned that Poland has now been defeated by a combination of Nazi and Soviet forces."

Sabrina could not believe how multiple disasters compounded themselves. First the Great Depression, then the continuing drought, now a war in Europe. She cut her talk about Levi Jackson short that day and raced home to tell Kirby and the Livingstons what she had just learned.

On her drive back to the Circle K she prayed that the United States would stay out of that conflict. It had nothing to do with America. She found Kirby working on the ranch gate.

"Kirby, Europe is at war! Some British folks just told me that Poland has fallen to Germany. Here's hoping this does not lead to another world war."

"I've been worried that this might happen," said Kirby. "Why can't those countries just get along with each other? At least we have a big ocean between us. I'll meet you at the house; just tightening these gate hinges then I'll be along."

The O'Briens and Livingstons gathered around the kitchen table for coffee and cookies.

"How did today's talk go?" asked Rachel.

"Our visitors seem absolutely fascinated by the life and times of Levi Jackson. That reminds me, Kirby and I had a nice conversation with Levi's grandson, Louis Jackson, a few months ago. He's doing well and learning a number of trade skills; seems to have a real knack for fitting pipes together, the kind you see used on safety railings and flagpoles, and that kind of work has led to water utility pipes and plumbing fixtures."

Jeremy remarked, "Good for him, that kind of training may become very useful in the future."

Sabrina changed the subject. "I just learned from a British couple visiting on the South Rim that war has broken out in Europe; even their country, as well as France, has declared war on Germany. Hopefully we will not be dragged into this."

"I share that sentiment," stated Kirby. "Hey, look out the window. I believe those are early snowflakes drifting our way. Maybe we'll have an early snowstorm this year. While we're all sitting here, I'm thinking we need a second autocar here on the Circle K. Our two seat Roadster is fine for three riders, the third being in the rear rumble seat, but Jeremy, you need something more than a horse and wagon when not on the ranch. What if we all want to ride up to the Canyon together? I'm thinking we should look into buying a used touring car. Perhaps Trails West has one for sale. I understand train ridership is down and private autocars are everywhere which makes me think demands for Trails West touring cars are also down."

"Jeremy, before you say anything, don't worry about the cost. I've got that covered," said Sabrina. "Kirby, this will make it much easier for running into Flagstaff for supplies. Our Roadster does not hold much. Good plan. Let's see what we can do."

"You folks are so good to us. Kirby, if you think we are looking at an early winter, I need to get back to repairing that north fence line. Good horse and wagon job for me."

"Okay, everyone, let's not worry about what's going on in Europe. We can't do anything about it anyway," concluded Sabrina. "Oh, one more thing, Teresa tells me sales of Monte's book are still going very well. In fact, the Park Service and Trails West got together and ordered a second printing from the New York publishing house, enough to supply their retail outlets at the two museums, the visitor center and hotel gift shops."

* * *

For most of his adult years, including his barrel-filling days at Arrowhead Spring and his network of cisterns catching water off the Grand Canyon Hotel roof, Kirby has been wrestling with ways to capture, store and deliver life-giving water. The continuing drought rekindled his interest in water resources.

One day he decided to drive to the Village and share his latest idea with Park Engineer Russell Cramer, even though he got off to a bad start with this persnickety engineer.

"Oh, you again; why don't you make an appointment like everyone else?"

"Because, sir, I'm not everyone else. You should listen to me. I have spent considerable time in this office providing design suggestions to your predecessor on the Black Bridge project."

Russell swiveled in his chair. "Do you have a degree in engineering or a background in civil or structural design?"

"No, nothing like that. But I witnessed the collapse of the swinging bridge and offered ideas on abutment anchor design and terminal access for the replacement bridge."

"Then you are wasting my time. I need to get back to solving Village water supply issues."

"That's what I am talking about!" Kirby's frustration with this bureaucrat's attitude approached the boiling point.

"Sir, you should know my wife is the benefactor for the new Pioneer Museum and we are both canyon pioneers dating back to the turn of the century."

"That's a beautiful museum. I did not realize you two were involved."

"Involved? We planned and staged all the exhibits and Sabrina financed the architectural design and the construction!"

"Okay, okay, what's your big idea?"

Kirby unrolled a sketch on how to capture the water resources on the North Rim.

"Take a look. My idea is to channel spring water gushing from a North Rim cave through a trans-canyon pipeline to the South Rim. It would be gravity flow all the way down Skeleton Creek via pipeline, across the river, and up to Canyon Gardens. There it would supplement the Canyon Gardens supply which is delivered to the rim by the existing pump station and the four-mile pipeline that the Santa Fe Railway recently constructed. That pipeline generally follows the Pioneer Trail and even services the rest shelters along the way, built by the Conservation boys. As you may already know, for over thirty years, before thoughts of any kind of pipeline, the Santa Fe hauled water to the Village by railcar."

"And exactly how do you plan to cross the river?" The engineer remained highly skeptical.

"Only two choices. Either a pipeline slung under the Black Bridge or a new pedestrian bridge dedicated to carrying precious water to the Village."

"Can I borrow your sketch?" With a wide smile, Russell said, "I think you are on to something, Kirby O'Brien. I apologize for my bad attitude and bad mood. I'm new here and under a lot of pressure. Please give my best regards to your wife. You two are welcome to visit anytime."

"Thank you, Mr. Cramer. You can keep my sketch if you promise to pass along any news about the Bridge Canyon Dam project or the cog railway proposal. I would like to stop by whenever I'm in the area. Sabrina and I live on a ranch straddling the old stage road, but we come here often. She is a guest presenter for the museum's weekly ranger program."

"Oh, one more thing, Russell, if I may call you by your first name, Sabrina also financed publication of the book, *Monte Bridgestone—Pioneer of the Grand Canyon*. It's not a biography; it's Monte's story about all the canyon pioneers. You can buy a copy at the Pioneer Museum gift shop."

Smiling again, Russell said, "I will do that, thank you, Kirby, if I too may call you by your first name. Again, you and Sabrina are welcome to visit anytime."

As Kirby turned to leave the annex, he had one more thought. "Russell, I have another idea for a Village water supply, rather far-fetched but I thought I'd run it by you. Perhaps snowmelt can be captured from high in the San Francisco Peaks and channeled into a gravity pipeline across the Coconino Plateau. At some point along the way, an in-line pump station or two may be needed to boost water to the South Rim."

After a long pause, Russell shook his head in doubt.

"Well, so much for that wild idea, probably unreliable for a year-round water supply. See you next time."

As he sat in the driver's seat of his Roadster for a few moments, Kirby sighed, hardly believing the rapid turnaround in Russell's attitude and composure. An old adage came to mind: smiles are curves that set relationships straight. He congratulated himself in taking the initiative on kindling a friendly relationship with the new park engineer.

* * *

When Kirby arrived back home, he found Rachel and Cody in deep conversation about how the Village developed. Rachel, not as knowledgeable as Kirby, asked for help.

"Here's the story, Cody. While the first canyon visitors stepped onto the rim where Monte Bridgestone and Clancy Jennings established early tourist enterprises, that area did not grow into a village. It simply served as the terminus for the stage line, but unfortunately not the railroad. The Santa Fe Railway solidified the location of Grand Canyon Village by touching the Canyon fifteen miles further west. And with the railroad came hordes of tourists."

"So that explains why the Village is where it is now," said Cody.

Kirby continued, "And here is how it grew. With the railroad came its subsidiary, Trails West, which became the principal concessioner in the park. Clint McCarty's questionable mining claims eventually gave way to village development. By the turn of the century, the Santa Fe-Trails West conglomerate built the luxurious Canyon Queen Hotel on the rim, and set back from the rim, the railyard and train station, and a mule barn across the way. Even McCarty established a hotel by relocating the stage line's Red Horse Station to a site between the tracks and the rim. Chad Sherman's Cliffhanger Studio continued to teeter on the edge and the Starlight Lodge integrated Buckey O'Neill's cabin into its lodging complex."

"Here's the part I remember," said Rachel as now the story reached her time at the Canyon. "Grand Canyon Village continued to grow with the addition of a clinic, schools, multi-purpose community building, curio shops, and Bergner's country store. McCarty's Hotel eventually housed the Village's official post office. When autocars began to siphon travelers away from rail transportation, the Park Service and Trails West, with tremendous help from the Civilian Conservation Corps, rushed to build motor lodges, a gasoline station, better roads and more parking lots."

"That's right, Rachel, and now with the drought that you experienced at your RB Ranch, the Park is searching for alternate water supplies." Cody, the door is wide open for a career in this branch of engineering. I realize you are still in your late teens but it's something to think about as you decide on a direction for your life journey."

Chapter Eight

WINDS OF WAR

I'll be coming home, wait for me

In the Spring of nineteen forty, German forces invaded Norway and Denmark, then began their assault on western Europe by attacking and conquering France, Belgium and Netherlands. That Fall, the United States, while still hoping to avoid entering the expanding military conflict, instituted the Selective Service Act requiring all men between the ages of twenty-one and forty-five to register for the draft.

Far from Europe, the war of dams at the Grand Canyon continued for another year and Park Engineer Russell Cramer continued to update Kirby on the Bridge Canyon Dam.

"Kirby, I finally received an update from the Bureau of Reclamation. It is dated August nineteen forty-one. After constantly finding no suitable site for the dam, the drill team pivoted and found four sites with excellent abutment rock although, from a construction standpoint, they reside in the rising backwater of Boulder Dam. The report touts the silt-trapping benefit that Bridge Canyon Dam would provide Boulder. The Bureau has set its sights on locating the dam at river mile two-thirty-six. A four-year construction period is anticipated."

"So, Russell, what does this mean?"

"Kirby, it means that if Bridge Canyon Dam is built, it will back water all the way into Lower Havasu Canyon and many miles into the Park."

"Ugh! Sabrina will not like this news," groaned Kirby.

"I would not worry about it. I have a bad feeling that it is just a matter of time before the war in Europe explodes into World War Two. Kirby, that's just my gut feeling, but tensions are rising, including in the Pacific."

On the drive back to the ranch, Kirby realized that Cody may soon be eligible for the draft. With war on the horizon, the Bridge Canyon Dam project will surely be put on hold. He will convey that sentiment to Sabrina when he reports on his meeting with Russell. In the water fight between Arizona and California, Arizona focused on becoming the sole proprietor of a canyon dam. Even if that plan materialized, another world war would stop it dead in its tracks.

Sabrina took the Bridge Canyon news very well. "I agree with Russell. If war breaks out in the Pacific, that plan is dead."

Changing the subject, Kirby announced, "Sabrina, our Roadster needs gas. Although winter is about to take hold, I think the roads are still clear. Let's drive into Flagstaff and fill the tank and perhaps have a nice Sunday dinner at the restaurant inside the Monte Vista Hotel."

"I heard they have steak dinner specials on Sundays. Let's get our heavy coats and head for town," beamed Sabrina, but adding, "The roads may be lightly snow-packed but probably okay in town."

At the gas station, a small crowd huddled around a wooden tabletop radio set in the station office, listening to Grand Canyon Broadcasting Company's news report. "What's going on?" asked Kirby. A fellow with his hand on the volume control answered, "The Japanese attacked Pearl Harbor, Hawaii this morning! It's bad, two aerial attacks on our Pacific Fleet, several battleships sunk, thousands of sailors and marines killed."

Sabrina entered the office. "What is taking so long?"

"You have been worried about war breaking out in the Pacific. It just did!"

"Oh no, how bad?" Sabrina couldn't believe it.

"Very bad, the Japs bombed our ships moored in Pearl Harbor and sunk battleships California, Utah and Arizona, and caused Oklahoma to capsize, and heavily damaged several more battleships and cruisers, and hundreds of warplanes at nearby airfields," said another of the listeners.

"No, not our Arizona!?" shouted Sabrina.

"Yes, she just arrived back in port yesterday. They say an armor-piercing bomb penetrated the forward ammunition bunker. The tremendous explosion lifted the ship half out of the water, then she quickly settled on the bottom, only her masts and turrets showing above the surface. They estimate the explosion and sinking killed over eleven hundred crewmen."

On that fateful day, telephone switchboard operators, newspaper presses, telegraph operators, and radio broadcasters poured out hundreds and hundreds of news stories from coast to coast. The next day the United States declared war on Japan and ordered its Army and Navy forces into action. A few days later, Germany and Italy declared war on the United States which in turn declared war on them. Enlistments surged as angry civilians, vowing retaliation, swamped recruiting stations which stayed open around the clock. Sabrina's worst nightmare became a reality. This unprovoked, dastardly, surprise attack propelled an outraged nation into World War Two. It solidified public sentiment on war and ended any support for neutrality. Americans quickly rallied to support their country; all other matters became insignificant.

"Sabrina, I'm no longer in the mood for a quiet dinner at the Monte Vista. We have a full tank. Let's get home and break the news to Jeremy and Rachel."

"I feel like the whole world is falling apart. Let's go."

On the drive back to the ranch, Sabrina broke the quiet, somber mood. "Kirby, don't you think it's ironic that the Arizona, California and Utah battleships are named after the same states impacted by controversial dam projects on the Colorado? The loss of Arizona is most disturbing. I wonder how many Arizonans went down with the ship. Another thought. Like our battleship, I wonder if the Bridge Canyon Dam project is now dead in the water."

Five minutes later, "And one more thought, Kirby. If the Japanese can successfully sneak up on Hawaii, attack Pearl Harbor, inflict so much damage on our naval fleet, and murder so many sailors and marines, plus innocent civilians, I wonder what prevents a similar assault on the United States mainland, especially our Pacific coast."

"Our nation is very much on guard now. I'll bet we have coast watchers staked out along both coasts. This attack on Pearl Harbor is an absolute disaster but I'm sure, in the end, we will win through to victory and our Arizona battleship and all the others will be soundly avenged," concluded Kirby. But deep down inside he harbored another worry, that Louis and Cody may be drafted into service.

* * *

Kirby and Sabrina filled in the Livingstons on what they heard on the Flagstaff radio station. With the country now in a state of war, the selective service would soon be sending out draft notices.

Sabrina asked Rachel, "How old is Cody?"

"He will be twenty-one in February," answered Rachel, with a worried look. "Upon registration, he could be immediately drafted into the Army."

Deciding everyone needed to get into the Christmas spirit, Sabrina announced, "Despite the war, I'd like to start planning for the holidays, our families plus Louis. Maybe Cody and his girlfriend Cora can bring a nice Christmas tree for our great room. Let's pack up all our troubles and worries and set them aside for a while."

Kirby agreed, "I'll drive to Grand Canyon Village to extend the invitation to Louis. I'm sure our country's entry in the war has foreshadowed the end of the Civilian Conservation Corps."

Indeed, with enrollment on the decline, Congress diverted the Corps budget to national defense projects, although some of the last Corps projects focused on military base improvements and training, without weapons, at conservation camps. The boys easily transitioned into military life; after all, the Army ran the camps and disciplined these civilians to work as teams.

Before Kirby had a chance to visit Louis at the Village, Louis visited the Circle K on a return trip from Flagstaff.

"Hey, that's Louis in a jeep coming through our gate!" exclaimed Sabrina. "What's he doing here? Perfect timing, we can invite him to our holiday celebration."

"Howdy, Mrs. O'Brien! I thought I'd stop by and update you on my plans. Our Corps funds are being redirected to the war effort and we'll be out of business in a few months. I just came from the Navy recruiting station and have a plan in the works."

Kirby motioned Louis to come inside. "It sure is good to see you. I planned to drive to the South Rim and invite you to join us for Christmas."

"Christmas with the O'Brien-Livingston gang would be perfect. The Corps is winding down and will soon be history. I borrowed that Army jeep out there for a quick trip to Flagstaff but wanted to stop on my return and update you on my own plans."

Sabrina served steaming cups of hot chocolate at the kitchen table. "Louis, you may miss the Livingstons on your quick stop here today.

They are visiting their old homestead and retrieving a few pieces of furniture and kitchenware that can be used here."

"Okay, Louis Jackson," added Sabrina, "let's have it, what are you up to now?"

Louis set his cup down, and to Kirby and Sabrina's surprise, shared a story about Teddy Roosevelt.

"One day I met Jacob Greenfield repairing cables at the south terminal of the first aerial river crossing, you know, that rickety cage on a cable. He told me about his encounter with Teddy Roosevelt when he used the cable crossing to reach North Rim hunting grounds. That trip, just before the First World War, reminded Teddy of an earlier experience aboard a Navy submarine named Plunger. Jacob said the President stepped aboard as the submarine bobbed in Long Island Sound's rolling surf; seawater splashed down the open hatch. Teddy climbed down the slippery ladder and entered the bowels of that steel tube. He spent an entire afternoon inside that submarine, marveling at its inner workings. For an hour, the submarine sat on the bottom with the President of the United States completely out of reach of Congress. Ever since hearing Jacob's story, I've dreamed about what it would be like to be submerged at sea."

Kirby asked, "Louis, where are you going with this wild tale?"

"I am enlisting in the Navy! The recruiter says my pipefitting experience with the Conservation Corps and the Park Service fit perfectly into the Navy's shipfitter rating. He thinks I would have a jump on others at age twenty-nine, being more senior than most recruits. I'll separate from the Corps in January and begin basic and shipfitter training at Norfolk, Virginia, followed by submarine training in New London, Connecticut. After that, I'll be assigned to a submarine in the Pacific Theater. That's where I can do my part as the nation shifts its manpower to the war effort."

"Submarines?" exclaimed Sabrina, "That sounds like very dangerous duty."

"That's why it is strictly voluntary but it's what I want to do. Submarines are packed full of hydraulic, water and air systems with pumps, valves, tanks, and other fixtures. A shipfitter's dream, and vital to a submarine's operation."

"Wow," said Kirby, "A lot can go wrong with all those systems; what a change from Grand Canyon pipefitting to service in Navy ships that sink on purpose!"

"The Japanese sank the Arizona on purpose. I intend to do my part in wreaking havoc on Japanese forces. It's my way of getting revenge and getting our nation back on a path to peaceful times," promised the future submariner.

"I do have one request, Kirby. I have no next of kin. The Department of Defense requires a family contact or close friend to notify in case of emergency. May I give them your name and address?"

"Certainly, but I hope they never have a need to contact us."

"Thank you. Now, I must hit the road. My supervisor is going to want his jeep back and I have the duty in the morning. I think the task at hand for my team is a leaky valve manifold on a storage tank. See you Christmas morning!"

* * *

Ten days before Christmas, Cody and Cora rolled through the open ranch gate with a nice-sized pinyon in the wagon.

"Whoa, Bernardo! This is the Circle K Ranch, Cora, where my parents and I are staying. Wait till I introduce you to the O'Briens, Kirby and Sabrina, the nicest folks you'll ever meet."

Besides the Christmas tree, Cody also borrowed some tree ornaments from Cora's parents, carefully packed in a cardboard carton with a shipping label indicating it once contained something for the National Park Service. Cody helped a beautiful eighteen-year-old lady, with long blond hair, from the wagon seat. No one in the household had ever met Cody's secret girlfriend.

"Mom and Dad, I'd like to introduce you to Cora Cramer," said Cody, "we met in the Village last year. Cora, this is my father Jeremy and my mother Rachel. And here are the O'Briens, Kirby and Sabrina."

Sabrina stepped forward and clasped Cora's hand. "Welcome to the Circle K. It is very nice to meet you, Cora. This is my husband, Kirby. I assume you already met Cody's parents or are you meeting them for the first time now?"

Jeremy clarified, "We have not met until now." Unable to take his eyes off Cora, he added. "So, you are the one who keeps drawing Cody to the Village." Rachel then chimed in, "Now I understand why Cody kept volunteering to run errands in the Village. Welcome, Cora."

"So, Cora, it seems you live in the Village?"

"Yes, ma'am, in park employee housing. My father is the park engineer."

"You are Russell Cramer's daughter?!"

"Yes, Mrs. O'Brien; do you know my father? We are fairly new at Grand Canyon. By the way, my dad says some areas in the park are about to close; most management gets to stay on even though Washington has cut the Park Service budget to the bone. It will look rather vacant soon. Male employees are flocking to Armed Forces centers, tourism is dropping like a rock, and all but the Canyon Queen Hotel plan to close—all due to the war.

"Why are we all standing out here?" asked Kirby. "Let's get out of the cold, come on inside."

Cora announced, "We brought a Christmas tree, fresh cut from the National Forest, plus a box of ornaments from my house."

"Cora, we are overjoyed to meet you and overwhelmed by the Cramer connection." Then glaring at Cody, "Your friend here, never mentioned your last name!"

"Cody, let me help you get that tree inside," offered Kirby. "With our ornament collection and the box you brought, we should have a spectacular Christmas tree."

With the tree inside, Cody went back to retrieve the box.

"Kirby," said Jeremy, "I spotted some boards in the barn, perfect for making a tree stand. I'll pick some out and get a hammer and nails." Sabrina cautioned the men not to put the tree too close to the new wood-stove.

The ladies retired to the kitchen to brew some coffee and prepare a light lunch.

When Jeremy returned with the makings of a tree-stand, he whispered to his son, "Wow, Cody, she is beautiful!"

All talk during lunch revolved around the war. Sabrina announced, "We just learned that Louis Jackson, Levi's grandson, is enlisting in the Navy. He wants to be a submariner!"

Jeremy and Rachel never broached the subject of Cody's upcoming draft registration for fear of upsetting Cora. "I prefer to keep my feet on dry land," said Cody.

"Me too," said Jeremy, "but someone needs to climb this stepladder and place this angel on the top of our Christmas tree."

Sabrina declared, "That honor goes to our special guest, Cora. To me the angel on high is a statement of the ever-popular phrase we hear every year about this time: Peace on earth, goodwill toward men. This year, with a world at war, it is especially important to say it out loud and often. It means we strive for a world without war, a society where we respect and help our friends and neighbors, a place where we protect and uplift those most in need."

And with that, Cora performed the honors. As she set the angel on the very top of that fragrant pinyon pine, she repeated the time-honored expression: "Peace on earth . . ." She almost lost her balance . . . "goodwill toward men."

Sabrina reminded everyone to be there Christmas morning.

"Louis will be here and Cody, I'm sure you will make sure Cora joins us. One more thing. It's Christmas, no more war talk."

* * *

During turkey dinner, all conversation steered clear of any mention of war. Louis summarized his time with the Civilian Conservation Corps, Cody confessed his Village visits also served as chances to see Cora, Jeremy proposed a toast to Kirby and Sabrina for inviting the Livingstons to live at the ranch, and Kirby discussed various park projects like the Black Bridge across the river. Sabrina expressed her joy in seeing her Pioneer Museum promise to Monte come to fruition. Cora explained that her family will be able to stay in park housing, but many employees are leaving; with visitation rapidly declining, their jobs are evaporating.

Sabrina broke her own rule and mentioned the war. "Kirby, let's leave the Christmas tree up until the war is over."

"Okay by me, but the needles may fall to the floor before our enemies fall to the ground." Then Kirby asked, "Cody, are you taking Cora home tonight?"

"Yes sir, in fact, we need to get going soon."

Cora interjected, "It may be dark when you and Bernardo need to head back here. I'm sure you can stay overnight at our house and start fresh in the morning."

"That sounds like a good plan," said Cody.

Sabrina had a question for Cora. "Your father knows Kirby and I live here at the Circle K Ranch. Does he know this is where you spent Christmas Day?"

"Yes, I told him the Livingstons also call the Circle K home."

Sabrina had an idea. "Cody, rather than having Bernardo trudge along with you and Cora bundled up in an open wagon, take our Roadster. It will be faster, safer and much more comfortable. And you can be back before dark."

Kirby added, "Her tank is full and she's ready to rumble."

"Thank you, sir."

"Yes, thank you, Kirby and Sabrina. A much better plan."

After saying their goodbyes and extending Merry Christmas wishes, Cody and Cora rolled out the gate, gears grinding as Cody shifted and swerved wildly as he struggled to get the feel for the Roadster's steering wheel.

Sabrina turned to Rachel. "Has Cody ever driven an autocar?"

"As far as I know, this is his first time."

"Rachel, let's not watch. We have kitchen work waiting for us."

"It's not that hard," added Louis. "I appreciate you letting me stay over a few days. I'm in limbo right now, with the Corps ending its jobs programs and the Navy not quite ready to conduct swearing-in ceremonies. Any odd jobs I can do in the meantime?"

Kirby could think of two. "Perhaps put Bernardo in the barn with some hay and bring in some more firewood from the woodshed."

Jeremy overheard that. "I'll take care of Bernardo and firewood. You two just sit tight."

"I meant bigger jobs. I need to earn my keep," responded Louis with a grin.

"Louis, let's just relax and enjoy the holidays while we can. Life in America is about to get much more difficult. I understand rationing will be a way of life soon."

Louis opened a conversation. "I just met Cody during this visit, but he seems rather quiet and unsure of himself. But he sure has a wonderful girlfriend. Cora is a real delight."

"How old are you now, Louis?"

"I'm twenty-nine, why?"

Kirby responded, "Cody will be twenty-one in early February. I think he's worried about being drafted into the Army and has not figured out how to tell Cora."

"He's right to worry. The Army is gearing up for a long fight in the European Theater. Many of my Corps buddies are already headed for training at Fort Benning, Georgia."

* * *

At ages seventy-eight and seventy-six, Kirby and Sabrina felt an overpowering need for some rim-sitting. While at the Canyon, they planned to check on the Pioneer Museum and visit with Teresa and Tomas. Also, it seemed a good idea to visit Russell Cramer to alleviate any potential awkwardness about his daughter's relationship with Cody Livingston and generally discuss the wild coincidence of meeting his daughter at Christmas.

"What's our first order of business on this trip?" asked Kirby, as they passed through the main entrance.

"I really need to just sit on the rim and ponder the world, and stare at our beloved Canyon. Let's go out to Summit Point for starters, and drop down the trail about a hundred feet or so, where our favorite sitting rock awaits. It's quiet and the views are spectacular."

Sabrina went on, "This world used to be full of goodness, kindness and gratitude. What happened, Kirby?"

"Several countries, far across the seas, decided they did not like us anymore. I wonder what Monte and Levi would think if they could see the turmoil in the world today. When I look down there at the Shooting Star Mine, I can almost visualize Monte packing select hunks of copper ore into canvas bags for me to haul up here."

"When I look beyond the mine and up the river, I visualize a nightmare, a huge concrete arch holding back water against its will. Have you ever seen Marble Canyon?"

"Just once, with Levi when we rode to the western edge of Navajoland and looked down on the river."

"What did you see?"

"It was an exceptionally clear day. The Canyon slept under deep blue skies peppered with fluffy white clouds. This is where the Colorado cuts deep into a sprawling plateau; its sides are steep with sheer, vertical, marbled walls and pockets for nesting ospreys. On that day, the river's vibrant green color contrasted sharply with eroded red slopes. I regret to say, Marble Canyon's topography really does lend itself to a dam and deep reservoir, but the scenery would never be the same."

"We should meet with Russell later today. I suspect all bets are off for any new canyon dams. It's crazy to think it takes a world war to put an end to any thoughts of damming the river and ruining the Grand Canyon."

After an hour or so on their favorite sitting rock, a huge slab of limestone under a leaning juniper, Kirby and Sabrina returned to their Roadster and motored into the Village.

"Sabrina, it looks very quiet. The museum parking lot is almost empty. Let's go see how Teresa is doing."

The main door creaked open. Mooney Yazzie looked up from her position behind the sales counter.

"Sabrina! Kirby! What a surprise to see you here, and a relief too. I think the Park Service is about to close us down."

"Mooney, good to see you too. Is Teresa here today?" asked Sabrina.

"Yes, she's in the office. We're working on our annual inventory. Let's see how she's doing."

Kirby gravitated toward the panoramic windows as the women engaged in rapid updates on each other's activities. There were no visitors in the museum; they had the place to themselves.

"Howdy, Kirby. I see we can't pry you away from the scenery," said Teresa.

"I really miss it. Don't get up here very often anymore. How are you and Tomas?"

"We think we both will be unemployed soon. Our museums are on the list for closing. The whole Village may be a ghost town the next time you see it. We're getting up in years but younger folks are diverting their energies to the war effort. Many are enlisting in the Armed Services. We also need to find a way to contribute."

Kirby looked at the woman, "We're all going to have to make adjustments. Cody just learned that the government is creating a system of rationing about twenty commodities, that is, limiting the amount of certain goods that a person can purchase. Supplies such as gasoline, rubber tires, butter, sugar and canned milk are on the list because they need to be diverted to the war effort. If you are still here in the upcoming growing season, Sabrina will have lots of vegetables to share from her Victory Garden. Let us know if we can help in other ways."

With that, the O'Briens climbed back into their Roadster and drove over to park headquarters, hoping to find Russell Cramer in the annex. Kirby noted two inches of snow covering Village roads and parking lots whereas Summit had none.

"Careful, slipping and sliding is not allowed," cautioned Kirby. "There's ice under this snow, the perfect combination for making very slippery surfaces." Fortunately, they found Russell in his office.

Russell looked up. "Well, it's a pleasure to see you two again. I hope you have had a joyous holiday season, despite a war going on. I understand you have met Cora, my precocious daughter."

"Russell, she is lovely and bubbly, and became the life of our Christmas party, including placing the angel atop our tree. By now you have had a chance to know her boyfriend, Cody Livingston. We took in Jeremy and Rachel, along with their adopted son, when their ranch failed," explained Sabrina. "They all live with us at our Circle K Ranch. At Christmas, when Cody introduced his girlfriend as Cora Cramer, we suddenly realized she is your daughter!"

"No need to explain," Sabrina. "I'm as surprised as you. Quite a coincidence. I find Cody to be quite a gentleman. Do you think their relationship is very serious? Cora is so young, only eighteen."

Kirby expressed a concern. "Russell, they appear to be very serious, but time will tell. I might say time apart will tell. Cora may not realize that Cody just turned twenty-one and, with the nation's call to arms, expects to be drafted."

"Well as you say, time apart will tell," concluded Russell. "If you came to get an update on dam-building, you no longer need to worry. Arizona has dropped its pursuit of becoming a sole proprietor of a dam on the Colorado and Bridge Canyon Dam is on indefinite hold. I expect Marble Canyon Dam will follow suit. As for Grand Canyon National Park, we no longer have sufficient funding or personnel to provide the customary services to the visiting public. Our concessioners are in the same boat. I'm part of a skeleton crew and my family will still be able to reside in park housing. The gates won't actually be closed, just unmanned, so you can still visit any time. Kirby, we'll have plenty of time to hash around water supply solutions. Nothing will be done until well after the war."

"Wow," exclaimed Sabrina, "How things can change, and virtually overnight!"

Kirby added, "We will continue to drop by, Russell; we may be travelling by old-fashioned horse and wagon, with gasoline being rationed."

"Before you go, here's a bit of interesting news I just read in our park news bulletin," stated Russell, clearly excited. "The Navy is planning to name a new ship Grand Canyon! It will be a destroyer tender. Construction will start in a few months in a northwest shipyard. So, we go from obstructing water flow on a wild river to a Grand Canyon namesake free to cruise the high seas!"

"That is exciting," said Kirby, "I'll pass that news along to Louis Jackson. He recently joined the Navy and is training to be a submariner!"

"Good for him; we need all the bright young men we can get to fight in this terrible war."

With all that good news, Kirby and Sabrina departed, but not without one more look at the Canyon. They walked over to the Canyon Queen and paused at the rock wall that Louis and his teammates built. Sabrina expressed a feeling that she had always carried in her heart. "So much in this world changes, but not this view, not this canyon of ours. We are so lucky to have spent so much of our life at her side."

"And me at your side, Sabrina."

Under The Canyon Sky: Guarding the Treasure

* * *

Several months passed after Kirby and Sabrina's last visit at the Canyon. Gas and food shortages changed American life for years. In May nineteen forty-two, gasoline rationing started and Americans received their first ration cards. Many supported the war effort by purchasing war bonds. Autocar manufacturers converted their factories to produce jeeps and tanks. Sixty percent of consumed produce came from Victory Gardens. By Spring, Sabrina and Rachel found themselves working every day in their Circle K Ranch gardens.

The Army swore in Cody Livingston. After receiving medical examinations and uniforms, he started basic infantry training at Fort Benning, Georgia. Two months later he completed his training and received orders to the European Theater. But first, he earned two weeks leave in Arizona.

Jeremy and Rachel had enough advance notice to arrange for Cora to be at the Circle K before Cody arrived.

"There he is!" shouted Cora. Kirby had saved enough gas for a few trips back and forth between the ranch and the Flagstaff train station.

A smartly uniformed soldier jumped out of Kirby's Roadster and ran to Cora.

"Cora, I have missed you so much," sputtered Cody. They hugged and walked hand-in-hand to the ranch house veranda.

"My soldier is home!" shouted Cora.

"Not for long," added Cody. "I only have two weeks and that includes travel back to Georgia where I'll be shipped overseas."

"Well, you are here now," said Rachel, "And that's what counts."

"And you're looking fit and trim," added Jeremy. "Kirby, don't we have some ranch work he can do?"

"Not on your life," said Sabrina. "Cody, don't let those guys coax you into odd jobs. This is your time to relax with family and a certain young lady who has been counting the days till you returned home. Besides rest and relaxation, what would you like to do most?"

"I'd like to borrow your Roadster again and visit the Canyon with Cora. I've been driving jeeps so I'm a much better driver now."

"That can easily be arranged, even tomorrow. Cora, if your dad has any gasoline saved up, the Roadster may be thirsty by the time you reach the park."

"I think he does," replied Cora as she and Cody moseyed over to the corral and behind the barn.

"Cora, I think you know I have fallen in love with you. I may be in harm's way for a year or two. You will be on my mind every day and every night. You will be my inspiration to survive this ugly war. These next words are most important: I'll be coming home. Wait for me."

"I will. I promise."

The next day, the two headed north to the Canyon. Sabrina opened the gate for them and watched the autocar speed up the old Stage Road. She then checked her mailbox, discovered a postcard from Louis, and rushed back to the house.

"Kirby, we have news from Louis. It is a card postmarked Fremantle; I think that is in Australia. Here's what he writes: I am serving aboard the submarine Squawfish. After refueling at Midway Island, we arrived in West Australia. This will be our base of operations for conducting patrols against Japanese ships in the Pacific Theater. My dream has come true, I'm in the Submarine Force! Love, Louis."

"Sabrina, Louis stopped briefly in Midway. When I picked up Cody at the train station, the town was buzzing with news of the Battle of Midway in early June. Midway is at the extreme western tip of the Hawaiian Islands, about thirteen hundred miles northwest of Pearl Harbor.

We sunk four of the six aircraft carriers that launched the attack on Pearl Harbor, a decisive victory and a devastating blow to the Japanese Imperial Navy. Newspapers are calling it the turning point in the Pacific War. Louis must have just missed that action."

Chapter Nine

DROPPING INTO A BLACK HOLE

That frothy, silt-laden water looked like a chocolate milkshake, but tasted like mud

Shipfitter Louis Jackson made several war patrols in Squawfish in the waters of southeast Asia in the Pacific Theater. The Army assigned Specialist Cody Livingston to the Fourth Infantry Division in western Europe.

Kirby had a suggestion for Sabrina. "With Louis, the submarine sailor, and Cody, the infantry soldier, in the war, maybe we should start a mail-order subscription to the *Frontier Times*. If we can receive a postcard from Australia at our gate mailbox, surely we can receive a newspaper from Flagstaff."

"Good idea, we need to follow the war news from overseas. I often feel we are out of touch with the rest of the country. Our trips to town or visitors returning from town seem to be our only link to the outside world," agreed Sabrina.

"That lack of communication could also be solved via telephone. There's a line just a mile or two west of us. Maybe we can tap into that line." Kirby added, "Even Monte had a telephone tap at the Coconino Basin Ranch."

"Kirby, I know where you are going with this. Telephone lines run on the same poles as power lines. You want electric power service for the ranch."

"Sabrina, we are using kerosene lanterns for light. Like gasoline, kerosene is being rationed. We are often in the dark because of insufficient fuel. Nowadays, electricity runs lights, motors, and heaters, even radios."

"No, if we get electricity, others will want it too, and then more; before long there will be powerlines all over the countryside and new demands for hydropower generation in the Canyon."

"Sabrina, thanks to the president's rural electrification program, everyone else already has electric power. We are the only ones without it! Your anti-electric stance is keeping us from moving into the modern era! Coconino Power Company could easily run a line to the house."

"I'll go for telephone, not electricity!"

The Livingstons could not help but overhear the argument, the first they had ever heard between Sabrina and Kirby, but hesitated to enter the fray.

"Jeremy, maybe I can convince Sabrina to change her mind. She's strong-headed about so many things, but I could try."

Rachel approached Sabrina in the kitchen.

"Stay out of this Rachel. This is between Kirby and I." Rachel backed away.

Kirby had more to say. "Sabrina, you enjoy lighted restaurants and offices; even Grand Canyon Village has its own coal-fired powerplant so your Pioneer Museum can have electric lights and ventilation fans. The coffee pot in Russell Cramer's office is electric. Our Roadster has electric headlights and a starter running off a generator and battery system. The radio set at the Flagstaff gas station where we heard about the Pearl Harbor attack runs on electric power. You cannot escape electricity; it is a marvelous invention that makes life easier, and I believe it is here to stay!"

"I am seventy-seven and set in my ways, very old-fashioned you might say. I have lived here on this ranch without electricity for half a century and watched the world change, not always for the better. Now the world is at war. Now there are those who want to dam the river and flood the Canyon." Sabrina paused for about ten seconds. "Louis told me when he was working on the walkway wall at the Starlight Lodge, there were unsightly power poles with three yard-arms and many wires strung along the rim. That's exactly what I don't want to see at the Canyon or here on the ranch."

After another pause, "Can electric and telephone lines be buried in the ground like waterlines so they do not ruin the countryside?"

Kirby sensed that Sabrina may be coming around, but did not want to push too hard. He decided to look into the feasibility of getting electrical service to the ranch house during wartime conditions and then report on his findings.

"Sabrina, I'm sure electrical utilities can be buried but that would require miles of trenching. I think that's why we see so many pole lines. Let's visit Coconino Power Company the next time we are in Flagstaff. We can check with the telephone company too and order a subscription to the newspaper."

"Okay Kirby, sorry for my dang attitude. I need to apologize to Rachel for my outburst. I think I'm feeling the tension of a world at war. And all is certainly not right in this country. Life used to be so much quieter and simpler than this. If the Canyon Queen is still open, maybe we could use a few days of vacation."

"I'm all for that," said Kirby. "At our age, I wonder if we could handle a hike or even a ride down the Summit Trail. On second thought, this is not the best time of year to venture below the rim. Let's think about it. Sitting at a shady overlook in our nostalgic reverie might be better."

Under The Canyon Sky: Guarding the Treasure

* * *

Kirby had booked them into the Canyon Queen, but not a suite like in past visits, just a regular room. Using their wartime privileges, a number of military personnel had taken all of the suites and a large number of park officials, Army Air Corps personnel, news reporters and spectators occupied the lobby and the dining room. Kirby and Sabrina may have stumbled upon an important event. It being late June, with the Allied invasion well underway in Normandy, perhaps the Canyon Queen invasion had good news to celebrate.

"Kirby, before we register, let's have a quick look at the Canyon," suggested Sabrina.

They walked over to the wall and stared out across the vast void, then down at the Pioneer Trail.

"Look down there, Sabrina!" said Kirby, as he pointed to a mule train coming up the trail. "Two wranglers, a heavily loaded pack mule, half a small metal boat on one mule, the other half on another, and three more mules with empty saddles. There's got to be a story behind that work party. Let's go register." Kirby took his place in line at the check-in counter.

"Sabrina, when I picked up our room key, the clerk apologized for all the commotion. Apparently, a bomber on a night training mission out of Tonopah Airfield in Nevada suddenly lost all four engines while cruising at twenty-thousand feet above the Canyon, somewhere south of Point Sublime. Three of the six-member crew—the navigator, flight engineer and bombardier—bailed out through the open bomb bay doors. After ten days below the rim, they were rescued. They are here tonight!"

"What happened to the others? Did the plane crash?"

"As the co-pilot and radioman prepared to jump, the pilot went back to the cockpit to try one more time to restart three engines. Success! and he managed to safely land the plane at Kingman Army Air Field. Maybe we can catch more details after this crowd disperses," surmised Kirby. "The lucky rescued airmen will be here a few more days."

At dinner, they overheard the bombardier describing his harrowing parachute descent into the pitch-black canyon. "I could see some town lights, which I later learned were the lights of Williams. I could also see our plane regaining altitude, banking and climbing, in a steep turn to the west, and disappearing in the night. Then, suddenly the scene went blank. Nothing but blackness. I apparently slipped below the rim, then my chute snagged a rocky cliff edge. There I was, still harnessed to my chute, dangling a thousand feet above the river. I felt like I fell into a deep black hole."

"Did you hear what that young fellow just said? What a harrowing experience," observed Kirby.

"Yes, and someone else mentioned a press conference in the main lobby in an hour. Let's listen in. For a long time, I have worried about airplanes flying over the Canyon."

Kirby and Sabrina finished their dinner and moseyed into the lobby, taking a position in a leather two-seater under a moosehead trophy.

"Ladies and gentlemen, this news conference is about to start but first I'd like to salute our three Army Air Corps survivors, Flight Engineer Frank Riley, Bombardier Lieutenant Gene Hutchins and Navigator Officer Scott Applebee; he's the one on crutches. Gentlemen, thank you for your service; also, congratulations to your heroic rescuers." The park superintendent then handed off the meeting to a military spokesman who opened the floor to questions.

"Where in the canyon depths did you land?"

"We three finally linked up on the North Tonto Plateau, somewhere below Point Sublime, but we did not realize that until daylight."

Bombardier Hutchins added, "I managed to climb up a talus slope by gathering three or four shroud lines together, planting my feet in soft, crumbly ground, seemingly sliding back down with every lifting motion, but arriving at the top just in time to see a dazzling sunrise."

"Then what did you do?" asked another reporter.

"Whenever something like this happens, we are trained to spread out our chutes so they can be seen by rescue planes. In fact, I spotted Navigator Applebee's chute below me. I staggered down a dry creek bed where we both reached the river. It was in flood stage. That frothy, silt-laden water looked like a chocolate milkshake, but tasted like mud. Applebee had a broken foot and felt shooting pains with every step through that rocky terrain."

"That's two of you, what about Flight Engineer Corporal Riley?" shouted a reporter in the back.

"He spread out his chute too. We tried following the river bank downstream, but then backtracked and returned to the plateau in hopes of getting spotted. That's where I cut a makeshift crutch for Applebee using an agave stalk. Being out in the open worked and another bomber dropped rations and canteens of water within our reach. And a while later, another dropped signal flares and a two-way radio."

Unknown to the bedraggled airmen, the Park Service initiated a rescue attempt from the South Rim. A mule party descended the Pioneer Trail and included a fellow with a line-throwing gun, a two-piece, fourteen-foot boat, and three extra mules. The party travelled across the South Tonto Plateau and down Sunset Creek to the river. After one look at the inner gorge relative to where the survivors waited high on the North Tonto Plateau and assessing the risk of a crossing in the churning

Colorado River, they abandoned their plan. Eventually a rescue party from the North Rim reached the thirsty, sunburned airmen.

"What caused your engines to fail?"

"We are not certain. One of our engines caught fire. In trying to cut off its fuel supply, the team in the cockpit may have accidentally cut fuel to all four engines. That's just conjecture at this point as an investigation is just getting underway in Kingman. I personally believe our quick-thinking pilot discovered the problem and restored fuel to the three good engines," surmised Frank Riley, adding, "This would account for all four engines losing power."

With that, the press conference ended, and folks began drifting out of the hotel lobby. Kirby and Sabrina remained seated, watching the crowd evaporate, and feeling absolutely amazed that they happened upon a story that will surely compete for headlines with the massive Allied invasion of Normandy. After a sunset stroll along the Village rim walk, they retired for the evening.

Following a hearty breakfast at the Canyon Queen Café, Kirby and Sabrina drove out to Summit Point for some quiet, morning views. They sat on some rocks near where the Grand Canyon Hotel used to stand. For a while, neither spoke, but the canyon view lured both into thinking about the good ol' days. Then Sabrina broke the silence.

"Kirby, what happened to all those sad-eyed burros you corralled into hauling copper ore and spring water?"

"Monte had me set them free, free to roam wherever their tiny feet took them. Those critters, originally imported from Africa, can easily fend for themselves, but they have obviously grown in numbers. I heard two park rangers saying some areas are overrun with papas, mamas and burritos. There's no market for burro steaks and they have no natural enemies; that is, if they stay on the Tonto and out of lion country."

"Sabrina! Look at that, another military plane. Looks like a fighter. There are two! No three! Why do they choose to train over this sacred land? This is a national park; it should be off-limits for training flights."

"Here comes three more!" exclaimed Sabrina, "And a third group of three! That's nine fighter planes, maybe enough to constitute a squadron. I guess the Park Service and the Army Air Corps have some kind of agreement. We should talk with Russell about this assault on the Canyon, spoiling her silence and solitude."

"I guess the intrusion is part of being at war," concluded Kirby. "Before heading back to the Canyon Queen, there's something else we should do while out this way."

"What's that?"

"We should check on the condition of Monte's Coconino Basin Ranch. He left it to us and we have yet to decide what to do with the property. It's one hundred and thirty-five fenced acres, largely unspoiled forest and open pastures. His abandoned ranch house and barns no longer do it justice."

"I had planned to check on how it is recorded with the County during a Flagstaff visit," remembered Sabrina. "If it really is in our names, then a visit with the Forest Service in Williams might be in order. Our hesitancy was based on the worry that they may require us to clean up, perhaps dismantle and remove, the ranch buildings before they would accept ownership, even if we donate the land."

"Maybe we should hold off doing anything until after the war," suggested Kirby. "But for now, let's run over there and see how it's holding up."

"Kirby, I don't have the gate key."

"Well, maybe we can hop the fence."

"Hop the fence? We're in our late seventies! I don't hop fences anymore," Sabrina stated flatly.

"Well, it doesn't matter. Look. The gate has been completely torn off its hinges. I suspect the work of treasure hunters. We can just drive right up to the house!"

Sabrina exclaimed, "What house? It's flat on the ground. Other buildings too. I think vandals have been at work on the dismantling job. And Blackie is gone! Who would want an old broken-down Hudson?"

"Now I definitely want to put this problem off until World War Two is over," added Kirby. "Let's go, this place is a lost cause."

Conscious of gas rationing, the O'Briens decided any further exploring would be on foot. After lunch, they strolled along the rim from the Canyon Queen to Inspiration Point, site of the two closed museums. They selected the bench with the best canyon view, no bombers or fighter planes flying about, no tourists along the rim, only a small herd of mule deer nibbling juniper twigs.

After a half hour, Kirby asked, "What are you thinking about?"

"Cody and Cora. She must be worried sick about him with all the fighting on those Normandy beaches. He could be on the front line of that siege. What are you thinking about?"

"Louis," confessed Kirby. "He's also in a very dangerous situation. I heard we have already lost thirty-three submarines in this war. Enough war talk, how do you like the view?"

"Stupendous! I could sit here for hours."

"Me too. Let's do it! And the next one who mentions war, gets to buy dinner. I'm planning on a big juicy ribeye steak!" announced Kirby.

"You know, we can see a lot of the Canyon from this bench. I can't see Kirby Tunnel," Sabrina grinned, "But the bridge and river are easy to spot. And we have a great view looking up the full length of Skeleton Canyon to the North Rim. And there's Angel's Gate to the east and her neighbors and Point Sublime far to the west. We have both spent many years roaming all those side canyons and plateaus and yet we surely missed a lot, even in this view before us."

"Sabrina, our wanderings are just a drop in the bucket. River runners report there's a lot more to see in Marble Canyon and far more between Dancing Ghost Ranch and Lake Mead behind Boulder Dam. By the way, Reclamation recently gave that monster a new name, Hoover Dam, after President Herbert Hoover who, as a mining engineer, helped conduct the surveys for that dam."

"Ah, Kirby, now you've gone ahead and spoiled it all by mentioning dams. I doubt we have heard the end of Marble Canyon Dam or Bridge Canyon Dam."

"Okay, new rule, whoever mentions war—or dams—again, buys dinner."

"I am so grateful for all the times I've had below the rim; especially the times spent watching a young miner fill water barrels from a spring below Windsong Mesa. Sure glad he followed me one day. That spring became our secret meeting place."

"It was no secret to Monte, Sabrina. He trained his binoculars on us many times. He could be watching us right now."

The couple started back along the rim trail toward the Canyon Queen, pausing on occasion to take in exceptional panoramas.

"Monte called you the Mystery Lady. He gave you that title and everyone picked it up. We all had fleeting glimpses of the Mystery Lady, on the stage road, on the Tonto, and in deep side canyons."

"And I thought I was doing well to remain undiscovered. Guess not." Sabrina changed the subject. "We should talk about the Circle K."

"What about it?"

"It is great that Jeremy and Rachel are living with us and can keep the ranch going while we are away, like now. I feel good about rescuing the Livingstons from their failing ranch. Now, I'm thinking ahead. The Livingstons are about ten years younger than us so we are all aging to a point where it becomes more difficult running the ranch. When Cody comes home from the war . . . dang, I said it, I'm buying dinner tonight . . . it is quite likely he and Cora will get married and possibly start raising a family. This is entirely up to Cody and Cora, but do you think they would be amenable to also living at the Circle K? They may not be comfortable living under the same roof as Jeremy and Rachel."

"I see your point; it could be awkward, especially if they begin raising children. As a new family, they need their privacy. We do not know if Cody wants to be a rancher like his dad or if Cora would take to ranch life."

"Your point about privacy gives me an idea." Sabrina smiled. "We could build a separate house, maybe one with the luxury of electrical service, for Cody's family somewhere on the property. And I'll go a step farther. We could will the entire ranch to Cody and Cora."

"Wow! That would make for an ideal situation. Should we broach this subject with Jeremy and Rachel when we get home, or hold up for a while?" asked Kirby.

"Definitely hold up until Cody comes home and we see if a marriage is still on the horizon. For now, let's plan to spend the evening at the Canyon Queen, and head home in the morning."

* * *

When Kirby and Sabrina pulled up to their gate, there was another postcard in their box from Louis Jackson, postmarked in Australia, and a letter from Cody postmarked in Bethesda, Maryland for Jeremy and Rachel! Sabrina read the card from Louis. "Hello again, O'Briens. After completing four successful war patrols in the Squawfish, I have been reassigned to the Catfish. She is a new submarine and is getting ready for her first patrol. This is the Silent Service and we're not at liberty to say anything about operations. But I can say what submariners like to say, Pride Runs Deep. Love Louis."

"Well, it sounds like Louis is doing well. He does not have many chances to correspond. I appreciate the few times he gives us an update."

"And Jeremy and Rachel will be relieved to get some news about Cody," added Sabrina. "But the postmark has me confused. Let's get up to the house."

Jeremy, feeding the horses in the corral, noticed the Roadster pull in.

"Hey, Jeremy, we've got a letter from Cody for you!"

The O'Briens and Livingstons gathered around the kitchen table. Jeremy slit open the envelope and handed Rachel the letter.

"Here's what Cody has to say. Thousands of American troops were killed or wounded at Omaha Beach in Normandy last week. Omaha is a code word for one of five sectors of the Allied invasion of German-occupied France and the day of the bloody siege at Omaha Beach will forever be known as D-Day. I have been serving in a combat-hardened infantry division. I'm among one of many wounded while facing German machine-guns on bluffs as our landing craft stormed ashore. Because I am carrying a German bullet close to an artery in my left leg, too risky to operate in a field hospital, I was shipped back to the states."

Rachel shouted, "He's been shot!"

She continued reading. "I'm recovering from surgery to remove the bullet this morning and resting in a temporary building at Walter Reed Military Medical Center. Don't tell Cora. I'll write to her separately later today. There is an overload of war-wounded here. The doctor is letting me keep the bullet. I'm scheduled for a medical discharge."

"What does that mean?" asked Rachel.

"It means our son is coming home!" answered Jeremy.

Rachel continued reading, "I'm so very anxious to see the Circle K Ranch again and to hold the girl I left behind. Love, Cody."

"Wait, there's a postscript!"

"This may not be known in Arizona yet, but Teddy Roosevelt's oldest son, Ted Roosevelt Jr., a 56-year-old Brigadier General and World War I veteran, fought gallantly at the adjacent Utah Beach. It is rumored he will be awarded the Medal of Honor! Teddy would be so proud."

Jeremy, relieved that Cody will survive the war, expressed what everyone had on their mind. Cora will be absolutely thrilled when she receives Cody's letter. It's probably already on its way.

"We received a postcard from Louis saying he has been transferred to a newer submarine and is about to embark on that sub's first war patrol," reported Sabrina.

Kirby had a closing comment, "It is amazing that we are receiving news from the warfront, from clear across both the Atlantic and the Pacific, without reading newspapers or listening to radio broadcasts. Cody is going to be home soon and Louis is doing what he really wanted to do, serve our country as an undersea warrior."

* * *

After much thought, Kirby and Sabrina decided against a Trails West touring car in view of its high gas consumption and gas rationing during the war. Instead, they visited several Flagstaff dealers and found one willing to grant a modest trade-in value on their aging Roadster on the purchase of a used nineteen forty-two Ford four-door sedan with more seating, a radio and a full tank. Because the government ordered a halt to civilian automobile production two months after the Pearl Harbor attack, that model carried the distinction as one of the last automobiles to roll off the assembly line. Finally, the O'Briens could comfortably seat four people.

While Kirby and Sabrina put their new automobile through its paces on the drive back to the ranch, Cora, letter in hand, blond braids flying, burst into her father's office screaming "Cody is wounded, already in the states, and coming home early!"

"What? Is he okay? Where is he?"

Cora calmed down. "He had surgery at Walter Reed Hospital in Maryland to remove a bullet from his leg. Cody is being medically discharged from the Army and will be sent home soon."

"I'm sure he did his share of fighting on those Normandy beaches. Have you told your mother yet? This is great news that you and Cody will be together again. By the way, I have reserved that surplus Army jeep, left by the Conservation Corps, for use by you and Cody. It is parked in the back. Check the gas tank. If it needs gas, tell maintenance I'm authorizing them to top it off."

"Thanks, Dad. That jeep will be a big help."

* * *

Cora paced back and forth during the next two weeks, waiting for news on Cody's Army discharge. Another letter provided the date and approximate time of arrival in Flagstaff. The night before that date, Cora drove the Army jeep to the Circle K Ranch where she stayed overnight. The next day, with Jeremy driving the O'Brien's new automobile, Rachel navigating in the front passenger seat, and Cora dreaming in the back, the journey to the Flagstaff train station began. They would soon learn that the other seat in the back would be occupied by a highly decorated staff sergeant.

The train screeched to a grinding halt. First to disembark, the twenty-four-year-old war hero emerged from the passenger car to loud cheers from the crowd on the station platform. Everyone noticed the Silver Star for valor in combat, the Purple Heart and other meritorious service medals pinned to his Army uniform. The station master assisted with Cody's over-stuffed duffle bag. Cora rushed to his open arms, nearly knocking Cody off his crutches.

"Wow, Cora, you are as beautiful as the day I met you! And, boy, did I miss you! Knowing you were here waiting for me, helped me through that horrible blood bath. I promise, I'll never leave you again." They hugged and kissed all the way to the car where Jeremy and Rachel joined the hugging. "Welcome home, son. Thank God, you have made it home safe." Rachel asked, "Does your leg hurt. Are you feeling any pain? We missed you so much, and so did this young lady you left behind."

"I'm fine everyone. It's a terrible war and it's not over by a longshot. It's hard to understand how men can turn on each other like this."

On the return to the ranch, with crutches strapped to the roof, Cody and Cora embraced each other so tightly no one could tear them apart. The Ford automobile tooted its horn as it cruised through the gate. Kirby and Sabrina came running out of the house.

"Cody, you are here!" cried Sabrina. Kirby added, "Welcome home Staff Sergeant Cody Livingston. We have prayed every day for your safe return. Let's go inside; Sabrina has prepared a feast to help celebrate your service and your survival."

During dinner, everyone wanted to hear about Omaha Beach. Cody cautioned that it is a gruesome, bloody story and not appropriate dinner conversation.

"If I tell you what it was like, it will be the only time I ever speak of it. Cora, this is going to be difficult for you to hear but here goes."

"We crossed the English Channel in countless landing craft and hit the six-mile-long beach known to Allied Forces as Omaha. The Germans were entrenched on one-hundred-foot-high cliffs and blasted us with deadly machine-gun fire, over twenty-four hundred casualties, some drowned in the surf, some were shot while wading ashore, the water was red with blood. With no shelter and mass confusion, Omaha Beach was a killing field of the worst kind. I saw five tanks sink in choppy waters; only two out of thirty made it ashore. Only ten percent of one unit in the first wave survived."

Cora, Sabrina and Kirby had horrified looks on their faces as Cody continued.

"Our Navy shelled enemy fortifications but that did little to kill the rain of bullets coming down from the cliffs. The beach was littered with destroyed landing craft and dead bodies washing up on shore. I sprawled on the sand to stay low but before I could fire a shot, I caught a bullet in my left upper leg. It stung like a thousand bees. There were hundreds of wounded men thrashing in the waves. Despite the stinging in my leg, I crawled back in the water seven times and rescued wounded soldiers screaming for help."

Cody reached into his pocket. "Here's the bullet that lodged right next to a major artery. I'll pass it around; feel how heavy it is. There's a lead core under the shiny copper jacket. Doctors in our Normandy field hospital felt the situation too risky to try removing the bullet in such rudimentary conditions, so they transported me to a captured airfield where transport planes rushed special wounded cases back to the states and Walter Reed Hospital. After successful surgery, I finally had a chance to write a few letters." Cody swallowed some water, cleared his throat, and continued.

"We paid dearly but we took that beach, we climbed those cliffs, and we charged inland. We had the Germans on the run. Cora, my love, you kept me alive; all I wanted to do is get back to the Grand Canyon and live the rest of my life with you. I must say, I fully expect visions of the Omaha Beach carnage will haunt me for the rest of my days. They haunted me in the airplane, in the hospital, and on the train. They haunt me now."

After a short pause, Cody added, "I just read in the *Frontier Times* that Brigadier General Ted Roosevelt Jr., who walked with a big stick, died of a heart attack just five weeks after the Utah Beach siege. He is being interred in an American cemetery in Normandy alongside his younger brother Quentin who was shot down by a German fighter in World War One."

Kirby commented, "I think all the Roosevelts carried big sticks and gave so much to our country, and so have you, Cody."

Cora eventually returned to Grand Canyon Village, leaving Cody to rest and relax in his old bedroom upstairs. Clearly, their plan to marry was on their mind, with date and location still unknown. Cody depended on Cora to drive whenever they visited the South Rim, but his recovery period went quickly and in true military fashion, he assigned himself to light-duty ranch chores. Deep down, he knew what he wanted to do—cattle ranching and raise a family with Cora.

One day, while Cody and Cora gazed at the Canyon from Inspiration Point, it occurred to Cody that he had not formally asked for Cora's hand in marriage. Sitting there, he silently tried composing and rehearsing a heart-melting proposal, one that promised Cora she will never be alone, that she is the only one for him, that their future will always be founded in love, laughter, joy, and peace. Then he decided to just ask the simple question.

Cora noted he was especially quiet. "What are you thinking about?"

"You, I'm thinking about how much I love you. Will you marry me?"

Cora looked at him with an impish smile. "It's about time you asked me that. My answer is yes, Cody, I will marry you and spend the rest of my days loving you."

They kissed and the calm and serenity of the Canyon evaporated as wedding plans went into high gear.

"There's a small chapel near the Pioneer Cemetery. I'd like to start our marriage there, a small wedding when it's cooler, say September."

"I don't have a ring for you yet. I'm thinking about using some of the metal in my bullet and having one specially made."

"I'll pretend it's gold and cherish it because it was once inside you. But I will not pretend my love for you – that is real and that I will cherish forever."

They returned to the Circle K to announce their engagement and plans for a small wedding ceremony at the Canyon in two months.

"What? A copper ring made from an enemy bullet?" cried Rachel. Kirby added, "I know all about copper; it corrodes and there's probably not enough of it in a copper-plated bullet to fabricate a ring."

"Kirby, that's not the point." Sabrina, as appalled as Rachel, offered a much better alternative, "Mooney's brother is a silversmith. He could fashion a lovely silver ring."

"Who's Mooney?" asked Cora.

"Moonflower Yazzie is a dear Navajo friend who works at the Pioneer Museum at Inspiration Point."

"Oh, we were just there, sitting on a bench and gazing at the Canyon," said Cora.

"Mooney's brother, Milton Yazzie, is a master silversmith in Willow Springs. He makes all sorts of hand-crafted Navajo jewelry. I've seen his work. It is fabulous."

Rachel added, "I like Sabrina's idea. Cora and Cody, wouldn't you prefer a silver ring made by a Native American rather than one from metal molded in a dirty German ammunition factory?"

Cody answered, "When you put it like that, there is no question about it. Cora, forget my crazy idea. I'm sure you would be much happier with a bright shiny silver ring than one made of mixed metals shot from a German machine-gun."

"Absolutely. Cody, we were not thinking straight. The ring is a symbol of our love and lifetime commitment, not a world war that will soon pass into history. Let's visit Milton Yazzie about hand-crafting matching bands."

* * *

Everyone gathered around as Reverend Dean Dixon, pastor of Flagstaff Presbyterian Church, began the simple ceremony. "Folks, welcome to the Chapel of the Ages. We have assembled here on this beautiful autumn afternoon at the Canyon to celebrate one of life's greatest moments, that is, to unite a man and a woman in marriage. I now ask, who gives the bride away?"

"I, Russell Cramer, have the honor of giving away my lovely daughter, Cora."

"Very well. Cora Cramer, do you take Cody Livingston as your lawful wedded husband to love, honor and trust for the rest of your life?"

"I do," confirmed Cora.

"Cody Livingston, do you take Cora as your wedded wife and promise that no matter what challenges lie ahead, you will face them together in love, in honor and in trust?"

"Yes, I most certainly do. Cora, with this special silver ring, I promise I will always love and cherish you," confirmed Cody.

"And Cody, this matching silver ring represents my commitment to love and cherish you forever."

"Then in witness of those present here on this special day, and with the power vested in me by the Presbyterian Church, I now pronounce you husband and wife."

The O'Briens and the Livingstons congratulated the newlyweds, wished them all the best in the years to come, and saw them off to a brief honeymoon at the Canyon Queen Hotel.

Chapter Ten

TRAPPED IN A BLIZZARD

The power to change the world may reside in radioactive rocks

With the war winding down, Kirby and Sabrina planned several major changes to the historic Circle K Cattle Ranch at Little Springs. Most important, Sabrina finally consented to electric utility and telephone service for the ranch. A visit to the respective companies in Flagstaff confirmed that taps can easily be made from the nearby power line.

Other than utility wiring, the ranch house needed few physical modifications. The original floor plan instituted by Gus and Martha Klostermeyer many years ago still worked well for the O'Brien-Livingston household, albeit, the Livingston branch needed to accommodate the newlyweds.

Sabrina called a meeting of all Circle K residents in the dining room. "As you know, the first floor of this house has a high-ceiling great room, this dining room in front, a kitchen in back, and a bedroom in back for you, Jeremy and Rachel."

"We are most grateful for that, Sabrina," said Rachel.

"The second floor has railings along an open hallway that looks down on the great room. The remaining upstairs portion of the house includes our master bedroom in the back opening to a balcony with a tremendous western view of the ranch, a vacant guest room also in the back, and a front bedroom used by Cody, back when he was young and single. That room has a balcony looking eastward over the ranch."

Sabrina continued, "Now here's my plan. I am offering that front bedroom to Cody and Cora until a new house can be built nearby. It would have electrical service and initially serve as the Cody family residence, but later as the bunkhouse for ranch hands. By the way, the barn would also be wired for electric lights."

"Wow, Sabrina, that is most gracious of you and Kirby. Thank you. I think you know Cody and I would love to stay on and contribute to this growing enterprise. We want to be ranchers too."

"Cora, you are most welcome but that is not all. Kirby and I are approaching our eighties. We will not always be here. When we journey to the big canyon in the sky, we would like you and Cody to move back into the big house where there is plenty of room to raise a family and care for Jeremy and Rachel, who, like us, are not getting any younger."

Sabrina had a closing comment. "I have one more matter of profound importance to present to you, Cody and Cora. If you two adapt to cattle ranching like I think you will, and if you want to stay close to our beloved Grand Canyon, Kirby and I plan to will the entire Circle K Ranch to you, and with all our blessings."

"The Circle K itself is a blessing," said Cody.

"It is also a real treasure," said Jeremy, adding, "Sabrina, as Rachel just said, we are most grateful and appreciative for your sharing your home with us."

Rachel asked, "How can we show our gratitude? Our whole world has changed. You have given us peace of mind, security, and a vision for the future. Our heartfelt thanks come from our thankful hearts."

Cody added, "Sabrina and Kirby, you have been most gracious and generous to my parents. And now to Cora and I. We never dreamed such good fortune would be coming our way. We will forever be indebted to you. God bless you. God bless America."

***

One hot July day, while relaxing on the Circle K deck, Kirby and Cody celebrated some good news from the European Theater. Germany surrendered unconditionally to the Western Allies and Nazi Party leader Adolph Hitler committed suicide. They raised their root beer bottles in a toast to our Allied Forces.

"Okay, Japan," exclaimed Kirby, "You are next!"

"About that, Kirby, while recovering from surgery at Walter Reed last year, I overheard two wounded Army officers discussing development of a new weapon that might bring an end to the war in the Pacific Theater. The hospital had us all jammed into a makeshift tent in the hospital parking lot. Only hanging white sheets separated cubicles but I heard most of their conversation."

Cody continued. "For several years, our country has been secretly stockpiling high-grade uranium ore from a mine in the Belgian Congo, a colony in Central Africa, a risky proposition since Germany had conquered Belgium at the beginning of the war."

"What's uranium?"

"I'm getting to that. Some physicists discovered a chain reaction called nuclear fission in nineteen thirty-eight. Two years later a German-born scientist named Albert Einstein, who became an American citizen, informed the President that concentrated uranium could generate an enormous amount of energy. This led to the establishment of a secret government laboratory in New Mexico with a mission to develop an atomic bomb. One of the officers confirmed we recently tested one at White Sands. Before he died of his wounds, he implied the test was so successful that work quickly proceeded in putting the finishing touches on two more bombs that might put an end to World War Two."

"So, this so-called bomb has uranium in it?" guessed Kirby.

"Yes, and it is radioactive, meaning it emits tiny particles. The ore is black and grainy, and is often found in sedimentary rocks with copper carbonates."

"Down at the Shooting Star Mine, we disposed of that kind of black rock at our dump on the east wall of Windsong Mesa. But I never saw any particles shooting out of our black rocks. And I never felt any hits either."

"Maybe they are too small to see or feel. The Army officer well on his way to recovering from his wounds, sounded rather optimistic; in fact, he predicted the power to change the world may reside in radioactive rocks."

* * *

On a hot sultry day in late August, Kirby and Sabrina sat on their shaded deck, discussing the future, now that the war in the Pacific seemed to be nearing its end. They watched a grey jeep ride through the open gate and park under a tree. Two uniformed naval officers stepped out and approached the O'Briens.

One asked, "Is this the residence of Kirby O'Brien?"

"Yes sir, I am Kirby O'Brien and this is my wife, Sabrina." Both had a bad feeling about this visit.

"Folks, we'll get right to the point. We regret to inform you that Louis Jackson, a member of the crew of the submarine Catfish, is missing in action and presumed lost."

"No, not Louis! All he ever wanted was to be a Navy submariner," cried Sabrina.

"I understand, ma'am; I'm a submariner myself. I can tell you what we know. On the last day of July, the Catfish left Fremantle, Australia, with eighty-four men on board, and headed back to the Java Sea to commence her third war patrol. On August sixth, she radioed that she had passed through the strait between the Indonesian islands of Bali and Lombok, traveling on the surface, and arrived in her assigned patrol area. That was the last message received from the Catfish. After two weeks, she has now been officially declared overdue and presumed lost."

Kirby asked, "What do you think happened?"

"I'm not a submariner like my associate here, but we have some intelligence data that may explain what happened. I should point out that it is very difficult to determine precisely which of the many Japanese anti-submarine attacks was the one that sank Catfish. However, reports reveal that at eight o'clock in the morning of August sixth, a Japanese Army plane bombed a submarine off the Bali coast with two direct hits, and then observed gushing oil and air bubbling to the surface. The submarine went down with all hands."

The submarine officer offered a concluding thought. "Mr. and Mrs. O'Brien, we submariners never consider our brothers lost at sea. Rather, because they went down with their ship in the service of their country and are now entombed in their final resting place beneath the waves, they and their boats are deemed on eternal patrol."

With that, the officers returned to their jeep and left the ranch, leaving Kirby and Sabrina in shock about the loss of Levi Jackson's grandson.

With the end of the war at hand, two atomic bombs obliterated Hiroshima and Nagasaki while two conventional bombs obliterated the Catfish, the last submarine, in fact, the last ship, lost in the war. Japan finally surrendered, bringing an end to World War Two.

Under The Canyon Sky: Guarding the Treasure

* * *

Because Teddy Roosevelt favored a former Rough Rider named Sam Thornton by personally signing his mine patent certificate, the government allowed continued operation of his copper mine one thousand feet below the rim, just a mile west of the Village. This lode claim became one of the last privately held pieces of land inside the park. Thornton did not know the black waste rock he discarded from his mine held a very special property.

Just in case his mine did not pay, Thornton also built a rudimentary tourist complex called Grand Canyon Trading Post and soon added a saloon and a cluster of cabins. He eventually sold his mine and tourist enterprises. But Thornton's mine would have a new lease on life.

A post-war uranium boom erupted in the sedimentary layers of the Colorado Plateau. The mineral, uranium oxide, drew prospectors in the search for the same black rock that plagued Thornton's copper mine. Armed with radiation detectors, instruments that can count invisible particle emissions from radioactive rocks, these modern-day prospectors scoured the countryside in surplus Army jeeps. They filed thousands of high-grade lode claims. Ideal locations included abandoned copper mines which already exposed various minerals. Uranium compounds are often associated with tailings such as found on the dumps of Thornton's copper mine and the famed Shooting Star Mine.

The atomic bombs dropped on Japan used enriched uranium and, after the war, scientists realized that this radioactive heavy metal could also be used for peaceful purposes—the fueling of nuclear fission power plants.

***

"Kirby, let's run up to the Canyon tomorrow. We could use some rim-sitting time before winter sets in and we have not seen Russell since Cora's wedding."

"We should do that. I'd like to talk to him about annoying overflights, uranium boom impacts on the park, and the impending post-war tourist surge. Oh, and we should tell him about the fate of Louis and his fellow undersea warriors."

October is one of the best times to visit Grand Canyon. The skies are deep blue, the air is clear and crisp, and there is very little wind. And the Canyon casts its spell on anyone willing to spend some time on the rim. For this visit, Kirby and Sabrina concentrated their activities in the Village.

"For starters, Kirby, let's pull into the Canyon Queen parking lot and order coffee-to-go at the Café. Then I suggest we sit on the wall that Louis and his crew built. I think about him all the time. He and Cody are true war heroes. Unfortunately, only one came home."

"Sabrina, let's not talk about the war. It's over and we won. Now we need to return to everyday living and put the horrible atrocities behind us. On a much happier note, I'm pleased how Cody and Cora are taking to ranch life. Cody is a huge help now that he has returned to good health. He and Jeremy repaired the entire fence line last week. He still has a lot to learn about the cattle business but that will come in time."

"And Cora, she and Rachel have relieved me completely of kitchen duties. She whispered to me yesterday that she thinks she might be pregnant. That's not confirmed so don't say anything, not even to Russell when we see him later today. You know, we do not know how much longer Russell will continue as the Park Engineer. He may be up for a transfer or retirement soon. The time is coming when the young bride's parents may not be as accessible as they are now."

Kirby added, "Well, that's all part of growing up. This might be a good time for a courtesy call with Russell."

The O'Briens left their Ford sedan in the parking lot and walked over to headquarters. They found Russell in a heated discussion about the uranium boom. His secretary advised returning in an hour or so.

"We've mostly been sitting this morning," observed Kirby. "Let's walk along the rim and cut down to the Pioneer Cemetery and pay our respects to Monte and Anna."

At Monte's final resting place, Kirby and Sabrina stood in a moment of silence and reverence. Always in the hearts and memories of the O'Briens, it seemed like well over a decade had passed since Monte and Anna Bridgestone departed this world.

Sabrina remembered Louis Jackson saying the Conservation Corps conducted the surveys for the cemetery and laid out the general pathways and reference markers. Then her mind returned to the present. "Monte helped make the world a better place although the world recently went astray."

Kirby added, "Time moves on and so should we. Perhaps Russell is now available for a courtesy call." They walked over to the annex.

"Greetings, O'Briens! My secretary tells me you stopped by about an hour ago. Good to see you again."

"Good to see you too, Russell. We bring sad news about one of our Navy sailors who used to work here before the war. Perhaps you remember Louis Jackson. He became a submariner in the Pacific Theater. While transiting on the surface, his sub was bombed by a Japanese Army plane on the very day we dropped the atomic bomb on Hiroshima. All hands were lost."

"That is very sad news. I do remember him and all the good work he did for the Civilian Conservation Corps and the National Park Service. We lost so many good men and women in that wicked war." He shook his head. "What a waste."

Russell changed the subject. "Sabrina, you would see this new issue, the so-called uranium boom, as another assault on our Canyon. I had to remind our regional director this morning that this is a national park and now it is under siege by a new breed of prospectors."

"But Russell, the park is no longer open to mining! They should be turned back," stated Sabrina.

"The problem is we have hundreds of open prospect holes, tunnels and shafts that expose the sedimentary rocks that may contain uranium. Even Thornton's old mine is getting a second look. Kirby, you probably know the location of many of those sites."

"I do, Russell; in fact, some of our penetrations in Windsong Mesa may have had uranium deposits; Of course, we were mining copper."

"Kirby, let me stop you for a minute. The Cramers and the O'Briens are very good friends now. Please call me Russ."

Kirby continued, "Russ, I remember some heavy rocks with black granular crystals that we discounted out of hand as having no value. They were not as hard as the black diamond rock that we eventually decided were also of no value. Is this regional manager directing you to open the Canyon to uranium exploration?"

"Exactly, and I refuse. We're turning these guys away at the park entrances. There are plenty of other places where they can wave their little crackling radiation detectors in search of uranium. I probably have not heard the last word from the Park Service on this matter but my job is to protect and preserve this wonder of nature, not reopen it to mining."

Sabrina congratulated him on his stance. "Good for you, Russ. You are doing the right thing. Since we are talking about threats to our Canyon, I'd like to broach the subject of annoying overflights. During the war, there were many military training flights through the Canyon, some below the rim. Now I'm seeing some commercial flights below the rim. They totally disrupt the silence and solitude that we cherish here."

"Sabrina, as usual, you are right on top of things. Now we are faced with scenic flights over the Canyon. We're going to develop an aviation management plan that sets aside a small part of the Canyon for commercial overflights and post restrictions over the bulk of canyon airspace. I may retire in a few years and let someone else deal with all these canyon threats. Another threat is the post-war surge in running the river in surplus inflatable rafts. We may need a river management plan as well."

Russ continued, "On the positive side, we are bracing for a surge in visitation. Last year, with the war still raging, we counted less than one hundred thousand visitors. We'll be reopening the museums and concessions soon. That reminds me, Kirby, more visitors mean more water demand. We still need to have our brainstorming session on future water supplies for the park. I'll do some research in our history files. Before we know where we're going, it's good to know where we've been."

"On another positive note," added Sabrina, "We are happy to report that Cora and Cody have adapted to ranch life extremely well. They are a pleasure to have living with us and have off-loaded many of the strenuous tasks from Kirby and I. We're both feeling our age now."

"Sabrina, I never dreamed Cora would become a rancher's wife. She is so happy, especially now that she is in a family way."

"We did not realize you knew she and Cody are expecting a baby, I think in May," confessed Sabrina.

"I just got the news from my wife, Mabel, a few days ago," said Russ. "I guess she and Cora were holding back until they knew for sure. We're going to be grandparents next year!"

And on that happy note, Kirby and Sabrina walked back to the Canyon Queen parking lot, pleased about their visits in the Village. Their trusty Ford automobile carried them back to the Circle K in comfort. With the war finally over, a good feeling of peace and prosperity hung in the air.

* * *

Several weeks passed before Russ and Kirby could set aside enough time to return to their discussion of water supply issues in the Village. During the interim, Russ explored park records dating back to the Santa Fe Railway's arrival at the South Rim.

"I know what you are going to say, Russ." Kirby grinned, "The first water supplied in bulk came by Santa Fe railcar, but I have personal experience in hauling water from springs below the rim. In my younger days, I drove strings of burros, each burro with two barrels of water strapped to its back, up the Summit Trail to the Grand Canyon Hotel."

"A great example of how we first supplied drinking water to early visitors. I'm sure burros also hauled water from the springs in Canyon Gardens too. As soon as rails reached the rim here in the Village, our records show it cost the Santa Fe three dollars per thousand gallons to deliver water by railcar."

Russ glanced at his open file folder and continued, "In nineteen twenty-four, the Santa Fe began looking elsewhere for reliable water supplies. Kirby, some time ago you mentioned the possibility of piping snowmelt from the San Francisco Peaks. That idea was thrown out due to concerns over water rights and the need for an exceptionally long pipeline. Another option was drilling for water south of the Park, the thought being that the land on the rim drains to the south, but several exploratory wells came up dry. The Santa Fe finally decided to develop the springs at Canyon Gardens. It was a four-year project but in the end a pipeline and a pump station began delivering water to the Village at a cost of a dollar fifty per thousand gallons. This system has met our needs until now, but it won't much longer. As post-war tourism surges, we'll not only need more storage, but we need to be thinking beyond that."

Kirby, tapping his feet and shifting his weight in the chair, seemed anxious to inject his idea into the discussion.

"With all due respect Russ, your research in what the Park did for supplying drinking water to its visitors before the war is commendable, but I'd like to return to a concept I broached earlier. When Sabrina and I visited Zuni Falls in a side canyon off Skeleton Creek, we heard about a much bigger spring-fed waterfall further upstream. Folks who had been there called it Echo Falls."

"Oh, I have heard of Echo Falls. I understand it is the primary source feeding Skeleton Creek," said Russ.

"Exactly. I believe these springs could feed a pipeline across the Canyon. I too have done some study. At the College in Flagstaff, specifically its geology department, I learned more about underground water reservoirs called aquifers. At the Canyon there are two stacked aquifers, designated the Coconino aquifer at one thousand feet below the rim and the Redwall aquifer about three thousand feet below the rim. They both feed Echo Falls. I believe this is the only reliable source of drinking water in the Park."

"Kirby, I'm impressed and now I see a need for another plan, a water resource plan, an in-depth study of a long-term water supply."

"That's not all, Russ. We're talking about a trans-canyon pipeline where gravity plays a major role. Echo Falls is at elevation fifty-two hundred feet. Canyon Gardens, where we already have a pump station and a pipeline to the Village, is at elevation thirty-seven hundred feet. That means there's hundreds of pounds of pressure to get water all the way to Canyon Gardens by gravity flow. It just needs a pump station, which is already in place, to give the Echo Falls water a final boost to your storage tanks."

"Kirby, are you sure you are not an engineer? You've gone way past water barrels on burros. I like your trans-canyon pipeline idea. It may require a second bridge across the river but the fact that it can utilize the existing pipeline to the South Rim makes the concept worth studying, even if the booster pumps need to be upgraded."

"No, Russ, I never studied engineering. My whole career has been dedicated to mining and trail-building here at the Canyon. I have no regrets as I have been able to spend most of my life in canyon country, and much of it with a most remarkable woman. Sabrina and I, now in our early eighties, cannot resist sitting on the rim and watching shadows glide across glowing red buttes."

"You both are remarkable and I'm so fortunate to have come to know you. Now, back to our water discussion. I'd like to schedule a meeting with you and my staff to further explore the trans-canyon pipeline concept. Can you come back up here in two or three weeks?"

"I'd be happy to continue brainstorming this concept and look forward to what your colleagues think about this wild idea. See you then."

In some respects, Kirby did have regrets. If only he had pursued an engineering career instead of the life of a wandering prospector and pick-and-shovel miner. Still, on his drive back to the ranch, he was pleased with his life journey, especially all the years with Sabrina.

* * *

To Kirby's surprise, Sabrina finally reached the point of contracting for electrical and telephone service for the Circle K Ranch.

"Kirby, while you were up at the Canyon, Cody and I drove the jeep into town to find out what it would take to extend electricity to the ranch before winter set in. The Coconino Power Company said they would need two weeks to extend their pole line. They estimated it would take twenty-four poles and would work with Mountain States Telephone Company to string a phone line to the ranch house."

"We learned that Coconino Power only runs electric lines to a terminal on the exterior of the house. They said their job ends with a transformer, meter and breaker box, whatever those things are. They recommend we hire Hartman Electric Shop in Flagstaff to wire the house for power and lights. We should run back to Flagstaff and firm up all the arrangements with Coconino Power, Mountain States Telephone, and Hartman Electric."

Pleased to see his wife ready to enter the Circle K into the modern era, Kirby jumped on the plan, exclaiming, "Let's go!"

In town, they signed the necessary contracts and made down payments on parts and labor, and at the telephone company, they came away with their assigned phone number, six-eight-six. To celebrate, Kirby and Sabrina finally had that special steak dinner they wanted at the Monte Vista Hotel dining room before war broke out.

By mid-November, the ranch house had lights that could be turned on and off with the flick of a wall switch and wall-mounted outlets where electrical appliances could be plugged in. The telephone installer provided instructions on how to answer calls and make person-to-person and station-to-station calls. Cora could now call her parents at the Village and everyone else in the house felt connected to the outside world for the first time, especially important in emergency situations.

Cora turned to Kirby. "Now you can arrange meetings with my dad by telephone. His number at park headquarters is nine-four-two. Let me write that down and post it near the telephone set. Because of distance, you may need to go through an operator but I'm not sure. Let's try it!"

"Not only try it, but I need to make an appointment for a follow-up meeting with your dad," stated Kirby.

Cora, having some experience in making calls while living in park housing, had a few more tips in telephone communications. "Be aware that telephone calls are not free. The charge for daytime person-to-person calls made Mondays through Saturdays is eighty cents for three minutes. It's cheaper on nights and Sundays, only sixty cents for three minutes. To make the call, for example, you dial the switchboard operator and tell her you want to call Russell Cramer at Park Headquarters and give her the number. By the way, we need to get telephone directories for Flagstaff and Grand Canyon Village. Again, my dad's number at Park Headquarters is nine-four-two."

Kirby made the inaugural call during business hours and through the office secretary set up a Wednesday afternoon meeting with Russ and his engineering staff to continue their trans-canyon pipeline discussion.

* * *

As Kirby arrived at Park Headquarters, he noticed darkening skies in the northwest but never gave them another thought. With his team assembled in the conference room, Russ introduced Kirby as a canyon pioneer, having helped build the Jackson, Summit and Pioneer trails and provided valuable input to the design of the Pioneer Museum and Black Bridge.

"Kirby, these petulant young fellows have been kicking around your idea for a trans-canyon pipeline and have some major concerns." Russ sat down and let the comments fly.

One engineer, twisting in his seat, obviously anxious to shoot down the project, spoke up quickly. "It's a crazy idea to run a pipeline down an active streambed known to have flashfloods! The force of rushing water will surely take out large sections of pipe."

The fellow next to him jumped in, "That's not all, rockslides will do the same kind of damage."

Yet a third man had another negative observation. "We engineers normally call for pipelines to be buried so that they are protected from mechanical damage. It will be very difficult to completely bury the line. In many areas it will be exposed which alone is aesthetically not acceptable in this protected landscape. All these negatives will add up to high maintenance."

Kirby, glancing at Russ and shaking his head, could not let all that negative talk kill the project before a pencil could draw the first line on a drafting table. "Fellas, I see you take your responsibility to the general public very seriously, and that's quite admirable, but you are also professional problem solvers. Start thinking positively. You see me as an unschooled old-timer, a non-engineer, if you will. That's fine. I never had the opportunity you had to get a formal education, but I can still be creative."

The last engineer who spoke had one more comment, rather derogatory at that. "That's right, you are not an engineer and should stay out of our business. We're the ones with the experience and credentials to solve problems, not you."

With that, Russ called an abrupt end to the meeting. When he and Kirby stood alone at the door, he apologized for his team's rudeness and contrary attitude.

"Russ, I still feel this plan is worthy of serious consideration. Your guys don't seem to want to give it a chance. We never got to the river crossing challenge or transitioning to the existing pipeline at Canyon Gardens. Too bad."

Kirby left the building, grumbling to himself and feeling unappreciated. He immediately found himself in a late-November blizzard. Blinded by snow and irked by his reception by the park's staff engineers, he unknowingly made a wrong turn and lost all sense of direction.

In trying to negotiate a sharp turn, his Ford sedan slid sideways into a snowbank that filled a deep ditch, so deep that Kirby could not open his doors. Destined to spend a frigid night in his car, his thoughts turned to Sabrina, surely alarmed by his delayed return. She probably telephoned Russ in a panic and learned he left the meeting about mid-afternoon, refusing an overnight stay as he was anxious to get home.

As she grew more worried, and making a second call the following day, confirming Kirby failed to return home, she probably asked Russ to dispatch a Park Service heavy-duty truck with a snowplow to cruise the roads in the area. Despite no news to report, his people would keep searching.

Kirby's Ford became buried deeper due to snow drifting overnight. He ran his motor periodically for heat and for melting snow. By hand-cranking the only working window partly open he could let in some fresh air and gather enough snow to make a little drinking water in an ash tray. He had no food and as daylight faded, Kirby headed into a second night in the car. He tried several times to open a door in hopes of walking away, but snow had him trapped. It mattered little; he had no idea regarding the direction to walk to safety, if he could get out. The wind howled and the storm raged on, burying the ill-fated automobile even deeper.

He muttered to himself, "Well, Kirby O'Brien, now you are in a real fix and there is no way out. By now Sabrina must be in severe panic mode. I shudder to think I may never see her again."

Kirby spent most of the night reviewing in his mind all the great years he and Sabrina had together, all their adventures, all their good times. He doubted he would make it through the night. Exhausted, hungry, shivering and cramped, he finally dropped into a deep sleep.

Chapter Eleven

HOLE IN THE PARK

Uranium may be at the core of future nuclear power plants but today it is at the core of a new attack on Grand Canyon National Park

On the third day of being held captive in his snowbound car, Kirby awoke to tapping on his window. A county snowplow driver discovered the weak, delirious driver.

"Hey, mister, can you roll down your window?" shouted Jorge Miranda. "I'm with the Coconino County Road Department."

"Uh, yes, sir, but only the one behind me and only halfway down. All others are frozen. I've been trapped in here for two or three days—can't remember how long—without food and very little water. My name is Kirby O'Brien and I'm lost."

Jorge trudged back to his plow and returned with water and half his box lunch. Kirby explained what happened and asked, "Where am I?"

"Don't talk, just drink and eat. My name is Jorge Miranda. You are on Anita Road, about twenty miles south of the Grand Canyon, not far from the old Anita copper mines and the water stop on the canyon railway."

"Jorge, I'm so thankful you happened along. I had given up on ever being rescued. I will be forever indebted to you."

"Mr. O'Brien, keep drinking while I get a shovel and dig for a place to attach a chain to pull you out."

After fifteen minutes of shoveling, Jorge attached his chain to the Ford's undercarriage. "How's your gas?"

"I'm very low. Shall I start the motor and try to go forward while you pull?"

"That's the plan, sir."

"Call me Kirby. I'm ready whenever you are."

Jorge put a strain on the chain, then started forward. In just minutes Kirby's car was yanked from the snowbank and pulled onto the open road. Kirby opened the door but could not move.

"Here, Kirby, let me help you out. Can you stand?"

"I'm so stiff I need to go slow. Please help me get upright. I forgot to turn the motor off."

"I'll do that; lean against the car. I have a spare can of gas which will partially replenish your tank. Where were you headed when you got so side-tracked?"

"My Circle K Ranch at Little Springs, on the old stage road."

"Wow, you were going way off in the wrong direction."

"My wife must be in extreme distress by now. I was due home days ago. Last night I dreamed I would never see her again."

"Just relax, walk around a little bit to loosen up while I try to get more snow off your car. You are lucky I came along. I rarely plow Anita Road. It's hardly used any more since the copper mines closed down. But after this storm, it seemed somehow warranted."

"Jorge, you saved my life." As he teetered a bit, Kirby added, "It's rather ironic; I am an old copper miner from way back; not around here, but in the Canyon."

Jorge may not have heard Kirby, but he returned from his plow with a hand-drawn map showing a route using recently plowed roads to help Kirby find his way home.

"Kirby, I need to get back to work. Do you feel up to driving home now?"

"Jorge, I'm okay. Thank you for sharing your lunch, water and most of all pulling me out of that monstrous pile of snow over there." He pointed to all the tire tracks and trampled snowdrifts, then shook hands with his rescuer. "Adios, Jorge Miranda!"

"Adios, Kirby O'Brien!"

* * *

With Jorge's route plan in hand, Kirby found his way home. Cora spotted his sedan approaching the ranch gate and shouted, "There's Uncle Kirby!" Sabrina rushed to the gate, tripped and nearly fell. The brakes screeched as the car skidded to a halt. Kirby, still very stiff, hobbled over to Sabrina's outstretched arms, leaving the motor still running. Intertwined in one big bear hug, tears streamed down their cheeks. Cora went inside to call her dad with the good news.

"I got lost in the blizzard. I'll explain everything later. I missed you so much."

"My heart has been torn in two; I thought I lost you. I feared the best part of our lives together was over," lamented Sabrina.

His throat dry, his voice gravelly, Kirby said, "You have always been in my heart and now you're back in my arms. Let's get out of this cold."

Jeremy parked the car as Kirby and Sabrina staggered into the house. Rachel handed Kirby a large glass of water. Kirby asked, "Where's Cody?"

"He's still out looking for you. He's put a lot of miles on the jeep, visited all your favorite spots on the rim—Canyon Queen Café, Summit Point, Inspiration Point—then backtracked to be sure he has covered all locations."

"I should go look for him."

"No way; you need to rest. And I have a new rule. The Ford does not leave the ranch without being provisioned with emergency supplies, food, and water."

"Speaking of food. I am famished. Do I smell a meat-and-potatoes dinner cooking?"

"Rachel and Cora are fixing it now, plus apple pie with coffee for dessert. And here comes the jeep! Cody can join you."

"Kirby, you're back! I've been cruising the Village and South Rim as far east as Monte's old ranch. What happened to you?" asked Cody.

"Unfortunately, Cody, I was far to the west, lost in the blizzard, about twenty miles from the Village, far from where you were searching. I'll explain my frigid ordeal and my rescue by a county road worker later."

After a hearty meal, and with no energy to climb upstairs, Kirby sprawled on the couch, and instantly passed out. Sabrina covered him with two blankets and sat nearby, thanking her lucky stars for Kirby's safe return.

* * *

"Kirby, wake up. You slept through breakfast and now it's almost noon."

"Oh, Sabrina I was just dreaming about you. I really needed that little nap. Trapped in the car for two days and two nights, I could not stretch out. I was huddled in a seat with my legs cramping every time I tried to shift position."

"Kirby, you still have not told us what happened," said Sabrina.

Everyone sat around the dining room table, building their own special sandwich, and listening to Kirby's long spiel on taking a wrong turn in a blinding blizzard, sliding into a deep snow-filled ditch, being trapped in the car, unable to open the doors or windows, hoping someone would come along. He described how Jorge Miranda of the Coconino County Road Department pulled him out of the snowbank and explained that the County only plowed the old Anita Mine Road on rare occasions, this big storm being one of those. Then Jorge drew a crude road map showing Kirby's current location, southwest of the Village, and a recently plowed route back to Little Springs.

After three days of rest and relaxation for Kirby, Sabrina suggested a visit to the Pioneer Museum. "We can sit inside where it's warm and view our Canyon through those huge panorama windows. Don't take this the wrong way, but I'm driving."

With plenty of water and a picnic lunch on board, the O'Briens headed north to the Canyon. It was a good time for a long talk.

"Kirby, while you were battling that blizzard, I reviewed our financials, budgeted eight thousand dollars for the new ranch house and another two thousand for extending water and electric utilities to the house. That leaves only five thousand in reserve. We've done a lot with those funds from the gold discovery but now we're getting low, especially after paying for the utility pole line and ranch house wiring."

Kirby offered a solution. "I suggest Jeremy and Cody, plus a couple hired cowboys from the Bergner cattle enterprise, round up and drive some of our beef cattle, say about one hundred head, to market this Spring. I understand the market price is about twelve dollars per hundredweight these days. That should bring in about ten thousand."

"I have no idea how you estimated that but okay, good plan. I have a few more things on my mind that I'd like to discuss before we reach the rim. We have several reasons to visit Flagstaff. We've been putting this off but we need to stop by the County Recorder's office and see if Monte and Jeremy's land are recorded properly."

Kirby suggested a visit to the County Road Department also. "By all means," said Sabrina, "Jorge saved your life and I need to thank him profusely."

"What do you mean profusely?"

Sabrina went on. We also should visit Bergner Construction and see if they can recommend a residential contractor. Kirby, we should build this Spring."

"When is Cora due?" asked Kirby.

"Sometime in May."

"Let's pick up a telephone directory while we're in town too," suggested Kirby, "I'll add that to our town list."

"Okay, we're coming into the museum parking lot. Enough discussion about things we ought to be doing."

After exchanging greetings with Mooney and Teresa in the museum office, Kirby and Sabrina headed straight for the bench at the center of the glass panorama. Sabrina noticed that Kirby seemed very stiff and awkward in his movements. They sat for ten minutes before Sabrina, who could not stop talking on the drive, broke the silence.

"I love the brilliant canyon sunrises, the sunsets and the stars but more than that, I love what lies under the canyon sky—cloud shadows gliding across the faces of crimson buttes and towers. Grand Canyon cast its golden spell on me a long time ago."

"Oh, on me too. In all my times below the rim, on twisting trails and in blind side canyons, I never lost my way, but after my meeting with Russ and his petulant staff engineers, I did indeed lose my way. I haven't mentioned this, but I was in a rotten mood after that meeting. All those guys could do is think of reasons not to build a trans-canyon pipeline. I was also perplexed why Russ let them ramble on that way, but he did apologize in the end."

Sabrina needed to put a positive spin on the project. "Kirby, your idea is sound. Just give those guys time to come to their senses. Looking up Skeleton Canyon right now, I can visualize a well-engineered pipeline delivering cool, clear water to millions of thirsty South Rim visitors."

"I reminded those guys that they are problem-solvers, not naysayers."

A few minutes passed. "Sabrina, either I'm still very stiff from being couped up in the car or I'm getting old. While just walking up here from the parking lot, I felt short of breath and unsteady on my feet, and now that I'm here, I feel I need a long break. What's it going to be like when we're in our eighties?" said Kirby with a grin.

"We both need a long break; you are finally feeling your age because you are eighty-two! I'm only eighty," teased Sabrina.

Kirby and Sabrina stopped talking and just sat there on that oak bench, gazing at the place where the earth radiates energy and inspires uplifting feelings. And the best feeling of all is being in the place where they first met so long ago.

* * *

The time had come to conduct some business in town. Despite clear roads, Sabrina insisted that she do the driving. They pulled into the County Recorder's Office. Monte's old ranch and the Livingston's ranch butted up to fences on opposite sides of Coconino National Forest. Sabrina wanted to see how the County listed the two properties.

"We may discover the Coconino Basin Ranch is still in Monte's name but we have his will in hand so we can get that corrected," said Sabrina. "Then we can decide if we want to donate it to the Forest Service."

A correction needed to be made. The clerk made sure the records now showed the property owned by Kirby and Sabrina O'Brien. As for Jeremy's old ranch, the clerk verified the property owners as Jeremy and Rachel Livingston. They could also decide its disposition later.

"What's next on our list?" asked Kirby.

"Coconino County Road Department. I think I remember where their garage is located. I need to thank Jorge Miranda for saving your life."

After some searching, they arrived at the garage, only to find Jorge spends his off days at the Flagstaff Orphanage. A worker at the garage provided directions and that is where they found Jorge.

"Kirby, it's you. You're still alive!" shouted Jorge.

"Thanks to you. Jorge; this is my wife, Sabrina. I think she wants to give you a big hug."

"Mr. Miranda, I cannot thank you enough for rescuing my husband. If you had not come along . . . well, I don't know if he'd be here today. Thank you, sir. Thank you from the bottom of my heart." An emotional Sabrina gave him a huge bear hug. Regaining her composure, "I did not know Flagstaff had an orphanage."

"Mrs. O'Brien, I wish more folks knew what we do here at the orphanage. We're all volunteers, running on a very tight budget to keep thirty-one children clothed and fed. We barely survived during the war years."

Sabrina again expressed her appreciation for saving her wayward husband and thanked Jorge for spending his spare time providing such a valuable community service. She donated five hundred dollars to the orphanage and handed Jorge the check while delivering another bear hug.

"Sabrina and Kirby, on behalf of all the children here at the orphanage, thank you very much." As a quick after-thought, "Sabrina, I see you are doing the driving; take care of Kirby there; he tends to drive off the road at times," said Jorge, snickering as he waved goodbye.

Walking back to the car, Kirby mumbled, "Very funny. Okay, what's next?"

"I'm hoping Harvey Klostermeyer at Bergner Construction can recommend a contractor willing to build residential homes in rural areas. Let's go visit him. This may be our last stop for the day."

"O'Briens! What brings you here? How's the Pioneer Museum holding up?"

"It's perfect, Harvey; your company did a fabulous job." Sabrina described their need for a single-story ranch house at the Circle K to first accommodate additional family and later to serve as a bunkhouse for ranch hands.

"Well, as you know, we specialize in commercial and industrial projects, but for what you have in mind, I highly recommend Timberline Homebuilders. I'll have my secretary give you the contact information. I'd like to talk some more but I'm on my way to a bid opening. Stop by again whenever you are in town."

Five minutes later, the secretary provided the name and telephone number for Ron Morgan, Timberline's foreman. Kirby stuffed the business card in his coat pocket and, noticing a small pile of telephone directories on a table, asked if they could spare an extra.

Kirby and Sabrina headed back to the ranch, all missions accomplished, and with a telephone book in hand as well.

* * *

Timberline Homebuilders started construction a few weeks after reviewing Sabrina's rough drawings and signing contracts. Foreman Ron

Morgan offered a ten percent veterans discount in appreciation for Cody's war service.

Jeremy noted the winter's heavy snowfall meant good grass for cattle grazing in the spring and summer months. He and Cody, with two hired cowboys, started the tedious operation of rounding up one hundred of their best beef cattle, weeding out calves and yearlings and paying no attention whether they carried the RB brand or the Circle K brand, then driving them to a holding pen on adjacent land of the Bergner Cattle Company. There the cattle would be merged with Bergner cattle on the long drive to market.

That Spring, a government scientist, Dr. James Klein, making the rounds to national parks throughout the Colorado Plateau, visited Russell Cramer and the superintendent of Grand Canyon National Park regarding the ongoing uranium boom. The park superintendent, remembering Abe Lincoln's saying that it is better to remain silent and be thought a fool than to speak out and remove all doubt, sat quietly listening to the conversation, totally relying on his chief engineer to capture the technical details and any actions that needed to be taken.

Dr. Klein started the meeting. "Russell, as the Park Engineer, I am loaning you a portable instrument called a Geiger counter and some extra batteries. It is designed to detect radiation emitted by uranium compounds, including their radioactive decay products like radon gas and radium. These may occur wherever you have ground water percolating through limestone formations. I'm not talking about placers where prospectors pan for gold. I'm talking about the layered sedimentary deposits you have here in canyon walls."

"Thank you, doc, we will make good use of it here. We have many copper mine tailings and open pits in our rock layers that need checking."

Dr. Klein added, "Believe it or not, even the junipers you have here on the rim absorb uranium from shallow deposits and outcrops in sufficient quantities to allow detection! But I would worry more about your mine tailings, prospect holes and open shafts and pits. It is there you are more likely to detect uranium, especially where, historically, prospectors have found minable copper compounds."

"One of our old-time miners, a good friend, Kirby O'Brien, tells me he recalled seeing freckled black shale mixed in with copper carbonates. He always discarded such rocks but maybe they were radioactive," explained Russ.

"That's exactly the kind of deposits you should scan with this Geiger counter," said Dr. Klein. "By the way, these counters read in counts per minute and there are selector switches to choose meter scales like times ten, times one hundred, etcetera. A normal background reading might be fifty counts per minute or less, five hundred is high, over one thousand is very high. Radiation detection and measurement is not an exact science, but the higher the counts, the more likely you are reading uranium emissions."

"Now let me explain what is happening in Washington. There is an act working its way through Congress to establish the Atomic Energy Commission. In this post-war era, the government sees an immediate need for uranium for future strategic weapons but mostly for non-military peacetime purposes. It believes the Colorado Plateau will be an important uranium source for years to come."

Dr. Klein added, "We understand you have a privately owned uranium deposit here on the South Rim, the Thornton Mine, I believe, but the most promising locations are the limestone formations near Grants, New Mexico and Marysvale, Utah. Still, we have Geiger counter-wielding prospectors roaming all over the Four Corner states, even though the uranium used in the Hiroshima bomb never came from the

Colorado Plateau. The new Atomic Energy Commission's primary emphasis will be enriching uranium and regulating its use in nuclear power plants."

"What we are concerned about here at the Grand Canyon," clarified Russ, "Is the potential radiation danger to the visiting public. The last thing we need in the park is uranium searchers mapping, drilling, trenching and even driving shafts like the Thornton Mine. In fact, mining is illegal in this national park and our job is to defend, protect and preserve this wondrous creation of nature in pristine condition for future generations."

Dr. Klein offered some concluding remarks. "Let's not get ahead of ourselves. Use this Geiger counter and check places where your rock layers were exposed when the Canyon was open to copper mining. Then report back to me and we'll jointly decide the next course of action, if any. And with that, gentlemen, I hand you my business card, and thank you for your time and interest in this new post-war development."

Russ, and especially the superintendent, seemed overwhelmed by the search for a mysterious mineral element that shoots invisible particles. The superintendent summed it up best. "Uranium may be at the core of future nuclear power plants but today it is at the core of a new attack on Grand Canyon National Park."

* * *

During the first weekend of May, Cora began to feel labor pains. The women decided it best to have the baby born in a hospital in case of complications. Early Monday morning, Cora climbed rather awkwardly into the Ford's back seat. At the last minute, Cody climbed in beside her. Rachel sat in the front passenger seat while Sabrina drove.

They arrived at the Flagstaff Medical Center as Cora's labor pains increased dramatically. Two hours later, she gave birth to a son, Josh.

"Congratulations Cora and Cody," said Sabrina, "You are now the proud parents of a baby son!" The day went so smoothly and with Cora anxious to get out of the hospital, the doctor agreed Cora and Josh could be discharged. They left town in plenty of time to arrive home in daylight.

Sabrina tooted her horn as they pulled up to the house. Kirby shouted to Jeremy, "Hey, look, I think you have a new ranch hand reporting for duty!" Cody jumped out first. Cora handed Josh to Cody and all went inside.

Cora announced, "Everyone, I'm both extremely happy and extremely exhausted. Cody, let's take Josh up to our room. All went well today but we could use some rest. And Uncle Kirby, I heard what you said. Josh is not quite ready for ranch work yet."

Sabrina called Russ and invited he and Mabel to meet their grandson, Josh Livingston. They would drive down in two days when Russ could take a day off work. It would be their very first visit to the Circle K Ranch.

* * *

Post-war automobile production put an end to the nation's pent-up market for new vehicles. Russ and Mabel's blue, four-door Chrysler Town and Country automobile typified the models rolling off the assembly lines. When it rolled through the open gate, the ranch house residents emptied into the parking area, with Cora, Cody and Josh leading the pack.

"Mom, Dad, meet your grandson!" cried Cora.

"He's so tiny! It's been years since I held a newborn baby!"

"That would be me, Mom."

"Congratulations Cody! And Kirby and Sabrina, it is so nice of you to invite us to your ranch. It's our first visit to this area and it's plain to see why you like country living. This place is beautiful. And Jeremy and Rachel, you too are now grandparents!" Russ seemed overwhelmed by the realization that he and Mabel had become part of a much bigger family.

"Folks, let's go inside," suggested Sabrina. "It may be Spring, but it's still chilly and the windy season is now upon us."

Russ went back to the car to retrieve a small leather case.

"What's that Russ?" asked Kirby.

"It's a Geiger counter."

"A what counter?"

"I'll explain as I have a lot to tell you about the uranium craze going on."

After celebrating Josh and the new parents and grandparents with cake and coffee, Russ jumped right into a discussion about radioactive rocks.

"Dr. James Klein just paid a visit to my office and loaned the Park this new instrument, a Geiger counter. It reads radiation in counts per minute. A normal background reading might be fifty but high readings can be five hundred or one thousand or even more, indicating uranium compounds are present."

Sabrina, with a broad smile, cautioned, "Don't get too technical with us, Russ. We're not engineers like you."

"This is typical of my father, Sabrina. He'd come home from work and regale mom and I with new project developments. Engineers like to do that. We just roll our eyes and put up with it." She flashed a broad smile at her dad.

"Okay, duly-noted, daughter, or I should say brand-new mother. I'll keep it short. We need to check the mine tailings, prospect holes, shafts and pits both on and below the canyon rim—the places where copper ore has already showed itself. Apparently, those exposed locations are also likely places where uranium ore can be found."

Russ continued although he doubted he had the women's undivided attention. "An Act of Congress will soon create a new government agency, the Atomic Energy Commission, to oversee uranium production for both military and non-military purposes. The latter involves constructing nuclear power plants. Dr. Klein, a geologist, is convinced the Colorado Plateau will be an important uranium source in the near-future. He's well aware of the Thornton Mine near the Village but is not really too concerned about uranium mining at the Canyon, but instead reports Grants, New Mexico and Marysvale, Utah as major mining locations."

Kirby's ears perked up. "Marysvale! I remember ol' Francois LaRue trying to promote a Denver and Rio Grande Railway extension from Marysvale to the North Rim!"

"I remember that too, Kirby, little did he know there were radioactive rocks at that proposed railroad junction," commented Sabrina.

Russ added, "Apparently a local prospector recently located a promising uranium deposit there."

"We've all been very worried about more dams in the Canyon to produce hydroelectric power for distant cities, but a viable alternative may be nuclear power plants," observed Sabrina. "I'm not sure the dam issues are completely dead yet but this new innovation could derail any further consideration of dams."

"That crossed my mind too, Sabrina," then switching subjects, "Kirby, are you still able to hike your old canyon trails?"

Before he could answer, Sabrina interrupted, "No way, Russ, we're both too old."

"She's right, Russ. We're just rim-walkers now."

"I figured that but had to ask. Jeremy, would you be willing to meet Park Ranger Tim Simmons at Summit later this week? I understand you are quite familiar with the Summit Trail and the Shooting Star mine. I'd like you and Simmons to check the tailings and tunnels with this Geiger counter and keep a log of your readings. Maybe you could check the Thornton mine too."

"Russ, I'd be happy to assist. Having helped build the trail and mine, I know all the places to check on Windsong Mesa but I'm not familiar with Thornton's operation. Whatever I can do to help."

"Thank you, Jeremy. I'll have Simmons call you and set a date and time. Be sure to bring the Geiger counter. Okay, that's enough technical talk. Let's get back to celebrating the arrival of Josh Livingston."

* * *

When Jeremy parked his jeep at Summit Point and walked over to the trailhead, he found the uniformed Ranger Simmons already there.

"Hello, Tim, I'm Jeremy Livingston. Have you hiked this trail before?"

"No Jeremy, I recently transferred from the North Rim to the Backcountry Office and so I'm still getting to know the South Rim trails."

"Well, this one is only about three miles long but no longer maintained. It was built over fifty years ago and is not in good condition," commented Jeremy.

"Who built it?"

"The master trail-builder was Monte Bridgestone. The rest of us just followed orders. That was Kirby O'Brien, my brother Dexter and myself, and several others. I assume you have a full canteen and are ready to go. I'm a lot older now so we'll be going slow."

Jeremy and Tim rested on flat rocks at the Coconino Saddle. Jeremy made sure Tim recognized the fine workmanship of the trail-bed and cribbing. Monte built the trail to last a century and Jeremy noted it looked like it has held up well so far.

"Tim, when we climb back up, you'll find you'll need more breaks. Going down is easy and from here to Windsong Mesa is even easier."

"When do we start taking Geiger counter readings?"

"We'll start by descending the east wall. There are two tunnel adits there, each with its own dump. One tunnel leads to a large cave-like chamber where we had a mysterious explosion, the other leads to a shaft that goes to the surface."

The men paused briefly on the mesa.

"Tim, let's take our first reading right here. This is where Monte did all his ore sorting and sacking work. The shaft opening behind him used to have a winch for hoisting ore buckets. I'm turning on the counter, get ready to log our readings. For the ore sacking area, I get thirty-eight counts per minute which is essentially a background reading. Okay, let's head down the east wall and I'll keep monitoring the counter as we go."

The descent led to the first tunnel. About fifty feet inside, Jeremy read seventy-two counts at the mineshaft and about the same on its dump.

"I'm real curious about the second tunnel. Here we found our best deposits, including a large vein of native copper. Okay, I need to switch to the times ten scale; write down five hundred and sixty counts. And three fifty for the dump."

"Jeremy, I guess your dumps were where you discarded waste rock over the side. It sure leaves an ugly scar, but I suppose that is one drawback of mining."

"It's not nearly as ugly as surface mining. If we have time, I'm going to take you to Prospector Flats. The landscape still looks like a pack of giant prairie dogs lived there. Okay, we need to go back and cross the mesa to the caves."

At the entrance to the caves, still boarded up, the miners cut a short trail above Cottonwood Canyon. Jeremy only measured background there.

"At one time these limestone caves drew as much tourist attention as the Canyon itself. I believe our work is done here. We did not get very high readings at our checkpoints or along the way, even though this mesa is a honeycomb of underground tunnels, cross-cuts and shafts. We can climb back to the rim and drive over to the Thornton mine."

After a few hours of climbing and a fifteen-mile drive to the Thornton mine, including a brief stop at a prospect hole behind the Cliffhanger Studio, the men realized much of the afternoon had already slipped by, but enough daylight still lingered. Prospector Flats would have to wait for another day; besides, it's outside the southern boundary line.

"Tim, log thirty counts for the Cliffhanger prospect hole. I'm not very familiar with Thornton's old copper mine. It appears abandoned. Let's walk around and take a series of surface readings. I'm turning on the counter. Whoa, it's pegged on the times ten scale; going to times one hundred. I'm reading seventy-five so Tim, write down seventy-five hundred at this shaft! And sixty-five hundred at this pile of rocks!"

The men walked over to the rim. Jeremy read eight thousand at a big pile of ore, part of which had slid over the side. Near a wood-frame building, perhaps the mine office, he read two thousand.

"Tim, are you getting all this? It appears there are radioactive rocks everywhere. I suggest you immediately report these findings to the Park Engineer. I don't know what happens when humans are exposed to radiation, but I recommend this entire mining claim be fenced off from the general public as a hazardous area, post radiation danger signs, and consider this site essentially off limits, like a hole in the park."

"I'll go over to his office now and show him our log readings."

"Here, you can also return his Geiger counter. It's turned off. If we used it correctly, I think we have a serious radiation problem at this mine. Thankfully, the Shooting Star seems relatively safe. I have a long drive home, hoping to get there before dark. Thank you for your assistance, Tim, nice working with you."

"And you Jeremy. I've already learned a lot about mining, but I'm as concerned as you are if we really have a uranium contamination problem here on the rim. See you again soon."

Chapter Twelve

TRAIN WRECK

It takes millions of years to build the Canyon, but less than a lifetime to destroy it

"Kirby, it's been two weeks since Jeremy completed the radiation survey. I wonder what's happening with that. I still do not understand how some rocks can be spewing tiny invisible particles while others sit minding their own business, being no bother to anyone."

"Sabrina, you sure have a way with words. I think we should call Russ on the phone and invite him to join us for lunch at the Canyon Queen Café. It would be interesting to catch up on any new developments, you know, things like river dams, cross-canyon pipelines, and radiation hazards.

"Good idea, I'll make the call right now," volunteered Sabrina.

* * *

Sabrina, still insisting on doing all the driving, even though there were no snowdrifts in sight, parked their sedan in the Canyon Queen parking lot. Arriving early, they took a few minutes to stare at the Canyon. This time, they caught her in a rare mood. A thin layer of clouds swirling around the tallest buttes, filling the canyon voids, and turning the entire abyss into a vacant sea of white.

A waitress seated Kirby and Sabrina at a corner table just as Russ arrived.

"Good afternoon, O'Briens. This is a great idea, getting me out of the office. I'm looking forward to a great lunch and no doubt some lively conversation as you two, lifelong canyon stewards always have heavy issues on your mind. By the way, thank you for a most delightful time at your ranch. I've never seen my daughter so happy. I feel like the Livingstons, Cramers and O'Briens are all one big close-knit family!"

"That we are, Russ. Let's order and then I'd like to see how things stand after Jeremy's radiation survey," said Kirby. "He was quite alarmed with the readings at the Thornton mine."

The waitress took their lunch orders, all specials of the day, ready in no time.

Russ explained. "Jeremy will be pleased to know I have borrowed Ranger Simmons from the Backcountry Office to conduct additional surveys, including mapping locations with high radiation levels. Besides the Thornton mess, Simmons is checking areas most frequented by backcountry hikers. He'll then prepare a report for Dr. Klein. In the meantime, we have fenced off the Thornton mining claim, even though it is private land. We're trying to contact the owners but so far, no luck. I never dreamed we would have a problem of radiation exposure here at the Canyon. Oh, I think I see our lunch coming."

He added, "I know what you're thinking, Sabrina, what else can threaten our beloved Canyon?"

"I do not understand radiation. Kirby and I are well aware of the mining potential when such a huge swath of the earth's crust is exposed but invisible rays from rocks? Very strange. Changing subjects, are the Bridge Canyon and Marble Canyon dam proposals dead issues now?"

"Well, I can tell you this," replied Russ, "Even though some studies continued during the war, I think Reclamation is losing interest in the Bridge Canyon Dam. Everyone is tired of arguing. I would not be surprised to see Reclamation quashing the project by estimating construction costs so high as to offset any benefits, thereby declaring the project not feasible."

"Will that kill it?" asked Sabrina, hoping for a positive response about her beloved Grand Canyon. "It takes millions of years to build the Canyon, but less than a lifetime to destroy it."

"Maybe. Perhaps you have heard of an environmental organization called the Sierra Club. John Muir started it back in eighteen ninety-two. These people are adamantly opposed to coal-fired plants, hydroelectric power plants, and I wouldn't be surprised if they oppose nuclear power plants in the future. These are the same good folks who advocated removing our national parks from Forest Service oversight. Despite the Sierra Club outcry against canyon dams, some Arizona politicians still support Bridge Canyon Dam. To me, that's outrageous. I can't imagine backing up the river ninety miles to Kanab Creek, creating lake frontage for the Hualapai, flooding the lower part of Havasu Creek, and drowning Anasazi pictographs and prehistoric artifacts."

"What about the other dam proposed for the lower end of Marble Canyon?" asked Sabrina.

"Sierra Club is just as opposed to that dam, backing up water forty miles to Lees Ferry and, shudder to think, submerging Redwall Cavern! It appears that project will lay dormant for quite some time. Arizona politicians, while wanting water supplies for the Phoenix area, are fighting California which wants to build dams below Hoover. I think you know the Colorado River Compact governs the allocation of river water rights among seven states. After twenty-two years of opposition, the Arizona legislature finally ratified the Compact. But I predict the differences between Arizona and California will continue for years," concluded Russ.

"So, the big water fight over the Colorado and the resulting threat to the Canyon continues," said Sabrina with a sigh. "I hope the common sense of younger generations prevails."

"Let's hope so," agreed Russ, sliding back his chair in a move to get back to his office.

"Wait Russ," said Kirby, "One more thing before you go. I keep thinking about your staff engineers and our discussion about harvesting water from Echo Falls. Certainly, more study is needed. You might direct your guys to build a model using a water hose to get a better understanding of hydraulic head and what it will take to marry up with the existing Canyon Garden system. They could also study ways to stabilize a partially exposed pressurized pipeline while minimizing the impact on the visitor's canyon experience. Just thinking out loud here."

"Good thinking, Kirby, as usual. I'll pass this along as a work assignment. Now I need to get back. Thank you for lunch. Now try to stay out of trouble and take care."

* * *

Kirby met Jeremy at the barn, feeding livestock and replenishing the water troughs.

"Hey, Jeremy. Good news. Our cattle sale brought in ninety-five hundred dollars less eight hundred for Bergner handling fees and cowboy services," announced Kirby.

"That's great. Maybe we can use a few hundred for some repairs on this old barn," suggested Jeremy, as he continued filling the horse troughs. "By the way, when I was working with Ranger Simmons on that radiation survey, he asked me about ranching in these parts. And that led to a discussion about a newly created agency within the Interior Department called the Bureau of Land Management. It was created by merging the General Land Office with the U.S. Grazing Service. That second agency was new to me. Anyway, Simmons says the mission of this combined agency is to manage public lands, mostly in western states, and to ensure healthy rangelands for livestock grazing. Apparently, they will soon be issuing permits and leases to ranchers like us."

"Jeremy, you are overflowing this horse trough! What are you thinking?"

"Besides turning the water off," said Jeremy, with a chuckle, "I'm thinking of Cody's future. We've assumed all the land between my old ranch and yours was Forest Service land, but I don't think we know that for sure. There are not enough trees out here to call the area a forest. If some of this rangeland comes under this new land management agency, and touches the RB and Circle K ranches, maybe we should consider applying for a grazing permit. In the long run, it would help Cody expand the cattle operation here. Wouldn't it be great if there were additional lands between ours for grazing cattle under a permit?"

"It would, Jeremy. Thanks for bringing this to my attention. I'll pass it along to Sabrina. I suggest you and Cody look into it further, including any applicable grazing fees. Maybe we can get in on the ground floor of this new program for ranchers."

"I'll do that Kirby, and let you know what I find."

* * *

All the grazing talk reminded Kirby about the Coconino Basin Ranch, Monte's old place, which now lies in ruins. He and Sabrina still needed to make some decisions about what to do with it.

"Sabrina, I've got an idea; let's visit the folks in the Forest Supervisor's office in Williams about possibly deeding over Monte's old ranch to them. We can show them the Forest Homestead certificate and

Monte's will, and just maybe they can show us their forest maps. I'm curious about the extent of the forest boundary and whether there is grazing land between Jeremy's old place and the Circle K."

"Well, we've been talking about that for some time, but why just now?" posed Sabrina.

"That involves part two of my idea and something I've always wanted to do. Since we'd already be in Williams, let's take the train to the Canyon, maybe stay overnight at the Canyon Queen, then return to Williams by train the next day and drive home. What do you think?"

"That sounds like a fun trip," said Sabrina. "I've seen the train many times but never thought about a train ride, probably because I've always regarded the engine as a grimy, smoke-belching monster spoiling the canyon ambience."

"Well, it is that, but the ride itself might be a different experience for us, say a once-in-a-lifetime adventure," offered Kirby. "Let's tell Jeremy and Cody what we are up to, and head out early tomorrow morning."

* * *

Kirby and Sabrina presented their case to the Forest Supervisor.

"Sir, the land we are talking about is one hundred and thirty-five acres wedged between the national park and the national forest. It was granted to Benjamin Bridgestone as a forest homestead. Here's the entry certificate signed by the president. Ben died in the Spanish Influenza pandemic and his estate went to his father, Monte Bridgestone. Before Monte passed away, he willed the property to Kirby and I. We are willing to deed it over to the Forest Service."

The supervisor advised, "We would need to visit the property before any decision could be made. In the meantime, let's look at our maps and get an idea of what it would add to our forest."

As the supervisor unrolled their map, Kirby noticed it covered land south of the national forest. He pointed to what they knew as the Coconino Basin Ranch butting right up to the forest boundary. "Here it is. This is the property we are willing to deed over to the Forest Service." He decided to say nothing about collapsed buildings and ranch debris cluttering the ranch house site.

"Okay, sir, I'll send a ranger out there in a week or two and we'll get back to you."

Sabrina jumped in. "Sir, your map goes a lot further than we expected. Many years ago, I bought the Klostermeyer Ranch. It served as the Little Springs waystation on the old stage road. Our home is here." She pointed. "We call it the Circle K Ranch, the K for Klostermeyer. It covers about six hundred and forty acres. Can you tell us about the land between your forest and our ranch? Is it government land, private land, or a combination?"

"Well, you can see from this color coding, it's quite a mixed combination. One of the biggest landowners out there is the far-flung Bergner Cattle Company but there's also public land that may soon become available for grazing under permit, not through us but through the new agency known as the Bureau of Land Management. I can leave this spread out so you can study it a while. I have a meeting starting in a few minutes. Thanks for your generous offer. If you would leave your telephone number with my secretary, we'll get back to you soon."

With that, the supervisor left the room, leaving Kirby and Sabrina time to study the map and make a few notes.

"Sabrina, this looks like Jeremy's twenty acres. And here's the boundary line between the Circle K and the Bergner land. They, and some others, are all colored red denoting private land."

"And Kirby, here's a big yellow area labeled government-owned whereas national forest land is shown in green and national park land in blue. Maybe, just maybe, the yellow land comes under the jurisdiction of the new land management agency."

With that, the O'Briens drove over to the train station, bought two four-dollar, round-trip tickets, and waited for the conductor to bellow his time-honored call, All Aboard!

The Grand Canyon Railway needed seven cars on this trip to meet the demands of the burgeoning post-war tourist season. Kirby and Sabrina selected seats on the right side of the third car back. Except for a few sidings for livestock loading, the entire sixty-five-mile line consisted of a single track. No one expected trouble at Quivira Meadows, twenty miles out of Williams.

All went well for the first ten miles but once in the open with few ponderosa pines, Kirby noted, "It seems this car is rocking back and forth too much and tending to lean to one side."

"I think it's the wind. Our spring winds are gusting terribly this year. It's like we have a severe weather front moving in from the west," suggested Sabrina.

Minutes later, a roaring blast hit the train broadside and lifted the wheels on the upwind side clear off the rails.

"Hang on, Sabrina, I think we may be going over!"

With the terrifying sound of squealing steel, the engine, coal tender and first two cars derailed. The third car coupler broke and suddenly Kirby and Sabrina had a horrifying view straight ahead where the forward cars separated and rolled over. The boiler burst open, releasing a gush of steam. The firebox split open, belching black smoke and spilling red hot coals onto the dry prairie grass, igniting a windswept wildfire. The engine settled atop a jumbled collection of splintered railroad ties. Most passengers in the two overturned cars suffered scrapes and bruises and likely a few broke some bones.

"Sabrina, are you hurt?"

"No, I don't think so. I see the engineer and fireman were thrown from the cab, dazed but okay. There's a siding out there with a small building. It's a telephone booth! The engineer is staggering over there to call for help. I'm going out there and try to help those with injuries."

"Me too. I see a rancher on horseback. He probably witnessed the wreck. Just in case the engineer's telephone call does not go through, I'll see if the rancher is willing to gallop into Williams and notify the railroad officials."

On his way back from talking to the horseman, who did agree to ride into town, Kirby noticed mangled cribbing where a dry creek passed under the tracks. If it had given way prior to the train's arrival, perhaps it contributed to the derailment. Kirby wondered how high winds alone could knock a heavy engine off the tracks.

By now passengers milled about, stunned and wondering how long it would take for help to arrive. A limping, overweight conductor tried to make chaos and confusion into some kind of order, but then collapsed to the ground, unable to support himself in the strong wind. The brakeman, thrown clear of the wreckage, lay writhing in pain. Kirby suspected broken bones. He called for help, hoping there might be a vacationing doctor or nurse in the crowd.

Sabrina assessed their situation. "Here we are, stranded at Quivira Meadows, with no first aid kits, no food, and no water. It may be hours before the railway gets notice of this train wreck and can dispatch a second engine to pull the five cars still on the tracks, crowded with angry, bruised passengers, back to Williams."

"Forget my idea of visiting the Grand Canyon by train," said Kirby.

"Consider it forgotten; we are very lucky to be alive." Sabrina watched a slinking coyote trot by, eyes darting from side to side, then disappearing behind the smoldering grass fire. "Maybe that coyote knows where we can find water."

No one said a word on the train ride back to Williams but moaning and crying filled every railcar. On their drive home, Kirby apologized over and over for suggesting a train ride to the Canyon. Sabrina, too busy to respond, tightened her grip on the steering wheel as gusts of wind tried to send their sedan into roadside ditches. Later the *Frontier Times* reported the railway would be shut down for at least four weeks while wreckage is cleared and tracks are repaired. As for the grass fire, it burned itself out thirty-five miles downwind, just short of the Circle K's western boundary.

* * *

Arriving back at the ranch, Kirby and Sabrina withstood a barrage of questions.

Jeremy noted, "You're early! We did not expect you back for another day. What happened?"

"Train problem," answered Sabrina.

"What do you mean, train problem?" asked Rachel.

"Train broke in half!"

"What?" shrieked Cora.

"Then the front half rolled on its side," explained Sabrina, rather nonchalantly. "We'll explain. We're lucky to be alive."

Kirby added, "Needless to say, we're not impressed with train travel. What was to be a new adventure for us, turned out to be a nightmare. You probably noticed we have a few bumps and bruises. The folks in the overturned cars look a lot worse than we do."

Everyone gathered around the dining room table as Kirby and Sabrina described their train ordeal.

"Grand Canyon Railway sent another engine up the line and linked to the passenger cars still sitting upright on the tracks. We essentially crowded the passengers of seven cars into five and made it safely back to the Williams railyard," explained Kirby.

Sabrina added, "As far as we know there were no deaths or serious injuries, but the engine is a wreck, and the tracks are a tangled mess. Before we embarked on our disastrous train ride, we had a very good meeting with the Forest Supervisor in Williams. So, on a happier note, we'd like to report on that as it involves all of us."

"We first broached the subject of Monte's old ranch," said Kirby. "Earlier we made sure Coconino County records showed Sabrina and I as owners. We are proposing to transfer the property to the Forest Service as it borders their property. After a ranger checks the land, they will get back to us on whether they will accept our offer. So, that's one piece of important business we discussed."

"You will find this next part very interesting," said Sabrina. "The supervisor broke out a big color-coded map of the area. It showed national park lands, national forest lands, and private land holdings including yours, Jeremy and Rachel, our Circle K Ranch which will be yours, Cody and Cora, plus the vast holdings of the Bergner Cattle Company."

Sabrina continued, "It also showed a large section between the RB Ranch and the Circle K Ranch reserved by the U.S. Government. The supervisor explained that land will soon be made available for grazing permits managed by the new Bureau of Land Management. Cody, it is most important that you closely monitor the grazing permit situation. If we can run our cattle on that land as well as the land we own, we, I mean you younger folks, have an opportunity to expand our ranching operations."

Cody had an observation. "I'll certainly watch for the grazing permit opportunity but I'm worried that Bergner may grab any permits before we have a chance. They are much bigger and more influential than us."

"But they are also good neighbors and we work well together," explained Sabrina. "They may already have enough land and don't need grazing permits. Let's broach the subject with their foreman and explore the situation. And perhaps the grazing permit office will favor a Silver Star war hero."

"And now I propose we break for dinner. It's been a long day," announced Kirby.

* * *

"Sabrina, half the reason for our train trip was to spend some time at the Canyon. Since we missed out on that, let's just drive up there today, stroll along the rim, and find a bench with a mesmerizing view."

"I'm all for that. I just want to stare at the red buttes and ridges and imagine what could be hidden in shadowy crevices. Kirby, if we were younger, I'd say let's venture below the rim but my legs tell me those days are over."

"Mine even more so."

Sabrina crawled into the driver's seat and Kirby sank into the passenger seat. Both seemed rather slow and awkward in their movements but at least they could get to the South Rim on their own. This time they chose to sit on a bench at the Geology Museum.

"Kirby, from time to time, I conjure up memories of my first encounter with Monte, Clint McCarty and another burly fellow whose name I cannot recall. It was right down there on the Tonto. I introduced myself as a woman prospector. Those guys could not believe their eyes. I got the feeling they resented my intrusion into their world. At the same time, they could not take their eyes off me."

"That I can understand. I could not take my eyes off you when we first met. Still can't. Boy, those days seem so long ago. I was working with Levi back then."

"They do indeed seem like ages ago. But we've had some great times together since then, well, except for yesterday's train disaster. I hope everyone recovers quickly from being tossed around in bouncing railcars and puts the whole trip out of their mind. I can't believe I'm talking about it. If I'm not careful, I'm liable to spoil the mood here on the rim."

"I also conjure up memories of my days down there. Every time I led a string of burros down to Arrowhead Spring, I dreamed you would be there waiting for me. You were quite a tease because you rarely showed. But when you did, it made my day."

"Then I shouldn't tell you that one day I turned back. I started thinking why am I playing this silly game. I was not being fair to you, keeping you guessing if I'd show or not. Later, I regretted turning back. I'm sure glad you followed me that time."

"I wonder how many couples can say the Canyon brought them together. There may be a few, but I bet they were not canyon prospectors at the time. I venture to say, we are the only prospectors to marry one another."

"Now Kirby, that sounds outlandish. This magnificent canyon sure sets our minds swirling and our conversation straying. We should probably start back."

Once on the road, Kirby and Sabrina talked about the construction of the second ranch house.

"When Cora, Cody and Josh want more privacy, it will be ready for them," said Sabrina. "Until then, they can continue living in the main house. For a newborn baby, that is probably best."

Kirby reported on his construction observations. "The plumbing and electrical work has been roughed in. Ron Morgan's Timberline team and their subcontractor Hartman Electric are doing a good job. Jeremy and Cody plan to do all the finishing work. And they plan to retrieve the woodstove and any useful furniture from the RB Ranch. I don't think Jeremy knows what he wants to do with their old ranch. At least most of it is good for running cattle."

"Well, that's up to Jeremy and Rachel. I'm just thankful they are able to keep the Circle K going. We're at the same point where the Klostermeyers were, aging and no longer able to run the ranch. They moved to town. We can't run this outfit ourselves anymore either. Besides, what good are we in helping with ranch chores? We keep running off to the Canyon on a whim."

When they parked their sedan at the house, Cody and Cora came running out.

"We've got some great news," shouted Cody. Cora is pregnant. Our second baby is due in April!"

"That is great news! Congratulations! We're very happy for you," said Sabrina. "The Circle K population is growing!"

* * *

The weather improved enough that Kirby and Sabrina could sit out on the veranda again. More mild sunny days signaled Winter finally giving way to Spring. A glance at the livestock in the corral sparked a conversation about burros, even though there were none of those cute creatures running wild on the Circle K.

"Kirby, we have talked about burros in the Canyon on several occasions. I never used them as pack animals but certainly you have. You told me Monte and other canyon prospectors left them to roam free, foraging on the Tonto and fending for themselves. And when needed again, these shaggy critters were easy to round up."

"That's right, and yes, I know burros very well."

"I heard a slightly different version of their use by prospectors. Legend says early prospectors believed a wandering burro would lead them to gold. If a prospector stopped following his burro and abandoned his search for gold, he would also abandon his burro. And this is how they became feral and thrived as living symbols of the Old West."

"Where are you going with this, Sabrina? For years I've heard complaints about burros creating a maze of trails and trampling vegetation."

Sabrina countered, "Coyotes, bobcats, mule deer and bighorns also create trails. I see that as a good thing. They create a path and consistently use the same path, thus reducing the impact on canyon vegetation."

She continued. "Now we're embroiled in a bitter controversy over whether feral burros competing with desert bighorn sheep for food are invasive creatures which should be exterminated like the gray wolves on the North Rim or should they be protected as a valuable part of canyon history. I believe the gray wolves belonged here naturally and should never have been hunted down or trapped to the point of extinction."

"Burros were introduced here several hundred years ago. Who knows? Someday maybe elk will be introduced in the park, and they would be competing with mule deer for food. Seems to me that would not be any different than today's burro situation," explained Sabrina.

"Lately, I've heard park rangers talking about shooting burros again as a means of population control. They might feel differently if they saw a burro foal. Those little darlings look like stuffed toy animals. I'm always amazed that burros can produce such cute offspring. I guess I'm just sorry to see burros treated with such distain these days."

"Okay, Sabrina, I see your point. I've always been fond of burros and found them to be of great help in my mining days. As for elk in the park someday, I doubt that would ever happen. But I bet mountain lions would welcome some variety in their venison diet!"

* * *

During a return visit to the South Rim, this time the Pioneer Museum, Sabrina learned that Moonflower Yazzie had not been feeling well. She has been worried sick about too many airplanes buzzing her beloved canyon and this has added considerable stress to the aging Navajo woman.

Sabrina asked Teresa, "Is Mooney here today?"

"No, but she was here. She has been missing many days of work lately," replied Teresa. "I'm very worried about her. She stopped by this morning saying she needs more time off. Apparently, Mooney spends a lot of time praying at Navajo Point and planned to spend today there. She may or may not report for work in the morning."

Sabrina turned to Kirby, "Let's run out there and see if there is anything we can do for our dear friend."

"Let's go. It's been ages since we've been to the Canyon's eastern reaches, where Monte served as unofficial guardian, first for the Forest Service, then for the Park Service."

On the drive along the East Rim, well past Summit Point, Kirby reminded Sabrina that Mooney used to talk about watching Ford Tri-

Motor airplanes take off and land at an airfield just north of Red Butte. The first commercial scenic flights over the Grand Canyon originated at that lonely outpost.

Kirby and Sabrina found Mooney sitting on the rim at Navajo Point where she enjoyed a view of the glimmering ribbon of the Colorado. One hundred miles to the northeast is the brooding Navajo Mountain, visible even on days with diffused sunlight.

"Kirby! Sabrina! How did you find me out here?"

"Teresa said you would be here and that you seemed very troubled these days," answered Sabrina.

"Whenever I feel down about these airplanes flying over this vast canyon, I come out here. I'm a very old woman now. I've counted over one thousand moons, about eighty-five years, and I never dreamed man would be flying around like the ravens. I'm worried about airplanes overcrowding the sky. I have frequent visions of a great disaster, a collision between two big airplanes, falling debris, screaming passengers, and fiery crashes into canyon buttes," explained Mooney.

"Since the late nineteen twenties, I've watched occasional airplanes take off from Red Butte airfield and land after circling over the Canyon a few times. There were not many sight-seeing tours here then; but now, there are far too many," lamented Mooney.

"Kirby and I have expressed this very concern to the Park Engineer. Mooney, he wants to develop a plan to help manage and regulate flights over the Canyon in hopes of preventing the very disaster you are worried about."

Mooney continued, "One spring day, I met a tall pilot outside the Red Butte hangar building. He gave me a walkaround tour of his silver bird. His name was Charles Lindbergh. He told me this airplane was the sister of the Spirit of St. Louis which he flew alone, without stopping, across the Atlantic Ocean the previous year. I did not believe him. How can an airplane fly that far without many stops along the way?"

Kirby looked at Sabrina. "I've heard of this Lindbergh fellow. I think he made the first nonstop, solo flight from New York to Paris."

Mooney added, "When I come here, I pray to Navajo Mountain and the sacred stone arch near its base which many call Rainbow Bridge. I pray for all the people in those airplanes and that they will not fall out of the sky."

Mooney resumed her prayers in Navajo as Sabrina motioned that they return to the car and head back. Then Mooney paused and looked up at the O'Briens.

"Red Butte airfield is seldom used now. Twenty years ago, the Forest Service authorized a landing field for commercial flights just outside the park's south entrance. It has since become the official Grand Canyon Airport. The flights I see now operate out of that new facility."

Just then a low-flying airplane roared across Navajo Point and dropped below the rim and into the yawning void. Kirby and Sabrina instinctively ducked.

"I'm getting very old. I may not be able to do this much longer," confessed Mooney. As her voice trailed off, she added, "I don't think I am long for this world."

Chapter Thirteen

LAST CANYON TREK

Life is not measured in days, months or years, nor in the number of breaths we take; it is measured by the moments that take our breath away

Sabrina received a late Spring telephone call from the U. S. Forest Service, accepting Monte's old place, and posting the transfer paperwork in the mail. Much to Kirby and Sabrina's relief, the volunteer group known as Friends of the Forest offered to handle any necessary clean-up and debris removal.

Although Kirby is stiff and slow-moving, he is alert as ever. He watched the mailman stuff a large envelope in the ranch mailbox, then grabbed his cane and hobbled down to the gate to retrieve the package marked important papers. Being short of breath, he paused before trudging back to the house. He found the envelope contained documents transferring ownership of Coconino Basin Ranch to the Forest Service. To complete the transaction, they just needed to sign and return the agreement.

In another land matter, Cody reported good news. "Kirby, the Bureau of Land Management granted the Circle K Ranch a ten-year livestock grazing permit! The fee, ninety cents per animal per month, is based on the amount of forage needed to feed one cow for one month. If the cow has a calf, that still counts as one animal!"

Cora overheard the conversation. "Cody, Uncle Kirby, that's great news. I also have good news to report. My timing may not be the greatest as it is mid-afternoon but I suggest we go for a drive. My labor pains are starting!"

In no time, the Circle K became a beehive of activity. Cody brought the car around. Rachel helped Cora slide into the back seat, then jumped into the front seat. Uncle Kirby, Sabrina and Jeremy became Josh's babysitting crew as the car sped out the gate—destination, Flagstaff Memorial Hospital. During the night, Jake Livingston arrived. The doctor released mother and son later the next day.

Cora, who slept most of the way home, woke up as Cody made a quick turn into the gate, all the while yelling, "It's a boy! It's another boy!" Jeremy and Rachel helped their daughter and new grandson out of the back seat.

Cora cast a stern look in Kirby's direction. "Don't say it, Uncle Kirby."

Kirby just could not hold back. "Cody, now you have two future ranch hands!"

* * *

"Sabrina, you will be surprised about what I'm about to say. I want to make one more trip into the Canyon, a mule ride down the Pioneer Trail and a couple days of rest and relaxation at the Dancing Ghost Ranch."

"What? At our age? Kirby, we have no business riding mules on steep trails at our age!"

"On the contrary, we have every business making such a trip. We are canyon pioneers. We helped open the Canyon so others could see what we've seen, what we've experienced, what we believe in preserving for all who come after us. I know we've told folks we're just rim-walkers and rim-sitters now, but I'd like us to make just one more journey to the river and back."

"So, you are proposing we drive up to the South Rim, sign up for mule rides—it won't be a self-guided tour like the old days; it will be a mule party with a wrangler—rent a cabin for two nights at the ranch, and then saddle up with a different mule train for the return trip."

"Yes, exactly. The Canyon is calling me, and I must go," said Kirby.

"Assuming there are no age limits for mule-riders, do you feel physically up for all that time in the saddle? Keep in mind, this is mid-July, the hot time of year at river level."

"That's why I suggest some rest time at the bottom and the cottonwoods there now offer plenty of shade. We can pretend we're regular tourists. No one, not even the trail guide, needs to know we're old hands at this business."

"Okay, Kirby, I'll call and make the reservations. It will be our grand finale below the rim. You may be the first eighty-five-year-old to make such a journey. I suggest we practice mounting and dismounting with Bernardo, Jeremy's mule. Otherwise, folks will think we are green as grass."

"And you, just a few years behind me, may set a new record in the book of woman trail-riders."

* * *

With Sabrina riding Susie and Kirby trailing on Victor, the mule train made their way to the Pioneer trailhead. Heidi Sherman photographed them as the mule train posed for its classic tourist picture. They mingled with fellow riders during rest stops, pretending to be novices, but deep down inside enjoying every mule step as a step back in time, a reminder of the early days when mule travel served as a necessity, not a frivolous vacation getaway.

It so happened that this final journey coincided exactly with Grand Canyon River Expeditions' arrival at Dancing Ghost Ranch. As they approached the suspension bridge, they noticed four cataract-style boats beached on a wide sandbar on the Skeleton Creek delta. The bridge itself offered a great view of the river party. After dismounting, Sabrina learned the river party also planned to spend three days at the ranch to exchange passengers and get resupplied for the next leg of their river trip.

The O'Briens approached one of the boatmen. "Hello, sir, we're Kirby and Sabrina O'Brien. We just came down the Pioneer Trail by mule."

"Greetings, O'Briens, my name is Ken Robinson. Most folks call me Doc. Have you met our leader, Nick Taylor? If not, I'd introduce you but he's engaged in conversation with a park ranger right now. This is Nick's sixth trip through the Canyon after their World War Two hiatus. You will find he's somewhat of a showman. He has a small airplane and has been known to fly under the Navajo Bridge!"

Kirby turned to Sabrina. "I think Dexter Livingston mentioned Nick Taylor several years ago."

Doc added, "He's now a self-proclaimed pioneer in commercial river running."

"Mr. Robinson, we're pleased to meet you and we hope to talk some more. We'll be here a couple days and would like to meet others in the Grand Canyon River Expeditions party as well. Right now, we are exhausted and need to check into our cabin," said Sabrina.

On their way to register, Kirby found his stiff and sore legs calling for a break. He missed his cane and started scanning the area for a strong stick. He learned that the ranch has a supply of walking sticks on loan during their stay. They spent the rest of the day sitting on their cabin bench, watching the river-runners splash in the swimming pool the late Louis Jackson helped build when he worked for the Civilian Conservation Corps.

I remember Louis saying the pool is eighteen feet deep," said Sabrina. "I'm immersing myself in the depths of the inner canyon but I'm not immersing myself in the depths of that cold water." She paused a moment. "Well, I might dangle my feet to cool off."

After a family-style dinner at the cantina, the O'Briens retired for the evening.

* * *

Waiting for the cantina to open for breakfast, Kirby and Sabrina ran into Ken Robinson again. "Good morning O'Briens, have you met Nick yet?"

"Not yet. We imagine he's a busy guy getting your river party outfitted for the next leg of your expedition."

"Here he comes now."

"Morning, Doc. I'll need your help today getting our new provisions stowed in the boats."

"Nick, I'd like to introduce you to Kirby and Sabrina O'Brien who are visiting here for a few days."

"Hello folks, let's go in and have some breakfast," offered Nick.

They settled at the table and started passing breakfast platters around.

"We're pleased to meet you, Mr. Taylor. We have a cattle ranch at Little Springs south of the Canyon and have spent a lot of time below the rim. We're feeling our age now and so this may be our last time at river level. A good friend of mine is Dexter Livingston who last reported he is building boats designed for running the Colorado. Do you happen to know him?"

"Know him? Kirby, I hired Dexter when we bought Western River Adventures. By the way, you can call me Nick. Ol' Dexter is a master craftsman and is in our shop at Mexican Hat right now," exclaimed Taylor, surprised he met a friend of Dexter here at this canyon outpost.

Sabrina added, "His brother Jeremy and his family live with us at our Circle K Ranch."

"Well, this is a small world!" said Nick. "Ah, finally, here comes the coffee."

Kirby had to ask. "Nick, one day, before the war, we paused on the bridge to watch three boats, similar to the ones beached here, pass underneath and then we rode down the River Trail to watch them run the rapids at Six-Gun Creek. Was that you?"

"It's not only a small world but you two really get around. Yes, that was us. We were testing our boats and trying to perfect better ways to run rapids. When you get a chance, come down to boat beach and we'll show you the boats Dexter has helped build."

"We'll do that, Nick. And thank you for the update on Dexter. It's been a long time since he last visited us at the Circle K. You obviously are keeping him very busy," remarked Sabrina. "When you get back to Mexican Hat, please ask Dexter to contact us. We'd like to congratulate him on his fine workmanship and complain about his lack of communication."

They parted ways, Nick to the boats, Kirby and Sabrina to sit under the cottonwoods by Skeleton Creek's swimming hole. Later that day, another mule train arrived with new overnighters. The O'Briens planned to join them on their return trip. A pack train also arrived to resupply the ranch kitchen. Before the temperature rose much higher, Kirby wanted to take up Nick's offer to see his cataract boats.

"Let's not go to the river yet Kirby; with no shade it will be blazing hot down there," said Sabrina. "Maybe hold up another hour."

The pool is lined with boulders. There is a ladder for climbing out and a building for changing clothes. On the roof is a flood lamp for evening dips. In the shade of cottonwoods there are folding chairs. Indeed, the pool area served as a canyon oasis.

As the sun slipped below the inner gorge walls and the temperature became more tolerable, Kirby and Sabrina walked down to the river.

"Ah-ha, the O'Briens! Come watch some of our river rats stow provisions in the watertight compartments of our cataract boats. Kirby, your good friend Dexter crafted these half-ton boats of marine plywood. The iron ore locks in the cockpit are positioned for the oarsman to make quick adjustments in roller-coaster waves. The splash guards were Dexter's idea."

"Nick, I like the green trim on the white hulls. Very attractive," commented Sabrina.

"When we watched your boats go bow first through Six-Gun's rapids, we thought going stern first would offer better visibility and reaction time," stated Kirby.

"Great observation, Kirby. We now go through rapids with the broad stern facing downstream," said Nick, "And if there is a passenger onboard, that person is sprawled out on deck, hanging on for dear life."

"Whew, that's not for me. You'd never catch me attacking monster waves in tiny boats," proclaimed Sabrina.

"Oh, but we wear lifejackets in case we capsize or get thrown overboard," said Nick with a grin.

Kirby added, "Nick, thank you for the tour but even if Sabrina and I were younger, we would not tempt fate like this." They shook hands and strolled back up to the cantina to await the dinner bell.

* * *

After a great night's sleep and a hearty breakfast, Kirby and Sabrina wandered over to the mule corral.

"Sabrina, is that you?"

"Do you know that wrangler, Sabrina? He seems to know you."

"That's Arnie Turner! Do you remember when Teresa and I rode down the Pioneer Trail? It was her first time below the rim. We helped rescue a young woman who fell off her mule and broke her arm. We abandoned our trip plan and escorted her back up the trail and to the clinic. The wrangler that day was Arnie!"

"Arnie, we're playing tourist on what will probably be our last trip below the rim. This is my dear husband, Kirby. You know we are well-experienced canyoneers but would you keep our tourist ruse secret? We'd rather not let on to your mule-riders that we've made many mule trips into the Canyon."

"No problem, Sabrina. Many years have gone by but I'd like to thank you again for your help on the trail that day. The gal, Bridget, sent me a thank you card saying her arm healed nicely but added she will probably stay off mules for a while."

Arnie assigned Kirby to Hopalong and Sabrina, coincidentally, rode Susie again. Even though the mule does all the work, Kirby found the climb to the rim grueling, the jostling motion of Hopalong's haunches aggravating, and the travel time excessive. Several times Sabrina, following behind, found Kirby teetering in the saddle. Others in the mule train whispered remarks about why Trails West allowed elders to be tortured on such conveyances as mules.

Finally topping out on the rim, Kirby, feeling rather lightheaded, needed assistance in dismounting Hopalong. But with his feet firmly planted on the caprock, he thanked Arnie Turner for a most successful grand finale. Sabrina helped him to the parking lot. On the ride back to the ranch, Kirby fell asleep. Sabrina made a mental note to have her

Flagstaff attorney draw up their last will and testament in the coming week, leaving everything to Cody and Cora.

At the ranch, everyone wanted details of their final inner canyon trek and their rare look into the emerging river-running industry. Jeremy welcomed the news of his brother, living and working in the San Juan River community of Mexican Hat as a master boat builder. Kirby enjoyed meeting boatmen Ken Robinson and Nick Taylor, both highly complimentary of Dexter's craftsmanship. Sabrina recognized Arnie Turner, their returning trail guide, from the time she and Teresa rescued an injured mule-rider. Both Kirby and Sabrina marveled at the Dancing Ghost Ranch swimming pool that Louis Jackson helped build. From Taylor's personal tour of the four boats beached on a wide sandbar, they learned about new techniques for running rapids. But most of all, Kirby and Sabrina, pretending to be tourists, just relaxed with other visitors gathered in the cantina or around the shaded pool. Their quiet times on their cabin bench and on strolls along Skeleton Creek allowed for plenty of reminiscing about their cherished times below the rim.

Throughout the summer, Sabrina and Cody shuttled Kirby to the canyon rim, sometimes to Summit Point, sometimes to the Pioneer Museum. It reminded Sabrina of the days when she and Kirby hauled Monte to the rim. On several occasions, Kirby startled Sabrina and Cody by falling into a deep sleep.

One day, further to the east, a ranger spotted a pony hitched to a juniper at Navajo Point. He then found a dead Navajo woman propped against a rock, facing the direction of the sacred Navajo Mountain, apparently having suffered a natural death. Checking a tag on her silver and turquoise necklace, he identified the woman as Moonflower Yazzie, a park employee at the Pioneer Museum. There was a second tag on Mooney's necklace with the words: *Tell me a fact, and I'll learn. Tell me a truth, and I'll believe. But tell me a story, and it will live in my heart forever – an old Native American adage.* Teresa notified Mooney's silversmith brother, Milton Yazzie, of her passing peacefully under the Canyon sky. She then telephoned Sabrina with the sad news.

Ironically, about the same time as Mooney's passing, a helicopter suffered a calamitous crash during takeoff at the Red Butte Airfield. Helicopters, still in their early stage of development during World War Two, saw very limited combat service. But after the war, they began seeing civilian uses, including special sling-load operations in the Grand Canyon.

A church ministry chartered one of the first helicopters certified for civilian use. The job called for transporting a military surplus Quonset hut to Havasu Canyon where it would serve as a chapel. The prefabricated structure of corrugated steel resembled half a cylinder laying on its side. The helicopter crashed a mile and a half northwest of Red Butte while attempting to lift the hut. Luckily, the pilot escaped injury and the hut suffered only minor damage. As for the helicopter living to fly another day, that remained unclear. No doubt, Mooney never dreamed such an aircraft could fly without wings or hover over the Canyon like a hummingbird.

* * *

Sabrina and Kirby stopped at a gas station in the small unincorporated community of Tusayan, just outside the park. The attendant filled their tank for just under two dollars. This trip to the Canyon, like many other recent ventures that summer, included rim-sitting at the Pioneer Museum. With Kirby's failing health, Sabrina selected a bench within easy walking distance to the museum entrance.

Kirby propped his cane against the bench, steadied himself on the arm, and landed with a thud on the hard oak seat. Sabrina set her picnic basket down and both gazed down into the immeasurably deep fissure in the earth, and the endless line of formations evoking shapes that only their imaginations could bring to life.

"I'm going to miss this ol' Canyon," uttered Kirby.

"What do you mean? Are you going somewhere? We have lots more visits ahead of us like this."

"Sabrina, I think I'll be leaving you soon. I believe life is not measured in days, months or years, nor in the number of breaths we take. It is measured by the moments that take our breath away, moments like now, sitting on the rim with you, the love of my life."

"That's enough of that kind of talk. Before cooler weather sets in, I plan many more visits for us on the rim. No more trips below. That last trail ride to the river two months ago was too hard on both of us." Sabrina started to be concerned about Kirby's mood, possibly a sign of early depression.

"How about some lunch? I brought sandwiches and your favorite drink?"

Kirby perked up. "Root beer?"

"Of course, it's the only kind of beer you drink!"

"Let's wait a while. Whenever we stare into this gaping abyss, we always get talking about the good ol' days. What comes to your mind when you see that stretch of river down there?"

Sabrina, relieved to see Kirby's mood change, thought a minute and then announced, "When you asked me to marry you. You promised me the moon and the stars. We had hiked down Clancy's Whiskey Trail to the river and I kept asking you what you wanted in life. You didn't answer. You were either not listening or you were being a tease."

"I was listening, but also stalling. I was so afraid you would say no. All the way down I was trying to figure out how and when to broach the subject of marriage. I'll never forget that night on the sand dunes."

"Let's drink to that night. I brought two root beers and some roasted beef sandwiches," said Sabrina as she popped the tops. Here's to this moment, and all the moments yet to come."

* * *

Kirby and Sabrina remained concerned about big hydropower dams on the river. They joined the public outcry and resolved to fight the issue to their deaths. On an early October rim outing at the Pioneer Museum, Kirby felt so weak he struggled to get out of the car. Sabrina set the brake and came around to help.

The stroll up the walkway to their favorite bench took twice as long as usual. Kirby dropped his cane twice on the way. They finally settled into their seat and into the exceptionally clear air under the blue canyon sky.

"Kirby, it seems some folks are willing to dam the river at Bridge Canyon and Marble Canyon because the back-flooding won't impact the river view where most visitors go. In other words, the resulting reservoirs won't be visible from the South Rim."

"Sabrina, I love you, don't stop fighting."

"I won't stop, but I'm not sure what the next move should be. What do you think?"

After a few minutes, "Kirby, what do you think we can do to stop this madness?"

"Kirby?"

Sabrina turned to Kirby. He sat motionless. His eyes closed. His hand on her knee.

"Oh no! Kirby? No, don't leave me!"

Kirby O'Brien died peacefully at the Pioneer Museum that bright October day. Sabrina rushed into the museum to find Teresa. "He's gone, Teresa, Kirby just passed away on the bench outside!"

Teresa telephoned Tomas next door for help. Several workers gathered around the old canyon pioneer and the broken-hearted Sabrina. Kirby died at the very edge of his beloved Grand Canyon. When Sabrina regained her composure, she spoke the words which would become Kirby's epitaph. "He loved the canyon sunrises, sunsets and stars, but more than that, he loved what lies under the Canyon sky."

Teresa drove Sabrina home to the Circle K Ranch. Tomas followed in Sabrina's sedan. When the two cars arrived, everyone knew something was wrong.

Cora spoke first. "Where's Uncle Kirby?" Cody, Jeremy and Rachel quickly joined her.

Teresa answered for the devastated Sabrina. "Kirby died this afternoon of natural causes."

Sabrina, in tears, finally managed to speak. "Kirby and I were sitting on our favorite bench at the museum. I asked him a couple of questions, but he did not answer. I turned to him and realized his eyes were closed but his left hand firmly grasped my knee. I then realized, the love of my life, having given his last full measure of love and devotion to me and our Canyon, was gone."

* * *

Sabrina and the Livingstons arranged Kirby's graveside memorial service at the Grand Canyon Pioneer Cemetery, adjacent to the Bridgestone family plot. Attendees included Jeremy and Rachel, Cody and Cora with sons Josh and Jake, Russ and Mabel, Tomas and Teresa,

Chad and Heidi, the park superintendent and several rangers. Dexter Livingston and Steve Baxter could not be reached in time.

Jeremy delivered the eulogy. "Kirby was my best friend and my mining and trail-building partner. He was an extraordinary humanitarian. He and Sabrina invited my family into their home when our situation became dire. I'll never forget our times below the rim with Monte. Kirby, I miss you already."

Cora followed with her own remarks. "I am the only one who called him uncle. I did not know Uncle Kirby long, but I knew he was a great man, a great canyon pioneer, and a devoted life partner to Sabrina. Thank you, Uncle Kirby, for all you have done to open this wondrous canyon for all to see, experience and protect."

Sabrina then addressed the group. "I miss him so much. Kirby and I were together fifty years but I thought we still had a few more years left together." Tears welled in her eyes as she struggled to continue; the small gathering reminded her of Monte's ceremony. "On Kirby's headstone you can read his epitaph: *He loved the canyon sunrises, sunsets and stars, but more than that, he loved what lies under the Canyon sky.* I think that says it all. But also, here are some of the last words he said to me, 'I believe life is not measured in days, months or years, nor in the number of breaths we take. It is measured by the moments that take our breath away, moments like now, sitting on the rim with you, the love of my life.' I will cherish those words forever."

Sabrina could not go on. Cody stopped her from collapsing, and then announced, "Kirby left a legacy and his pioneering spirit carries on in all the lives he touched along his trail through life. Thank you everyone for paying tribute to Kirby O'Brien."

As friends and family parted ways, Heidi Sherman, the renowned canyon photographer, handed Jeremy a framed print. "Jeremy, at the appropriate time would you give this to Sabrina. It's an enlargement of

Kirby and her starting on their last trail ride, part of my traditional mule party view on that special day."

* * *

A week after Kirby's memorial service, Clint McCarty, now an old man, returned to his old stomping grounds. Exhibiting an air of privilege by having a young female chauffeur, he learned of Kirby's recent passing while visiting the Pioneer Museum.

"Hello ma'am, I am . . ."

"I know who you are Mr. McCarty," explained Teresa. "My name is Teresa Garcia, museum manager. Your exploits are well documented in our exhibits here and in our book *Monte Bridgestone—Pioneer of the Grand Canyon*, now in its second printing. I assume you have the book; after all, Sabrina O'Brien arranged for you to write the foreword."

"Teresa, I must confess, I do not have the book yet but I'd like to buy a copy now. It looks like Sabrina did a fine job bringing Monte's story to life. Would you mind giving my driver, Eva, instructions to her ranch? I want to express my sympathy and condolences on her loss of Kirby."

"Her Circle K ranch is on the old stage road at Little Springs. I know it's been decades but you should remember that old stage stop," explained Teresa. You may recall I was a stage driver back in those days."

"I do recall that. You and Roscoe used to alternate days for those stage runs."

"Mr. McCarty, Sabrina does not like surprises, especially while she's in mourning. If you don't mind, I think I should call her and let her know you plan to visit."

"That's the right thing to do, Teresa, thank you. Please tell her I'll drop by tomorrow, probably late morning. And thank you for Monte's book and all your help."

Sabrina cringed at the news that Clint McCarty planned to visit. She dreaded having to deal with him at this particular time, or for that matter, any time. Meantime, Clint had his driver drop him off at the Pioneer Cemetery and wait for him in the parking lot.

"I'll be less than an hour, Eva, I want to pay my respects to four old friends."

Clint walked over to the infamous canyon storyteller, Clancy Jennings. "I miss you, and your wild tales, Clancy. Things in the world have changed a lot since you've been gone. You could never accommodate the millions that visit today. You would not have nearly enough stories to go around. Rest in peace, my friend."

"Stuart Casey, like I was telling Clancy here, the South Rim is very crowded now. We are so fortunate to see the Canyon before it became a national park. Ah, those were the days. I trust you have found canyons in heaven. Rest in peace, Casey. I'll probably be along soon myself."

On his way to visit Monte, Clint paused at the fresh grave of Kirby O'Brien. "Sorry I missed your memorial service, Kirby. I will be expressing my sympathies to your grieving bride tomorrow. You are so very lucky to marry the mystery lady and spend a wonderful half-century together. Rest with the angels, my friend."

"Monte, I have come to pay my respects and to apologize for my reckless behavior during our mining days. I regret trying to control the Canyon's development. I was wrong to manipulate our mining laws for personal gain. I was wrong to file all those river claims in hopes of selling them to dam builders who would then flood and destroy much of our beloved canyon." A few tears dropped on Monte's grave. "Please forgive me, Monte. If I make it to heaven, and if our trails cross again,

I hope to atone for my poor judgement, my disrespect for National Park Service officials, my insatiable greed, and turning my back on my fellow canyon pioneers. May you rest in peace for all eternity."

* * *

There is some irony in that this man, Clint McCarty, who manipulated the national mining laws and who sought to single-handedly control the destiny of the Grand Canyon, became a lawmaker and accomplished some good things for Arizona. But Clint seemed to breed charges of impropriety. He enjoyed being at the center of swirling controversies, defying the government of which he had become a part. With his vindictive attacks on the Federal agencies plaguing him for years, he tarnished his reputation as a bulwark and defender against what many regarded as dangerous encroachments by the Federal government. And yet many Arizonans remembered Clint McCarty as a significant and colorful canyon pioneer.

Sabrina did not view him as good for Arizona. She did not trust him and she found him exceedingly self-centered and devious. She and Jeremy awaited his arrival. In all likelihood, Clint would not get a good reception.

"Jeremy, help me control my temper. I need to accept his condolences and sympathies but he'll get little sympathy from me. I'll thank him for coming all this way and then he'll be on his way," explained Sabrina. "It's late morning. I expect him any time now. I never thought we would see him again. I wonder what he's been doing all these years. It's awkward knowing he has a female chauffeur. I wonder if she'll wait in the car. I think we'll just meet out here on the veranda."

Jeremy felt the tension building. He hoped for a civilized meeting but he himself remembered Clint's endless demands for more copper ore because he always seemed to be low on cash.

Another hour passed, then a big black chauffeured sedan pulled into the driveway. Sabrina hardly recognized Clint. He had aged considerably and walked with a cane up to the house.

"Sabrina, I'm so very sorry for your loss. Kirby was a fine man and will be greatly missed. Please accept my condolences and my apologies for my poor timing."

"Thank you, Clint. Do you remember Jeremy Livingston from your mining days on Windsong Mesa? He and his family live here on the Circle K."

"Jeremy, it's been decades! What a pleasure it is to see you both again. If only it was under different circumstances."

"Clint, it's still a pleasant October day, would you like to sit outside on the veranda with a cup of coffee? Your driver is welcome to join us," offered Sabrina.

"Eva will wait in the car, but I'd certainly like to join you for coffee."

Jeremy went into the house to ask Rachel to join them with coffee and cookies.

"Clint, I hope you don't mind if I speak my mind. I'm going to say a few things that have bothered me for years and years. As you must know, Kirby and I became best friends with Uncle Monte. He was your friend too but you abandoned him. You hoped he would not leave the Canyon as there were few living landmarks left but it is you who left him and the Canyon. I would just like to know why."

"Sabrina, our mines were failing, the copper market soured, and I had many other business dealings away from the Canyon," confessed Clint.

"I know about those dealings and your attempts to control development of the entire Canyon, of your stance against the Grand Canyon becoming a national park, of your questionable mining claims that gave prospectors and miners bad reputations, and what galls me the most, your crazy schemes to sell fraudulent claims to naïve eastern companies intending to build dams and ruin the Canyon."

"Sabrina, I apologize for my wild schemes, my apparent greed, my misplaced treatment of fellow man, and especially my disagreements with Monte. I ruined our friendship."

Sabrina decided to hammer Clint on another issue that nearly jeopardized the Pioneer Museum. "Clint, as a canyon pioneer, you are not held in high esteem by the Park Service. We almost lost our museum location because of your reputation with park officials. For months they held back site approval because you were going to be featured with our other pioneers in the museum exhibits. You have no idea how close we came to losing the museum because of you."

Just then, Rachel arrived with a pot of fresh-brewed coffee, cups, and a tray of cookies. Jeremy changed the tone of the meeting. "Clint, I'd like to introduce you to my wife, Rachel. We are grandparents now. Our adopted son Cody, a Silver Star war hero, married Cora, the park engineer's daughter. They have two very young boys."

"Very pleased to meet you, Rachel. Kirby and the Livingston brothers were our hardest workers in our mining and trail-building days."

Sabrina reentered the conversation. "Let's have some coffee and I'll try not to be so rude and outspoken. Clint, before you leave, I want to talk about the dams proposed for Bridge Canyon and the lower end of Marble Canyon."

"You know about those? I do not think I am finished apologizing," said Clint. "Rachel, this coffee is great, thank you."

For a while, no one had anything to say. Sabrina wondered if she should advance her arguments any further. She looked at Jeremy who seemed eager to challenge Clint on the negative impacts of river dams on the Canyon.

"Clint, if Kirby were here, he would lambast you for advocating hydropower dams on the Colorado River. It's too late for Hoover Dam, but he and I have been leading public outcries against building more dams. Their mistreatment of the Canyon and the Colorado River is criminal. Dams upset the balance of the natural world. I blame you for planting the seeds that have grown into dam proposals! You started this mess when you filed so many fraudulent mining claims that spanned the river! You even claimed thirteen million miner's inches of water in the river! Your schemes would have back-flooded the part of the Canyon that we have all come to love and cherish. Thank goodness your schemes failed but there are still those who want to dam the river. Kirby fought this madness to his death and I will do the same. That's all I have to say."

Clint profusely apologized for instigating the ongoing dam controversy, but to no avail. He put down his coffee cup, stood up and expressed his regrets to Sabrina for the trouble he'd caused and for the loss of the great canyon pioneer, Kirby O'Brien. He clumsily snatched the last cookie, knocking Rachel's tray to the veranda deck, then hobbled over to his waiting car, shoved his cane through an open window, and climbed into the front seat. He shouted "I'm very sorry, Sabrina" but these final words fell flat on the deck like the cookie tray. Clint McCarty fled Circle K Ranch, never to be seen again.

Chapter Fourteen

CANYON OF DREAMS

National Park Service protects the Canyon while Bureau of Reclamation proposes more dams that will flood the Canyon

Ron Morgan of Timberline Homebuilders informed Sabrina about the status of construction. "My crew is just about finished with its work on your new ranch house."

"That's great news, Ron. Now Jeremy and Cody can pick up the pace on the interior work."

"You need to do that, Sabrina, if you want to move in soon. The general feeling is that winter is coming early this year," said Ron as his men rounded up tools and construction debris.

Rachel overheard the conversation and agreed with Ron's assessment.

"Sabrina, I believe Jeremy and Cody still need to retrieve the woodstove and some remaining furnishings at our old cabin. I'm starting to think Cody and Cora, especially now with two very young boys, should hold up until Spring before moving in. This year's *Farmers' Almanac* predicts a very rough winter for northern Arizona. I'm a regular subscriber and its predictions are surprisingly accurate. I also hear the Havasupai are seeing an abundance of pinyon nuts this year."

"Rachel, what do pinyon nuts have to do with predicting weather?"

"About every seven years or so, pinyon pines produce a bumper crop of nuts—a sign that very cold temperatures and heavy snowfalls are approaching," explained Rachel.

"I've heard the same prediction from some of my Navajo workers," said Ron as he continued to direct construction clean-up operations.

"If this is true, we need to cut more firewood for winter," concluded Sabrina.

* * *

Sabrina called a ranch meeting of all residents. They gathered around the dining room table. With winter coming, several chores needed attention. Before getting into details, Cora asked how do we know when it is time to prepare for cold weather.

"That's easy," answered Sabrina, somewhat facetiously. "When you see Navajo gathering firewood; when you see Havasupai moving off the rim and down to Supai Village in the Canyon; our Native American friends just seem to know when it is time."

"Okay, let's get to some serious ranch business," said Sabrina. "Today, I am naming Cody as our official ranch foreman. This job not only includes overseeing our cattle enterprise; that is, branding, round-ups, hay cutting and storage, and managing raucous cowboys, but also caring for our senior residents, Jeremy and Rachel, and the lonely widow too. Yes, I'm slowing down and some days I lack energy and feel rather weak."

"Jeremy, I understand yesterday you finally received a letter from your brother in Mexican Hat, Utah. Would you share that with us?" asked Sabrina.

"Of course, but I must warn you it is not very good news. Dexter reports that Nick Taylor and his wife perished when their small airplane crashed. Apparently, the engine failed while taking off from the Mexican Hat airfield."

Sabrina interrupted, "This was Mooney's biggest worry about airplanes, that they might crash. Did Dexter say anything about what happens to Grand Canyon River Expeditions? Will the company continue its commercial river operations in the Canyon?"

"No news on that, but he did say the company is extremely concerned about what Marble Canyon Dam could do to their river-running business. Dexter also said rumors are flying about another dam construction project proposed upstream of Marble Canyon, in fact, at the Navajo Bridge. It would be called Glen Canyon Dam and its reservoir could flood the sacred stone arch near the base of Navajo Mountain."

"Folks, I won't live long enough to fight all these dam proposals. I hope the younger generations will carry the torch," bemoaned Sabrina.

"I will," exclaimed Cora. Cody grinned at her sudden outburst.

Sabrina had another matter to discuss. Tapping her finger on a Bergner Ford advertisement in the *Frontier Times*, she announced, "This ranch needs a truck. Bergner is introducing Ford's all-new, post-war F-series design for the modern age. Cody, I think you and I should go to Flagstaff. I have two errands in mind. We should determine if this new truck is right for Circle K ranch work and we should stop by our bank and get you put on our account, the sooner the better."

"I'm ready when you are. My main concern will be the low suspension on today's trucks. Some of our country roads, including forest roads, are potholed and rutted," said Cody.

"Okay, moving on. Jeremy, do you have anything else to report? Some good news, perhaps?"

"Yes. Rachel and I have decided to keep our RB Ranch. Our twenty acres, which borders on the Bureau's land, will serve as additional livestock grazing and our old log cabin can serve as a line-camp or bunkhouse for summer use by wranglers as I'm sure our newly appointed foreman will continue to build this cattle enterprise. While miles from

Circle K Ranch headquarters, its rooms for cooking, eating, sleeping, and storing ranch gear can easily be adapted as an outlying cowboy bunkhouse."

That's a great plan, Dad," commented Cody. "Good forward thinking too. It also reminds me that we need to retrieve some things from that future bunkhouse before winter sets in."

Rachel added, "Sabrina, if it's okay with you, we think it best that the new Livingston family, Cody, Cora, Josh and Jake, postpone moving into the new ranch house. This will allow the interior work, including installation of the woodstove for heat, to continue through the winter months."

"Another good plan!" agreed Sabrina. "Rachel just mentioned woodstove. It reminds me of another task that needs immediate attention and that's firewood. Jeremy and Cody, could you gather deadwood from the national forest, haul it out by wagon, or truck if we buy one, and split the logs here at the ranch?"

"Sabrina, we'll tackle the firewood issue right away," promised Jeremy. "I have one more thing to bring up. I've been waiting for the right time when we're all together like this. Sabrina, at the end of Kirby's memorial service, Heidi Sherman gave me this framed enlargement to pass along to you at the appropriate time." Jeremy held up the photograph and then passed it to Sabrina. "It features you and Kirby on mules at the Pioneer trailhead just before you two made your last descent into your beloved Grand Canyon."

"Jeremy, thank you so very much, and all of you for your love and support. I miss Kirby so much." Tears welled in Sabrina's eyes as the ranch meeting ended.

* * *

Jeremy scheduled a day hike down the Summit Trail to Windsong Mesa and back for Cody and Cora, a first for the young couple. Rachel stayed behind to take care of Jake. They parked the car at Summit Point while Sabrina waited on the rim with four-year-old Josh.

Jeremy provided a short indoctrination on what to expect. "Okay, this is a six-mile round-trip hike. The trail drops twenty-five hundred feet to the mesa. In our knapsacks, Cody, you will find mom has provided water and a light snack. The trail is not maintained and is quite rough in some places. It starts out with thirty, very steep switchbacks but it gets easier halfway down. Any questions?"

"Will we see the mines where you and Uncle Kirby worked?"

"Yes, Cora, but we won't go in. Too dangerous, especially now that uranium has been detected in and around the mines. Now let's get started. Oh, one more thing. Don't try to view the scenery while trudging down the trail. Stop, then look. And keep your hats on and use your walking sticks; they are like having a third leg."

Sabrina and Josh sat on the caprock where early tourists chiseled their names, initials, or dates of visit in the limestone. Like in those days, visitors had the same stunning view of the Canyon. It reminded Sabrina of her many excursions below the rim, especially those with Kirby. Josh, who took quite a liking to Sabrina, pointed to a raven gliding along the rim on morning air currents.

"Josh, you won't understand what I'm about to say but many years ago a dear friend and canyon pioneer said to me 'Only the rocks live forever' and I've never forgotten that." Josh pointed to a rocky outcropping and said "old rocks."

"Yes, very old rocks," commented Sabrina. Just then a party of four reached the trailhead, groaning and huffing from their grueling slog up the trail.

"Hello there. Did you happen to pass a gentleman in his seventies guiding a young couple down the trail?"

"Did the young woman have long blond braids?" asked the fellow in the lead.

"Yes, she and her husband are on their very first venture below the rim," answered Sabrina.

"We crossed paths where the cribbing at a switchback had partially given way; seeing daylight through cracks gives you quite a queasy feeling. We all made it but we had quite a traffic jam there for a while. The trail is in bad shape. A sign here at the trailhead says a fellow by the name of Monte Bridgestone built the trail about sixty years ago."

"The elderly fellow you passed is Jeremy Livingston," added Sabrina. "He helped Monte build the trail. They were hoping it would last a hundred years. Sounds like it might not make it."

Meanwhile, resting at the saddle, Jeremy regaled Cody and Cora with more information on the trail's construction. "Using juniper logs and stone blocks, Monte, Dexter and I built this trail in eighteen ninety-two. We either blasted the trail out of the rock wall or we hung it on the wall with steel cables attached to rods jammed into drilled holes. You probably noticed the cut slabs of limestone that were fitted edgewise into the trail-bed—a durable, engineered tread of interlocking precision-cut cobblestones. This Summit Trail first served our rich copper mines on Windsong Mesa. We used pack mules and burros to haul high-grade ore to the rim. Later the trail served Monte's tour guide business."

"I'm really impressed," said Cody. You were master trail-builders!"

"How much further to the mines?" asked Cora, as she looked down the trail.

"Two more miles but the trail levels out so the going gets much easier. When we reach the mesa, you will experience the immensity and beauty of this Canyon and you will see some remnants of our mining operation. Except for the stone cookhouse, all the buildings and equipment are gone but the shafts and tunnels that perforate Windsong Mesa are still there, harboring empty promises of a hidden copper bonanza."

They covered the remaining distance to the mesa, a leisurely walk along the red dusty trail, in just over an hour. Jeremy guided them to a stone foundation where an open-air building once served as an ore sorting station. He noticed something new since his last visit, a radiation danger sign on a steel post.

"Keep in mind our ascent will take twice as long as our descent so our time here will be quite limited. Our rest place here is where Monte spent his days sorting ore and packing the good stuff in canvas bags for our burro strings. The rest of us worked underground in the Shooting Star Mine." Jeremy pointed. "That open shaft over there had a hoist for raising ore buckets to the surface. Kirby and I retrieved some of that equipment and now it resides at Sabrina's Pioneer Museum. We'll walk down to a tunnel on the east wall where we salvaged an ore cart and some track for the museum."

As they journeyed down to one of the mine tunnels, Cody asked if the Shooting Star Mine made a profit. "Dad, was it worth digging this high-grade copper ore? I imagine it was available in paying quantities but the pick and shovel work was only the first step in the process, right?"

"Cody, you bring up a most important point. First the ore had to be dug, sorted, sacked and packed on burros. Then it had to be hauled to the rim and loaded into wagons. Then the wagons had to be driven to Flagstaff on the old stage road. Then the ore had to be transferred to railcars and shipped to distant smelters, usually the ones in El Paso. Every step in the process costs money. So, unfortunately, the answer is the Shooting Star Mine was never a profitable business."

Cora chimed in. "How sad. Uncle Kirby, the Livingston brothers, and all the other miners worked so hard but gained so little. At least you were able to spend time in one of the most beautiful places in the world. Just look at the views from this mesa and what a feeling it is to be down here, inside the Canyon. It's mesmerizing! Living in the Village, I have viewed this wonder of nature many times from the rim but from down here you get a much different perspective. I could stay down here for hours and hours, maybe even days."

"Not today, Cora. Remember this is a day trip and we'll need four or five hours to trudge back up to the rim," said Jeremy. "In fact, we need to get started very soon. While we eat our snacks and drink some more water, I'll mention a delightful story about Sabrina and Kirby. Below the tunnel we just visited is a vibrant spring. This is where Kirby made regular water runs for the mine and the Grand Canyon Hotel near the trailhead. It is also where he met Sabrina on one of her prospecting excursions."

"Wait, Sabrina was a prospector?" asked Cora.

"Yes, she roamed these side canyons for many years. Other prospectors referred to her as the Mystery Lady. As I was saying, Kirby followed her across the Tonto one day and they arranged to meet but she never set a location or a date. Kirby assumed she would meet him at the spring but he never knew when she would show so he volunteered to make all the daily water runs. Indeed, she did show. She would watch him fill water barrels and load them on burros. Eventually a romance blossomed and the rest is history. And with that, let's be on our way."

The threesome started up the Summit Trail. The closer to the saddle, the more switchbacks. But the steepest switchbacks came after the saddle. Cora needed many rest-stops in this section of the trail. Cody too, as his old war injury sometimes caused him to pause. Jeremy too, having reached his mid-seventies, started feeling his age. The trail cut through cross-bedded Coconino sandstone and reached one of the best viewpoints in the Canyon, especially when colored in dazzling reds and oranges by the late afternoon sun.

"There you are!" shouted Sabrina. "How was your venture below the rim?"

Cora answered, "Excruciating, bordering on torture, but the most exhilarating and exciting journey of my life! I have a new appreciation for trail-building and mining below the rim. And Sabrina, I learned that you once roamed the Canyon as a prospector. Men must have been shocked when they came across a woman prospector—the Mystery Lady!"

"These two did great, Sabrina. They are now honorary canyoneers and deserve a certificate of completion for their arduous odyssey below the rim," stated Jeremy. "How did you two do waiting hours and hours for us?"

"Josh took a long nap and I reminisced about all my canyon odysseys over the years. But we're ready to head back to the Circle K if you are."

"I'm quite ready!" proclaimed Cora. Cody and Josh repeated the sentiment. "Well, Sabrina, I'd say we hit the road," concluded Jeremy. As they strolled over to the car, Josh had the final word, "Goodbye, old rocks!"

* * *

After a visit to the Ford dealer in Flagstaff, Sabrina decided not to invest in a truck at this time. She agreed with Cody about the low suspension. Wagons, with their large wheels, raise the wagon bed enough to clear ruts and holes so prevalent in forest roads. Jeremy and Cody decided to use their horse-drawn wagon to haul firewood.

"Cody, I have a place in mind with a nice mix of ponderosa, cedar and pinyon," said Jeremy, as they drove along a forest road. "Several years ago, a windstorm toppled a number of trees, cut a swath right through the forest. I propose we focus on that deadwood, cut to length to fit in the wagon. We can do the rest of the cutting and splitting at the ranch."

Fifteen minutes later, "Here we are, grab your ax and saw and let's get to work."

After two trips with full wagons, and having off-loaded them in the barn to keep them out of the weather, Jeremy suggested one more trip. As they cleared the forest on their third return, it started snowing. By the time they reached the ranch, they had blizzard conditions.

"Cody, jump down and open the barn doors so we can get the horses and wagon out of the storm. Then we can unhitch and put the horses in stalls. We can unload later."

"Whew!" sighed Cody. "That was close, Dad. I hope we have enough. This heavy snowfall will close the roads. Now we need to worry about our cattle."

"Sabrina tells me the Circle K has suffered heavy stock losses in the past, but has always pulled through," said Jeremy. "Our big challenge now is to minimize the losses. The predicted rough winter is now underway; I am sure glad that we'll all be safe and warm in the big house."

"This will be my first big challenge as foreman. It's going to be a busy winter season with cattle feeding, firewood cutting and finishing the new house interior."

Cody added, "There's another matter we keep talking about and that is visiting our old cabin and retrieving the woodstove and some furnishings mom wants. Maybe after this storm we can visit the old place and load up on things worth keeping. The hardest part will be removing the woodstove and all of its chimney parts. We'll need a ladder to get on the roof."

"Cody, I think there is still a ladder there, and maybe some stray tools. We should ask mom to make a list of things she wants us to retrieve."

* * *

Three weeks passed since the big blizzard. Most of the snowdrifts shrank to small piles and the County cleared their roads, but not the more primitive forest roads. Cody had a chance to assess the impact on their Herefords but had yet to break the bad news. Sabrina, curious about any new developments regarding canyon dams, had made an appointment with Russ Cramer at Park Headquarters. She asked Cody to drive.

On the way to the Canyon, Cody revealed his findings on their cattle situation. "Sabrina, I'm sorry to report the blizzard took the lives of seventeen cows, including three yearlings. One of Bergner's ranch hands told me they lost eighty-one cows."

"Cody, we got off easy. I've seen worse winters and bigger cattle losses."

After a long silence, Cody brought up another subject. "We should clarify ownership of the surplus Army jeep that I think was loaned to us. Initially it was for Cora's use but we've had use of it for five or six years. Let's ask Russ when or if he wants it back."

"That gets back to needing another vehicle for the ranch. I wish Ford would build a bigger, heavy-duty truck, one that is higher off the ground and has much more carrying capacity." Sabrina decided to leave the question of needing a more capable ranch vehicle up to her ranch foreman.

Cody asked, "What time is our appointment with Russ?"

"Ten o'clock. Looks like we'll be right on time. I hope Russ has some good news to report on stopping actions to hijack the river. It is nerve-wracking to see one part of the government, the National Park Service, charged to protect the Grand Canyon and its river while another part of the government, the Bureau of Reclamation, determined to dam the river and flood portions of the Canyon. And what's worse, the two agencies both come under the Department of the Interior! It's crazy!"

The secretary for the Park Engineer Office offered fresh coffee to Sabrina and Cody. "Russ will be ready to see you in a few minutes." They no sooner sat down with their cups and Russ called them.

"Welcome!" shouted Russ from down the hallway. As they entered his office, Russ said, "I've got two quick questions before we talk about dams. Cody, how are Cora and my two grandsons doing?"

"Russ, they are all doing very well. Josh is growing quickly and I'm sure Jake will follow his older brother. And Cora is amazing, especially helping us all get through that blizzard a few weeks ago."

"Sabrina, that's my second question. How did the Circle K hold up against that storm? I hear many ranchers lost hundreds of cows."

"Russ, Cody just completed a count. Unfortunately, we lost seventeen."

"Sorry to hear that. I've got some news that may cheer you up. Funding for investigative studies and conceptual design for Bridge Canyon Dam is about to be cut to zero, much to the chagrin of Hualapai tribal council members, but to the delight of our united front that has been adamantly opposing this dam. Thanks to you and the intense public outcry, all work is coming to an abrupt end on that project."

Sabrina let out a cheer. "Hurrah! This is very good news, Russ."

"We here at the Canyon agree. What a relief! At least that part of the Canyon will be spared. However, now we are worried that Reclamation's interest will shift to Marble Canyon. Somewhere around river mile thirty-nine, that's about twenty miles upstream of the Little Colorado confluence, test-drilling in the Redwall limestone is rumored to begin this spring, despite tremendous public outcry."

"Russ, a dam at the lower end of Marble Canyon would back water all the way to Lees Ferry, flooding the only river-level access in two hundred and seventy miles! It would ruin the whitewater river-running industry on the Colorado!" Sabrina could hardly believe this sudden switch to the proposed Marble Canyon Dam.

Russ added, "Construction site access alone would be a huge challenge. They would need a three-thousand-foot cableway just to get down there. That's assuming the Navajo and Hopi would give them access. Such intrusion into the Canyon would be a nightmare. The enormous Redwall Cavern in the towering limestone cliff would be no more. Like you, Sabrina, I am running out of energy to fight the very government I work for. I am so exasperated by federal idiots clinging to the need for more dams that I'm thinking about retiring from the National Park Service. Mabel and I may move to Sedona later this year."

"Russ, I'm eighty-five. I too am running out of energy. I'm at a loss for what to do."

Cody changed the subject. "Russ, we still have the jeep you set aside for Cora. It dates back to the Civilian Conservation Corps days. I guess the Army gave it to the Park Service. I'm still using it but I'm not clear on who actually owns it. Do you want it back?"

"Cody, keep it. There's no record of a surplus jeep here anymore. It's been forgotten. If it still runs, remove the outdated license plate and confine it to ranch duty. I'm pleased to see the Army jeep in the service of an Army veteran."

"Thank you, Russ," said Sabrina. "Like me, it's getting up in years. We'll keep it running as long as we can."

"Sabrina, I must thank you for your years of support. You and Kirby kept us all thinking straight and for that we are most grateful. Cody, I assume you are the designated driver. Take care on your return to the ranch. There may be some slick patches on the road."

Russ watched Cody carefully guide Sabrina to their car. He felt the good news on Bridge Canyon and the bad news on Marble Canyon cancelled each other out. No doubt, the dam fight at Grand Canyon would go on for years, maybe decades. He said to himself, "The more I think about it, it is definitely time to retire."

"Cody let's stop by the Pioneer Museum before heading back. Despite the extreme cold, it's a beautiful clear day, still and quiet. I'd like to sit inside for a spell, where it's warm at Kirby's window panorama."

With her spirit deflated and her energy exhausted, Sabrina gazed out the giant windows. Cody wandered around the museum while she sat before her Canyon of Dreams. She thought to herself: *"Kirby, I'm about to join you in the big canyon in the sky."*

Cody, after an hour of touring, returned to the panorama. He put a hand on Sabrina's shoulder. "We should get going soon." Sabrina suddenly jerked. "Oh, Kirby, I mean Cody, I must have dozed off. I had no intention of sleeping through this great view. Yes, we should go."

Sabrina fell asleep again on the drive back to the Circle K. Once home, she felt so exhausted, she announced she would skip supper and retire early. Cody expressed concern about her being so overly tired and feeling rather melancholy at the museum.

The next morning, when Sabrina failed to show for breakfast, Rachel checked on her. She was still asleep. Jeremy joined her in the master bedroom. They quickly realized Sabrina had died in her sleep. Jeremy and Rachel paused halfway down the stairs and announced to Cody and Cora that Sabrina passed away peacefully during the night.

"No, that can't be!" cried Cora. "She seemed fine yesterday."

Cody interjected. "Cora, she was not fine. She was extremely tired, totally devastated by never-ending canyon dam issues, and missing Kirby more than ever. We stopped at the museum yesterday afternoon where she sat in front of the panoramic windows and became lost in the canyon world that she and Kirby shared. I think she knew her time was coming. May they both now rest in peace."

Coming to grips with the passing of two great canyon pioneers, Cora concluded, "So Uncle Kirby and Sabrina are together again."

"But their legacy must go on," said Cody, who just inherited the Circle K Ranch. "This will not be easy. As Sabrina often noted, there is a paradox within two Interior Department agencies—the National Park Service is charged with protecting the Canyon while the Bureau of Reclamation is proposing more dams and reservoirs that will flood portions of the Canyon."

* * *

National Park Service volunteers buried Sabrina next to Kirby at the Grand Canyon Pioneer Cemetery. The epitaph on her headstone simply read 'She loved what lies under the Canyon sky' and of course her name and dates. Those attending her memorial service included Cora, Cody, Russ, Mabel, Jeremy, Rachel, Dexter, Tomas, Teresa, Chad and

Heidi, but also Tim Simmons, Harvey Klostermeyer, Ron Morgan and the deputy superintendent.

Unbeknownst to everyone except Cora, Uncle Kirby had prewritten Sabrina's eulogy and entrusted Cora with the envelope containing his tribute. She had instructions to keep it secret and to not even look at it herself until Sabrina's graveside service. The time had come for delivery.

Cora stood before the small gathering and announced, "Family and friends, I have the distinct honor of delivering Sabrina's eulogy." She paused, clearly nervous and shaking. "That is not quite correct. Uncle Kirby wrote Sabrina's eulogy and gave it to me for safekeeping. In effect, when I speak, it is really Uncle Kirby paying tribute." Cora wiped some tears away and began to read.

"Today, we are honoring, celebrating, and remembering Sabrina O'Brien, my wife of fifty years. From the moment I met her, I knew I had finally found the love of my life. She was shy and wary of strangers back then, and yet quite a free spirit. Her early life was fractured and complex, but she was a survivor."

Cora paused, looked up, and confirmed she had everyone's undivided attention. Although feeling awkward and uneasy in her unique role, she continued.

"Sabrina was a woman of courage, adventure, energy, and ambition, with a stubborn streak that surfaced whenever she set her mind to a controversial situation that was just not right. We shared everything—our hopes, our plans, our dreams—most notably our canyon dreams."

A few tears dropped from Cora's watery eyes onto the papers she held.

"Our undying, loving relationship involved a third party—the Grand Canyon. The three of us were very close, especially when one of us, the Canyon, came under siege. Sabrina accomplished much in her long fights to save the Canyon from the most unlikely combination of assaults—corporate greed, misguided government agencies, cableways, river dams, overflights, and a uranium boom. She was a strong fighter to the end."

Cora looked up to see her father, the park engineer, and the deputy superintendent, both high-level officials of a government agency, solemnly staring at the ground. Everyone else focused on her.

"Sabrina was my best friend, my partner, my confidante, and I cherish every moment we had together. She was beautiful and fun, generous and caring, always looking beyond herself. She had a heart of gold and a magical way of touching the lives of folks around her, bringing joy and humor into any situation."

Clearly, Kirby's eulogy to his beloved wife touched everyone at the memorial service, perhaps Cora more than anyone else. She dabbed her eyes with her sleeve. A glance at Cody gave her courage to continue reading Kirby's tribute to Sabrina.

"When you commit to spending the rest of your life with someone, you hope to be together, side by side, to the very end. But inevitably one partner's life journey ends before the other. I knew I would be first."

Cora swayed slightly, almost losing her balance. Cody went to her side for comfort and support. She, essentially Kirby, continued.

"Sabrina would not want us to dwell on grief and sorrow; instead, she would want us to focus on our lifetime of happy memories and special adventures. My life's best years were spent with Sabrina. Like me, she loved the canyon sunrises, sunsets, moonrises, moonsets, planets and stars, but more than that, she loved what lies under the Canyon sky."

Cora read Kirby's final words: "Now my beloved Sabrina is with me again, for all eternity."

The gathering of Sabrina's fans stood in awe, teary-eyed and most impressed by Cora's handling of Uncle Kirby's special request.

Cora had a closing comment.

"Folks, as you know, Sabrina left a legacy for this Canyon of Dreams. It needs to continue. Cody and I vow to carry on Sabrina's legacy, to raise our two sons in hopes that they too will continue the legacy to love, honor and guard our national treasure—the Grand Canyon of the Colorado."

About the Author

Dick Brown has always been fascinated by western history—mountain men, wagon trains, gold rushes, cattle drives, notorious outlaws, ghost towns, and transcontinental railroads; however, he has concentrated much of his recent writing on one region of the American West in particular—the Grand Canyon. He has spent decades researching the early pioneers and the Canyon's bumpy road from unbridled backcountry to a national park. It is the venerable pioneers of the late nineteenth century, with their struggles to survive and thrive on the ragged edge of this tremendous abyss, that inspired Dick to write this historical novel.

During his writing career, Dick has authored and co-authored six award-winning books and has been published in numerous periodicals. He is a retired systems engineer and past president of the Grand Canyon Historical Society. As a former Navy submariner, he is a regular contributor to the journal *The Submarine Review* for which he has won three literary awards. He is also past editor of the magazine *Ballooning*. Dick lives in the forested mountains of central New Mexico, enjoying retirement with his wife and two feral cats.

Now Available!

DICK BROWN'S

UNDER THE CANYON SKY SERIES
BOOK ONE – BOOK TWO

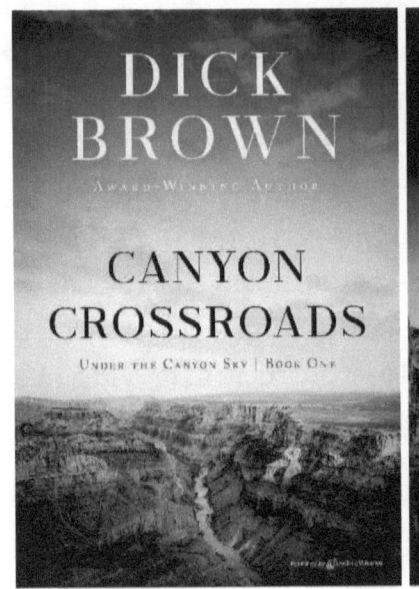 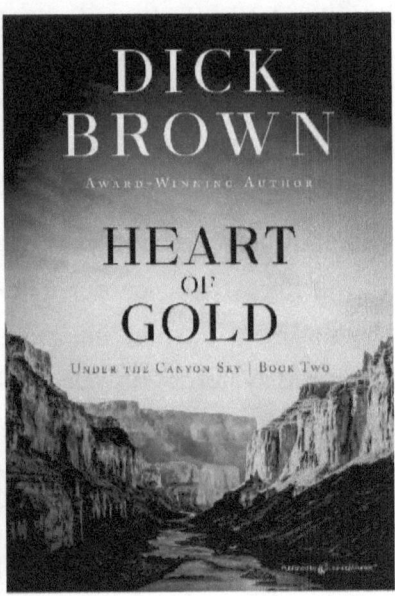

**For more information
visit: www.SpeakingVolumes.us**

Now Available!
JAMES D. CROWNOVER'S FIVE TRAILS WEST SERIES
BOOKS 1 – 4

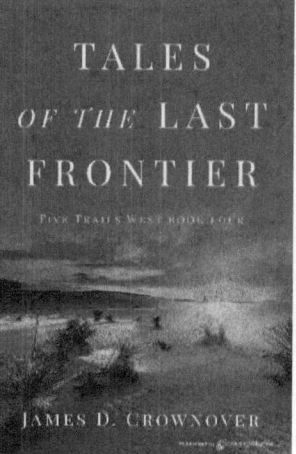

For more information visit: www.SpeakingVolumes.us

Now Available!
ROBERT WESTBROOK'S
HOWARD MOON DEER MYSTERIES
BOOKS 1 – 9

 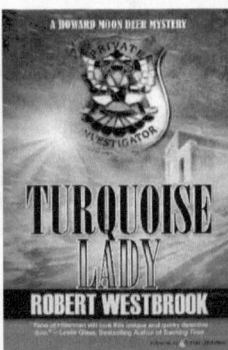 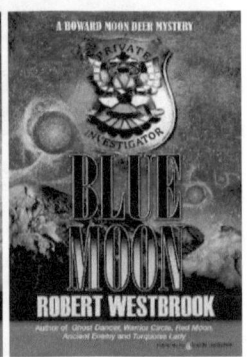

**For more information
visit:** www.SpeakingVolumes.us

www.ingramcontent.com/pod-product-compliance
Lightning Source LLC
LaVergne TN
LVHW091631070526
838199LV00044B/1025